ABANDONED and Protected

THE MARQUIS' TENACIOUS WIFE

BY
BREE WOLF

BREE WOLF
author

This is a work of fiction. Names, characters, businesses, places, brands, media, events and incidents are either the products of the author's imagination or used in a fictitious manner.

Any resemblance to actual persons, living or dead, or actual events is purely coincidental.

Cover Art by Victoria Cooper
Copyright © 2016 Bree Wolf

Paperback ISBN: 978-1539153696
Hardcover ISBN: 978-3-96482-110-2

www.breewolf.com

All Rights Reserved

This book or any portion thereof may not be reproduced or used in any manner whatsoever without the express written permission of the author except for the use of brief quotations in a book review.

To My Mom, who Taught me how to be a Mother

Acknowledgments

A great big heaping mountain of thank-you to everyone who lent a helping hand in the development of this book: my family, friends, beta-readers, proof-reader, avid readers, feedback givers, reviewers, hand-holders, muses and many more.

To name only a few: Michelle Chenoweth, Monique Taken, Zan-Mari Kiousi, Tray-Ci Roberts, Vicki Goodwin, Denise Boutin, Elizabeth Greenwood, Corinne Lehmann, Lynn Herron, Karen Semones, Maria DB, Kim O'Shea, Tricia Toney, Deborah Montiero, Keti Vezzu and Patty Michinko.

ABANDONED
and
Protected

Prologue

England 1781 (or a variation thereof)

The rain pelted on the roof as her mother's screams woke five-year-old Henrietta Turner from a rather fitful sleep. With wide eyes, she stared up at the dark ceiling, her hands curled into the blanket. Dark shadows danced around her as she lay listening.

The sounds of the storm raging outside her window almost drowned out her father's lamentations as he berated her mother once again, his drunken slur raising goose bumps on Henrietta's arms.

Closing her eyes, Henrietta rolled onto her side. If only she could go back to sleep, then everything would be all right!

Most nights, the small hunting cottage lay in silence as her father slept off his drunken stupor. However, that night was not one of them.

Something had roused him. Worse, something had angered him.

A chill crept up her small limbs, and Henrietta's jaw began to tremble as she gritted her teeth against the onslaught of sounds. Her mother's voice reached her ears, pleading, begging as she did her best to evade his anger. Her father, however, seemed oblivious to the fact that it was not an enemy he was advancing on, but his own wife.

Their voices mingled into an all too familiar dance of pain and hatred that sent Henrietta from her bed.

Despite the raging storm outside, she did not feel safe in this house, never had. For the only reason, her father, Rupert Turner, Viscount Elton, dragged his family out into the woods to the small hunting cottage on the outer border of their estate was that it gave him free rein over his family.

Out here, he did not have to hold back. Out here, he could do as he pleased. Out here, there was nothing and no one to stop him.

Least of all himself.

In her short life, Henrietta had seen it many times. In society, even with only servants around, her father did his utmost to portray the image that was expected of him. Despite his shortcomings in character and intelligence, few had ever seen him at his worst.

That privilege was reserved for his family.

Staring out into the storm, Henrietta squinted her eyes. Was that the shadow of a man? She wondered as a soft whinny mingled with the howling wind.

Then she closed her eyes. How often had her mind conjured a saviour who would come and stop her father and protect them? But he had never come, and he never would.

No one would protect her, not even her mother.

"Tristan," Henrietta whispered, and her eyes went wide as her heart hammered in her small chest.

Tiptoeing across the wooden floorboards, she cracked open the door, relieved that the pelting rain drowned out the soft creak of old hinges.

Instantly, her father's voice slammed into her as it echoed up the stairs from the small parlour in the front of the cottage.

Henrietta closed her eyes and took a deep breath. Then she stepped out into the dark hallway and silently walked toward the far door at its opposite end. Sliding it open, she stepped inside, her cold feet carrying her toward the wooden crib by the window.

Standing on her tiptoes, Henrietta peered down at her sleeping baby brother, safely swaddled in a soft blanket, his tiny chest rising and falling with each breath. He was the image of peace and trust, and in her little heart, Henrietta knew that she needed to protect him.

Though tall for her age, Henrietta had to drag over a chair in order to take him out of the crib. Resting his tiny head against her shoulder, she cradled him in her arms, holding him tight as he slept peacefully.

Then Henrietta opened the door once more, straining her ears. Her mother's frightened sobs reached her heart, and for a moment, Henrietta closed her eyes. As much as she wanted to help her, she knew there was nothing she could do. She glanced down at her brother.

Him, she would keep safe.

Approaching the stairs, Henrietta glanced over the banister into the small front room. When all remained clear and her parents' voices did not drift closer, she hugged her brother to her chest and silently slipped down the stairs. Glancing out the window, Henrietta knew she could not take him outside into the downpour, and so she tiptoed past the front door and toward the back where the kitchen was located.

The smells of fresh bread and savoury stew reached her nose, and Henrietta breathed in deeply as she entered the room. She rounded the working table in the middle and walked toward the small pantry. Stepping inside, she closed the door, then pulled aside a heavy crate of potatoes and slipped behind it, pulling it back into place.

Her back resting against the wall, Henrietta sat down cross-legged, her frozen feet like ice against her warm legs. Looking down at her brother, she wrapped him tighter in his little blanket, hugging him to her chest to keep him warm. When he slept on peacefully, Henrietta rested her head against the wall and closed her eyes, her parents' voices echoing in her ears.

A tear ran down her cold cheek at her father's angry shouts met by her mother's whimpering sobs.

Then her brother stirred, and Henrietta's head snapped up.

Gently rocking him in her arms, she began to hum a lullaby. After a while he quieted down. Relieved, Henrietta continued to hum under her breath, afraid he would wake and alert their father to their whereabouts. What would he do if he found them?

Henrietta didn't want to know.

After a while, her eyelids began to close and her head sank back. Henrietta immediately tightened her hold on Tristan, pulling up her knees to steady him, afraid her arms would slacken and she would drop him.

For a long while, only her mother's occasional sobs reached her ears, but other than that, the house fell silent. Only the storm still raged outside, the rain drumming on the roof as the wind howled through every crack, reaching inside with cold fingers.

Out of nowhere, a scream pierced the rhythmic drumming of the rain, and once more Henrietta's head snapped up.

Her mother.

Straining her ears, Henrietta listened, but she could not make out her mother's voice. Or her father's, for that matter.

Again, the house lay in silence.

An eerie sense of foreboding crawled up Henrietta's skin, and she swallowed, her only relief the peacefully sleeping baby in her small arms.

A shot rang through the dark, and Henrietta flinched.

Her heart hammered in her chest as she stared at the closed door to the pantry, afraid of what was happening on the other side. Had her father fired a shot? She wondered. He only used his rifles for hunting. Why would he...?

Henrietta swallowed before she stepped out from behind the box of potatoes and approached the door. Her arms trembled with the effort it took to hold her brother clutched to her chest, and her legs felt like pudding, wobbly and weak.

Cracking open the door a little, Henrietta peered out into the dark kitchen, but for the moment, all remained quiet.

Then footsteps echoed from the front parlour before they hastened up the stairs, the boards creaking under their weight.

With her eyes raised to the ceiling, Henrietta followed their sound as they stepped into one room after the other before finally returning downstairs. As they reached the front room, an angry growl echoed through the silence as the door was yanked open, inviting in the raging storm for but a moment before it closed once more.

The footsteps were gone.

For a long time, Henrietta stood by the door, peering through the crack. Straining her ears, she held her breath, trying to determine where her parents were. Had they left?

Henrietta felt utterly alone.

Swallowing, she pushed open the door before her courage could fail her and walked back the way she had come. As she approached the doorway to the parlour, Henrietta swallowed before peeking around the corner, hoping her father wouldn't see her.

The moment her gaze fell on her parents, her eyes went wide and she almost dropped her little brother.

Staring at their lifeless bodies, Henrietta couldn't help but wish that her father would yell at her, that he would glare at her with blood-shot eyes or even slap her across the face. Anything would be better than...this.

However, he never would again. He was no longer a threat to her or her brother.

Only, he had taken their mother with him when he had decided to leave this world, and Henrietta would never forgive him for that. A sweet-tempered woman, her mother had always submitted to his wishes, and yet, it had done her no good.

Henrietta would always remember the pain and hopelessness in her eyes, and she would never forget the cold disdain in her father's.

If she wanted to live, she needed to be strong.

For only the strong survived.

Chapter One

A HEART'S DESIRE

Twenty-Four Years Later

Feet apart to keep her balance on the soft ground of the clearing, Henrietta squinted her eyes as though focusing on her opponent. Then she lunged forward, extending her right arm at the same time, and her foil shot through the air, piercing the heart of her imagined enemy.

If only he were real. Henrietta thought, moving back into position.

A soft breeze blew through the trees bordering the small clearing, its coolness tickling her neck and soothing her heated skin. Henrietta sighed, enjoying the moment.

There were far too few of these.

With her ash-blond hair pinned up, she stood in the tall grass, her legs wrapped in loose-fitting breeches that she had taken from her brother's closet long ago. Unhindered by her skirts, Henrietta moved across the clearing, attacking and retreating, her eyes focused, her heart beating with purpose.

Despite her frail appearance, Henrietta's limbs were used to the exertion. She had long since passed the time when they would tremble with exhaustion, begging her to stop and rest.

With a foil in her hand, she felt strong, powerful and in control, and she cursed the day her uncle had discovered her ability.

Years ago, when her little brother had reached the age to be instructed, Henrietta had begged him to pass on to her what he learnt. Despite his initial reluctance, Tristan had complied because he loved his big sister dearly, and they had spent many wonderful days out in the woods, practising.

However, one day, their uncle had returned home unexpectedly and discovered them. He had been shocked out of his wits to see Henrietta in boys' clothes and forbidden her from ever touching another blade.

Although Henrietta had endured her uncle's harsh words, they had neither broken her spirit nor her determination to master the art. Tristan, however, had refused to practise with her ever again.

Ever since their father had killed not only himself but also their mother, Tristan had grown up with the sole memory of his uncle's disapproving gaze no matter how much he worked to excel at the tasks given him. Nothing was ever good enough, and yet, Tristan desired nothing more than his uncle's approval, the only father he ever knew.

And so he had turned from his sister, knowing that her rebellious ways would not serve him.

Rationally, Henrietta could understand why he had made that decision. Her heart, however, ached with betrayal every time she thought of her brother. All her life, she had given everything to protect him, and now, he had turned his back on her.

As anger surged through her veins, Henrietta moved across the clearing, her foil slicing the air in angry thrusts. Sweat ran down her temples, and heat burned in her limbs, but she could not stop. She would go on and on as she always did, to the point of physical exhaustion. Only then could she be satisfied with her progress. Only then could she be certain that she had done everything within her power to prepare herself.

Never would she allow herself to be treated the way her father had always treated her mother: like a possession, a worthless possession that he could use every way he chose.

No, she could not rely on the men in her family to keep her safe, especially not when they were very likely the ones who would seek to hurt her.

Cursing her brother's name, Henrietta groaned. If only she had a real opponent to practise with!

After days spent travelling in carriages with his legal adviser endlessly lecturing him about the importance of etiquette when appearing before parliament in order to claim his father's title, Connor Brunwood, future Marquis of Rodridge and new chief of the clan Brunwood, was ready to shoot himself.

The muscles in his legs trembled with the need to be off, to move and shake off the burdensome stiffness that had claimed them days ago. Ignoring Mr. Granten's shocked expression, he swung himself into the gelding's saddle in one fluid motion as the gigantic horse pranced nervously, its flanks heaving with anticipation. "Ye needna look so worried," he chuckled, shaking his head. "I assure ye I will meet ye in London before nightfall."

Then he loosened his hold on the reins, gave the gelding a swift kick and they were off racing across the meadow toward the tree line. As the wind whipping through his dark hair and brushed over his face, Connor closed his eyes for a moment, trusting the gelding to find its way, and enjoyed the feel of freedom he had missed dearly these past few weeks.

Not three months ago, his father, Ewan Brunwood, chief of clan Brunwood, had died rather unexpectedly in his sleep, leaving his worldly possessions, including his titles, to his only son while Connor's uncle, Hamish, tanist or second-in-command in the clan, had immediately become chief. Unexpectedly, Connor had been named his uncle's tanist although he had never expressed a desire to be burdened with the responsibility. His cousin Alastair had long since been thought to follow in the line of clan chiefs, and to this day, Connor had no idea what had gone wrong.

Unfortunately for many reasons, Hamish had followed his older brother to the grave within a month, effectively sealing Connor's fate.

Knowing that he was not cut out for the more tedious aspects of his newly-acquired duties, Connor had immediately chosen his cousin Alastair as tanist before agreeing to his mother's urgings to finally travel to London and claim his father's titles.

Although he knew his duty to his family, his people, his clan, Connor was far from accepting the changes in his life. With everything that needed to be done, he had had no time to mourn his father and uncle, two men who had shaped his life like no others. Their wise words and strong hands had taught him all he knew, and a part of Connor feared he would not be able to honour their memory by being the clan chief everyone expected him to be.

Reaching the tree line, his gelding slowed down, reluctantly picking his way through the thicket of the forest. When they came upon a well-travelled path though, his horse lunged forward as though a shot had been fired, eager to run and stretch its legs.

Connor knew the feeling.

Never in his life had he sat in a chair as much as he had in the last few weeks. It was unnatural, and Connor deeply regretted the turn his life had taken. The boredom and monotony that would now burden his days would slowly squeeze the life from him. He was certain of it.

Cursing under his breath, Connor sighed. If only a little excitement would come his way!

Chapter Two
A PROMISE GIVEN

As the sun rose higher in the sky, Henrietta felt fatigue wash over her limbs; yet, her heart would not let her rest. Who knew when another opportunity would present itself for her to slip away and return to her sanctuary? With her uncle currently in residence at her family's estate, Hampton Hall, his watchful eyes following her wherever she went, Henrietta's days were filled with countless proper activities fit for a lady.

Grunting under her breath, Henrietta lunged forward once more. Why was it that women were generally taught mind-numbingly useless things?

Nevertheless, a deep smile lifted the corners of her mouth as she pictured her uncle's shocked expression should he find her like this: dressed like a man, her hair tugged up and hidden under a hat, which currently lay in the tall grass where she had tethered her horse.

If she were lucky, his heart would give out and he would die on the spot!

A chuckle escaped her throat, and she brushed a sleeve over her forehead, her sweat staining the fabric. It was not lady-like, and yet, it made her feel more alive than anything she had ever done!

A horse's whinny echoed across the clearing, and Henrietta spun around.

Scanning the tree line, she felt the breath catch in her throat as a rider on a tall, dark horse emerged from the forest. For a moment, he stopped, head turned in her direction, before continuing towards her.

As her heart pounded in her chest, Henrietta forced herself to focus. Above all else, she must not allow him to see that she was a woman!

Returning to where she had tethered her mare, Henrietta snatched her hat off the ground, placing it firmly on her head and tugging away any loose strands. Then she slipped on her brother's coat, hoping it would conceal the small curves of her female figure.

All the while, her eyes never left the approaching rider.

As he came closer, she could make out his broad stature, thick legs and muscular arms that spoke of strength and power. Black hair framed his face, a matching beard darkening his features, and despite his normal attire, he seemed out of place, wild somehow as though he did not belong.

Taking a deep breath, Henrietta squared her shoulders and raised her head before she remembered that it might not be a good idea to meet his eyes and allow him to look into her face. Although no one would describe her features as soft and feminine, they still might be enough to arouse suspicion.

"Good day, Sir," the rider greeted her in a foreign slur as he pulled up his beast in front of her. "May I enquire what ye're doing so far out here? From afar, it looked a wee bit as though ye were dancing?" A slight chuckle shook his raspy voice as dark green eyes darted to the foil in her hand.

A spark of relief went through her at his address, and her hand on the foil's hilt relaxed a little. However, his derogatory remark irked her to no end, and she could barely keep herself from lifting her head and meeting his eyes. Instead, she glanced at him from under the rim of her hat. "A good day to you as well, Sir," she said, a touch of anger in her voice. "I was merely practising my footwork. However, I suppose from a distance it could have appeared...differently."

Henrietta gritted her teeth; conceding when she wanted to attack nearly drove her mad.

The stranger nodded as his eyes slid over her, a hint of curiosity in them. "I apologise. Allow me to assure ye that I meant no offence." While his gelding pawed the ground restlessly, its rider sat calmly atop its back, the expression on his face one of honest interest. "Even from afar, I could see ye're a fine swordsman." He nodded his head in compliment.

Pride surged through Henrietta at his words. No one, except for her brother, had ever given her such a compliment, and before she knew what she was doing, her head rose and a deep smile came to her face.

The second she met his penetrating eyes, Henrietta knew she had made a mistake.

But it was too late.

Connor frowned. There was something strange about this young man.

When he had come upon him, Connor had been surprised to see him train out in the woods all by himself. Would it not be easier to train on his estate? Judging from the young man's clothes-although they hung rather loosely on his body-they were of good quality, suggesting that he came of money and could well afford other means. The foil, too, looked to be of excellent craftsmanship.

A hint of regret filled Connor at the thought that despite the man's ability, he would never become a formidable fighter. Tall and slightly-built, he lacked the muscles and with it the strength to overpower an opponent. If he had not, Connor would have offered himself as a training partner. However, he did not wish to humiliate the young man.

And so Connor extended his honest compliments and was rather surprised to see such delight on the man's face as he lifted his head.

Instantly, Connor's eyes narrowed, and his gaze swept the young man's soft features and pale blue eyes, which widened in answer, staring back at him in shock.

When Connor leaned forward in the saddle, the young man dropped his gaze to the ground as though embarrassed, his hand tightening on the hilt of his foil.

He was hiding something! Connor knew he was, and so he dismounted determined to find out what. "'Tis a fine day," he observed, walking closer, his gelding trailing behind him. "D'ye come here often to practice?"

"Yes, I do," the young man answered in a strangely low voice as he took a step backwards.

Since the young man had lowered his chin almost to his chest, Connor could not see his face any longer. However, the way he moved was just as telling. There was a touch of gracefulness and pride, which Connor had never before seen in a man, and he remembered his earlier thought that the young man had seemed as though he had been dancing. "D'ye always practice alone?"

The young man stopped and straightened his shoulders as though he had decided not to run anymore. "I do what I must in order to maintain my skill."

Connor nodded, taking another step closer. "'Tis commendable," he remarked, stopping only a step away from the man's shoulder. And while the young man kept his head down, determined not to look at him, Connor's eyes swept over his thin shoulders, scrawny arms and long legs, and a suspicion began to form in his mind.

Connor leaned closer then, breathing in the soft scent of honeysuckle only slightly masked by sweat and a hint of panic. He also noticed the man's rapid breathing, not from exertion but rather fear, as his hand curled around the hilt of the foil, a slight tremble in his arm. "I forgot my manners," Connor called in feigned surprise. "Allow me to introduce myself." He inclined his head, his eyes still trained on the young man's posture. "Connor Brunwood, future Marquis of Rodridge."

"It's a pleasure to make your acquaintance," the young man forced out through gritted teeth, his voice not as low as it had been moments ago.

"And ye are?" Connor asked with a chuckle.

The young man cleared his throat. "My name is...eh...Henry... Henry Smith."

"Pleased to meet ye," Connor said, then shook his head laughing. "What are ye doing out here without an escort, *Henry*?"

The young *man* froze. "I beg your pardon."

Reaching out, Connor swiftly pulled off the hat, and although most of her blond tresses were pinned up in the back, a few loose strands tumbled down, framing her shocked face. Round eyes stared back into his, and Connor had to draw in a deep breath as his gaze swept over her, now knowing she was a woman. "A bonny lass," he whispered, smiling at her.

All noise was drowned out by the blood rushing in her ears as Henrietta stood in the clearing, staring at the bear of a man who had just now unmasked her, a delighted smirk on his face. His eyes slid over her in frank perusal, touching not only her lips and the curve of her neck but also venturing lower.

Refusing to be intimidated, Henrietta took a deep breath and squared her shoulders, her right hand coming forward, bringing the foil with it.

Instantly, his eyes snapped up to meet hers. "Correct me if I'm wrong, but is it not unusual for an English lass to ride out on her own?" he asked, amusement curling his lip., "And with a weapon no less?"

Henrietta's mouth pressed into a thin line as her eyes narrowed. "Maybe you are less acquainted with English customs than you think, *my lord*."

Smiling, he took a step closer, his eyes drilling into hers. "I doubt that," he whispered, and his breath brushed over her skin, making her shiver. "Ye've done yer best to conceal that ye're a woman," he continued, his eyes sweeping over her form as though trying to glimpse beneath her clothes, "which means that someone would be verra displeased with ye if he were to find ye this way." He met her eyes. "And yet, ye are here." He nodded. "This is important to ye."

Henrietta swallowed, suddenly acutely aware of the powerful man towering over her. Although she was tall for a woman, he seemed like a giant, and Henrietta had to admit that she was no match for him. That thought coincided with the realisation that they were, indeed, alone.

What she had considered an asset had now turned into a threat. What did he want?

"There's no need to be scared," he said, his eyes never leaving hers. "I mean ye no harm."

"I am not," Henrietta hissed, forcing herself not to take a step backwards. "However, I would appreciate it if you got back on your horse and left."

Again, a smile curled up the corners of his mouth. "Ye're willing to let me leave? Are ye not afraid I might betray yer secret?"

Henrietta tensed. Would he? Or rather could he? After all, she hadn't even given him her name. So, how on earth was he to find her? "You are not from these parts," she mumbled, considering her options.

He laughed. "What gave me away, Lass?"

Gritting her teeth, Henrietta fought the urge to run him through. And yet, despite his mockery, his words felt like a caress, and she shivered at the term of endearment.

In all her years, no man had ever unsettled her the way this brute did. From what she could tell, no man had ever wanted to. Curt words and harsh replies had always been her best defence against the opposite sex.

Maybe in his country, people did not consider civility a requirement for proper communication.

"Have ye made up yer mind?" he asked, clearly amused with the situation.

Raising her gaze to meet his once more, Henrietta took a slow step forward, her eyes cold as steel as she spoke. "Leave. Now." She lifted her foil, just barely, but his eyes caught the movement, and instantly, his hand shot out, twisting the foil out of her hand.

Henrietta gasped as he dropped the weapon to the ground and grabbed her. Forcing her chin up, he looked deep into her eyes. "Ye still have a lot to learn," he whispered, his gaze dropping to her lips, "but I'd love to teach ye."

As a shiver went through her, Henrietta swallowed and forced herself to remember what she had taught herself. "I demand that you release me immediately," she snarled, ignoring the amused gleam that came to his eyes.

To her relief, he did as she had asked and took a step back. "Ye should head home," he said, picking up the foil and handing it back to her hilt-first. "A storm is brewing."

Glancing at the sky, Henrietta noticed that the clear blue sky had turned dark, heavy with grey clouds. Then she took hold of her foil and stepped back, eyes on the man who had just taught her a valuable lesson.

Complacency would be her end. She needed more practice, real practice. What she needed was a real opponent.

"Farewell," he said, back on his black horse as though rider and steed formed a strange symbiosis. "Until we meet again."

Mounting her mare, Henrietta stopped as his words reached her. "We will not meet again," she snapped. "I can assure you that I will do everything within my power to avoid a future meeting."

A smile on his face, he nodded, then softly kicked his horse and came toward her.

Henrietta drew in a deep breath and swallowed as he stopped beside her, his knee touching hers.

"We *will* meet again," he said, his eyes holding hers, a promise in them that shook Henrietta to her very core. "I will find ye, Lass." He nodded. "Be assured of *that*." He held her gaze for a moment longer, then spurred on his horse and shot past her, galloping across the clearing like a warrior ready for battle.

And for the first time in her life, Henrietta was at a loss.

As London came in sight, Connor slowed down his gelding, watching the sun set on the horizon as it cast a warm glow over the city. Drenched from head to toe, he smiled. The downpour had been exactly what he had needed, and for the first time since his father had died, Connor looked into the future with a happy heart.

He had asked for excitement. He had gotten more than that. A lot more.

Yes, he would ride into London. He would do as Mr. Granten had instructed, and he would claim his father's titles.

However, before he returned to Scotland, he would claim something much more valuable to him than anything he had ever laid eyes upon.

Remembering the fierce look in her eyes, Connor chuckled. She was a wildcat, not a proper lady, and he wouldn't have her any other way.

Despite his slightly advanced age, Connor had never been married, and although his parents' match had been arranged, they had developed a deep love for one another, and, therefore, they had never pressured him to choose a bride let alone chosen one for him.

As was customary in his family, marriages were often arranged between cousins, and before today, while he had not been looking forward to wedding his cousin, Connor had had no objections.

Today, however, had changed everything.

Chapter Three
GRIEVANCES

A knock on the door roused Henrietta from her gloomy thoughts.

"Enter," she called, sliding the only letter Tristan had sent her since leaving the house back into the small mahogany box where she kept her most treasured possessions.

"Do you have a moment, Dear?" her aunt asked, closing the door behind her.

Forcing a smile on her face, Henrietta nodded, knowing that her efforts were not enough to convince her aunt as the woman's eyes slid over her, a concerned frown drawing down her greying brows.

A sympathetic smile touched her aunt's face as she came forward and reached out her hands, drawing Henrietta's into her own. "I know you miss him," she whispered, giving Henrietta's hands a gentle squeeze.

Drawing a deep breath, Henrietta blinked, willing the tears back down. "I do, yes." Then she withdrew her hands from her aunt's and walked over to the window, looking down into the gardens. "Is there something I can help you with, Aunt Clara?"

Her aunt cleared her throat. "Actually, I came here because I have news."

Henrietta's head spun around, and her heart constricted painfully as an old fear swept through her. "Of Tristan? Did something happen to him?"

As long as he had been under his uncle's strict supervision, Tristan had always been one to follow the rules and never acted out. However, ever since he had come of age and left his uncle's house, he had more than once taken a stroll on the dangerous side of life.

For a second, her aunt's eyes widened before she shook her head. "No. No, it has nothing to do with Tristan." She sighed. "I am sorry for frightening you."

"It's all right." Henrietta swallowed. "What is it then?"

A careful smile on her face, Aunt Clara stepped towards her, once more reaching for Henrietta's hands. "I have news of the Duchess of Cromwell."

Henrietta drew in a deep breath as the muscles in her body tensed. "Anna? Is she all right?"

Her aunt smiled, and Henrietta felt herself relax. "She just had a little baby girl."

For a moment, Henrietta closed her eyes as contradicting feelings surged through her.

Anna had a little daughter. She was a mother, and she would be a good mother; Henrietta was sure of it. After all, Anna was strong, not weak like Henrietta's own mother had been, and yet, she couldn't help but wonder if Anna would be strong enough to protect her child should her husband ever turn against them.

Henrietta sighed. Despite her misgivings, she hoped with every fibre of her body that Anna would never have to find out, that she was justified in thinking her husband a good man. With all her heart, Henrietta wished that she had been wrong to caution Anna the way she had, nevertheless, she knew she could not have acted any other way. What kind of a friend would she have been if she had allowed Anna to continue down a treacherous path without doing her best to warn her, to protect her?

Henrietta knew she had done all that she could. However, her sense of duty to her friend had cost her that very friendship.

"You miss her, do you not?" her aunt asked, squeezing her hands. "Do not deny it for I can see it in your eyes."

Henrietta sighed, once more fighting tears.

"You used to be so close," Aunt Clara continued, her gentle eyes searching Henrietta's face. "Whatever it was that you two quarrelled about, was it really worth losing each other over?"

Shaking her head, Henrietta sighed. "I had to," she whispered. "I couldn't just stand by and..." She met her aunt's gaze. "It's who I am. I had to protect her. I had to at least try."

Once more, Aunt Clara squeezed her hands, her soft brown eyes searching Henrietta's. "Not every man is like your father," she whispered, and Henrietta felt like she had been slapped in the face. "Most men are truly honourable. They make mistakes, yes, but don't we all?" Gently, she cupped a hand to Henrietta's face. "I know you've seen things no child should see. But you're not a child anymore. You are a grown woman, and you've robbed yourself of a future by allowing your past to rule your life."

Stepping back, Henrietta brushed off her aunt's hands. "What future? On the contrary, I have done everything I could to assure that my future does not turn out like my mother's."

Sighing, her aunt nodded. "Yes, you do not have a husband who beats you when he's drunk. But neither do you have a husband who watches over you when you are sick, who comforts you when you are sad, who smiles with you."

Henrietta snorted, "Are you trying to say that Uncle Randolph does these things for you?"

"No," her aunt sighed, a hint of sadness in her eyes. "He does not. We cannot all be fortunate enough to marry a man who truly loves us. But your uncle keeps me safe. He provides for me and my son. He never beats me." Her eyes looked into Henrietta's imploringly. "He is kind and caring, and for me, that is enough."

"I am happy for you, Aunt Clara, but I am not you."

"Do you never dream of a husband?" her aunt asked, curiosity marking her face. "Of love even? I did when I was young." A soft smile came to her face. "Do not all young women imagine the man they would one day marry?"

Henrietta shook her head, her lips pressed in a tight line. "I never did. Not once. All I ever thought about was how to protect myself from the man who would one day turn against me should I agree to marry him!"

Her aunt sighed, "As long as you only see the bad, you will never be happy."

"But I will be safe," Henrietta insisted, despite knowing her aunt meant well. However, the life Aunt Clara lived, always subservient to her husband, was none that Henrietta longed for.

Her aunt nodded, and a hint of resignation rested in her sad eyes. "That is good," she whispered before turning to the door, "but maybe you should go and see her." For a moment, she met Henrietta's eyes. "Do not waste your time clinging to grievances. What good is a life spent alone?"

After the door closed behind her aunt, Henrietta sank into the armchair under the bay windows, tears flowing freely down her cheeks.

A fortnight passed, and Henrietta's heart still ached with the losses she had suffered and been reminded of so unexpectedly. Although she had to admit to herself that she wanted to see Anna, Henrietta could not bring herself to visit her. Deep down, she knew it to be a sign of surrender, proving her wrong in her fears. And although Henrietta hoped for it to be true, she did not believe it, and she could not act against her own convictions.

Swallowing, Henrietta put Anna out of her mind and instead focused her energy on Tristan. Months had passed since she had last seen him, and even then, they had parted in disagreement.

Tristan was forever torn between complying with his uncle's wishes and being his own man. Often, he tried so hard to set himself apart from his uncle's expectations that he became reckless, and Henrietta constantly feared for his safety. When she had challenged his motivations, he had been outraged and stormed out.

A part of her had hoped that eventually he would come to see her, but he hadn't, and Henrietta began to wonder if he ever would. After all, he was her brother, and they shared the same stubbornness that so often ruled her own decisions.

However, he *was* her brother, and she could not allow such a minor disagreement to tear them apart for good. After all, he was all she had left.

Her uncle was a distant man, always disapproving of everything she did. Neither Tristan nor Henrietta had ever been able to develop an affectionate relationship with him. Her aunt was different; however, she often echoed her husband's opinion, which only strengthened Henrietta's resolve to keep her distance. And her cousin Matthew was merely a younger image of her uncle.

Tristan, her mind thought, and her heart ached. Would he want to see her if she went to London? Or would he send her away?

Her aunt's voice echoed in her thoughts. *Your uncle keeps me safe. He provides for me and my son.*

Who would provide for her once her aunt and uncle passed on? As a woman, Henrietta's options to provide for herself were severely limited, and at her age and with her disposition, Henrietta doubted that an offer of marriage would ever be made to her, not that she would accept it should one be made.

Her mind made up, Henrietta hurried down the stairs. She needed to see Tristan, whether he was still angry with her or not. After all, he was her baby brother, the only one she had ever truly loved without caution and restrictions.

"Henrietta, wait!" her aunt called in a hushed voice as she hastened after her down the corridor toward her uncle's study.

Stopping, Henrietta turned around. "What is it? I need to speak with Uncle. I've made up my mind; I need to see Tristan."

Her aunt nodded, but still took her hand and led her past the study and into the front parlour. "That needs to wait. Your uncle has a visitor."

"A visitor?" Henrietta frowned, aware that her uncle rarely conducted business on the family's estate. "Who is it?"

Her aunt shrugged. "He did not look familiar, and he had a strange accent. He must be a foreigner."

At her aunt's words, Henrietta's blood froze in her veins as the man's description echoed in her soul. Catching her breath, she swallowed, then turned to her aunt. "Was he tall, with broad shoulders, black hair and a beard covering his face?"

Aunt Clara's eyes widened. "How do you know?"

For a moment, Henrietta thought she would faint. What was he doing in her uncle's study? Was it a coincidence? Or had he discovered her true identity after all and was at this very moment informing her uncle of her unladylike behaviour? But why would he? What did he have to gain from betraying her secret?

Sinking onto the settee, Henrietta waited for the verdict.

Chapter Four
AN ANTAGONISTIC WOMAN

"Then we are in agreement?" Connor asked, eyeing Mr. Turner's delighted face with a hint of apprehension. Something about the man struck him as odd.

"We are indeed," Mr. Turner said as he rose from his chair and offered Connor his hand. "I am quite pleased with our deal."

Deal? Connor wondered, thinking it quite an odd way to describe the agreement they had reached, and yet, Connor himself felt a hint of guilt for allowing her uncle to dictate the terms. It was quite dishonourable. However, he could not ask her. Without a doubt, he knew that she would refuse him, and he could not risk that.

First rule of warfare: Know thy enemy...or, in this case, rather thy enemy thou regret thou have.

Leaving the study, the two men walked down the corridor toward the front hall. All the while, Mr. Turner marvelled at his good fortune, assuring Connor that they would be on their way within a fortnight.

Connor nodded, his eyes sweeping the rooms they passed as he wondered where she was. What would she look like with her hair down and wearing a gown instead of breeches?

As they stopped in the front hall, Mr. Turner bid him farewell, once again assuring him that all would go according to plan.

Frowning, Connor nodded. "I appreciate that, Mr. Turner. Please give my regards to the ladies of the house."

"I certainly shall," Mr. Turner assured him.

After bidding each other goodbye, Connor walked down the front steps and mounted his horse, a stab of regret in his chest that he had not even caught a glimpse of her. However, when he pulled up the reins, a curtain was pulled back from one of the windows in the parlour and before he knew what was happening, clear, blue eyes looked into his.

Angry, blue eyes, to be exact.

Connor could not hide a smile as he saw the confusion on her face as she searched his, clearly worrying about why he had come and possibly how he had found her.

A part of him wanted to go to her and lay everything open; however, he knew she would be furious and not yield easily. Better leave that to her uncle. He would speak to her later and explain himself...when they were alone.

As she stood by the window, glaring down at him, Connor's eyes swept over her, comparing what he saw to the memory he treasured. While the deep azure gown accented her eyes, it also made her look pale; however, part of that could possibly be attributed to the shock at seeing him invading her home. Although he had often pictured her in his thoughts with her hair flowing over her shoulders, Connor thought he liked her better with her hair pinned up, revealing her graceful neck.

Holding her gaze, he marvelled at the twists and turns of fate. Had his father not died when he had, had Connor not been delayed to travel to England in order to claim his title, had he not felt the urge for a hard ride after spending days locked in a carriage, he would never even have met her!

And what a tragedy that would have been! A tragedy he wouldn't even have been aware of!

Never before had he laid eyes on a woman who managed to stir his soul with a single curl to her lips. A woman who challenged him. A woman he could see riding by his side.

Chuckling, Connor nodded his head to her before he reluctantly kicked his gelding and they sped off down the drive.

Still, despite her unusual allure, Connor couldn't help but wonder how he had ever fallen for that twig of a girl!

A shiver ran down Henrietta's back that echoed into every fibre of her being as that man's soul-searching eyes swept over her, touching places that were quite improper for him to notice.

He was a stranger, a foreigner even, and yet, he acted as though they were intimately acquainted. Very intimately.

When his black beast sped down the drive, Henrietta's eyes stayed with them until they disappeared from view, and she wondered if she would ever see him again.

"Uncle Randolph!" she called, forcing herself to abandon her post by the window. After all, there was nothing to see anymore. "Who was that man? What did he want?"

Walking out into the hall, Henrietta stopped as her uncle came toward her, a satisfied smile on his face, a smile that had taught her to be cautious. Whenever her uncle looked immensely pleased, someone usually had to suffer for it.

Henrietta could only hope it wouldn't be her.

As though patting himself on the back for an achieved victory, her uncle straightened then glanced from her to his wife before raising his chin and saying, "That was the new Marquis of Rodridge."

Henrietta swallowed. "What did he want?" Judging from her uncle's face, she doubted that the marquis had betrayed her secret. Surely, her uncle's reaction would have been far from pleased. However, she had to know what was going on and why he had sought her out. After all, this could not be a coincidence that the same man who had come upon her in the woods would have business with her uncle.

Chuckling, her uncle met her eyes, and a cold shiver rolled down Henrietta's back. "In fact, he came here to ask for your hand in marriage."

That simple statement knocked the air from Henrietta's lungs, and for a moment, she thought her knees would betray her.

"What?" her aunt whispered, her eyes widened in stunned surprise. "He did?" Her gaze turned to Henrietta. "How do you know him?"

"I..." Closing her eyes, Henrietta tried to focus. He had asked for her hand? Why on earth would he want to marry her? She looked at her uncle's delighted face, and a dark sense of foreboding settled in her stomach. The marquis had asked for her hand, but surely, her uncle wouldn't...

Yes, he would.

As resignation flooded her being, Henrietta asked, "What was your answer?"

Her uncle scoffed. "What was my answer?" he echoed as though her question answered itself. "Naturally, I agreed. Anyone in their right mind would have." He took a step forward, and his cold eyes fixed her with a commanding stare. "These past twenty-odd years, you have been a burden."

"Randolph!" his wife objected, but he ignored her.

"Always arguing. Always disrespectful. Always antagonistic." He shook his head, his mouth an angry snarl. "But no more. Every endeavour I have undertaken to find you a suitable husband, any husband really, you have thwarted with your improper conduct, but not now."

Henrietta swallowed. Never before had she felt so alone in the world, abandoned by everyone who had ever meant anything to her.

Pointing out the window, her uncle continued, "*He* is bent on having you for his wife. I don't know why, and to be frank, I do not care. But I doubt there is anything you can do that would change his mind." He chuckled, triumph reddening his cheeks. "Finally, it seems that you have met your match, dear Niece." Holding her gaze for a moment longer, her uncle turned on his heels and started down the hall.

Never had Henrietta thought it would come to this; however, she had always wondered if her uncle would force her to marry against her wishes should an opportunity arise. Now, she had her answer. "I will not marry him," Henrietta said to his receding back.

At the sound of her voice, he stopped, turned and came toward her in measured strides, anger plainly visible on his face. "Yes, you will," he snarled.

"Randolph, listen," Aunt Clara interjected, placing a hand on his arm. "Maybe we should-"

"Leave us!" her uncle commanded, his eyes never leaving Henrietta's. "Now!"

Swallowing, her aunt glanced at her, an apologetic look in her eyes, before she bowed her head and walked away.

The second her aunt had left, her uncle's hand shot forward and his fingers curled around Henrietta's arm, pulling her closer. "Never will you speak to me this disrespectfully again! Do you hear me?" His face turned red with anger, and his breath came in rapid heaves. "Your brother left because of your impossible behaviour. Do you truly believe what you do does not affect your family as well? How is he to make a good match if you stand in his way?"

Tears came to Henrietta's eyes at her uncle's hurtful words. A part of her cautioned that her uncle was lying, that he was merely involving Tristan because he knew that her brother was her Achilles' heel. However, in that moment, Henrietta had no fight left in her. After everything she had lost, her strength finally failed her.

"You will marry him!" her uncle snarled into her face. "For once in your life, you will do as you're told. However, should you refuse, I swear I will send you from this house. You will no longer be family and forced to make your own way." He scoffed. "Although you're still unmarried, I suppose at your age, you are aware of the only way a woman can earn her own keep." He chuckled. "If you consider that preferable to marrying the marquis, then make your choice."

Releasing her arm, her uncle stepped back. "We will leave in a fortnight." Then he turned on his heel and left.

Listening to the echo of his footsteps, Henrietta stood in the large front hall, hoping that any moment now her maid would wake her from this nightmare.

However, she did not.

It was real.

By God, this was truly happening!

Chapter Five
A DUTIFUL WIFE

As though caught in a fog, Henrietta wandered the halls of her family's estate, unseeing, blind to everything around her. Reality had finally sunk to the core of her being, and yet, she could not believe it to be real. Moving through the day as though guided by an unseen hand, Henrietta found herself in her bedchamber as her aunt gave careful instructions to her maid on how to pack her niece's belongings.

"Your personal possessions can be added to the top of the trunk that holds your books," Aunt Clara told her before turning back to the maid.

Glancing around her bedchamber, the very room she had spent her life in since her parents' death, Henrietta felt anger begin to boil in her veins. How dare her uncle make such a decision for her?

"I know what you're thinking," her aunt said, jolting Henrietta from her inner turmoil. "However, I advise you to accept your uncle's decision. I assure you that he is acting in your best interest and would never have agreed to the marquis' proposal had he not believed it to be the right course for you."

Shaking her head in disbelief, Henrietta snorted. "Aunt Clara, you are a fool if you believe that!"

At her harsh words, her aunt's mouth fell open in shock. However, before she could regain her composure, a knock sounded on the door and Hampton Hall's butler entered.

Turning toward the door, Henrietta ignored her aunt's hurt face. "Yes, Harrison, what is it?"

"You have a visitor, Miss."

Henrietta frowned. A visitor? Who could possibly want to see her?

"The Duchess of Cromwell," Harrison elaborated. "She is waiting in the back parlour."

Henrietta swallowed. "Thank you."

Harrison nodded and left.

"Did you send word to her?" Aunt Clara asked, apparently having recovered from her niece's insulting comment.

"I did not," Henrietta answered her, nevertheless, her feet carried her out the door and down the staircase.

Apart from Tristan, Anna was the closest she had to family, and no matter what had happened between them, Henrietta wanted to see her before she would be shipped off to marry a barbarian from the North. Who knew if they would ever see each other again?

As Henrietta entered the parlour, she found her friend facing the tall windows that opened the room to the gardens. Her fiery hair pinned in the back, Anna sighed, and for a moment, her eyes closed and a hint of sadness fell over her face.

Swallowing, Henrietta stepped forward. "It has been a long time."

Spinning around, Anna met her eyes, and a deep smile came to her face. "It has," she whispered, taking a careful step forward. "It has been too long." She swallowed, then took a deep breath. "I have missed you."

Feeling her resolve waver, Henrietta exhaled deeply before her lips pressed into a thin line. "What brings you here today?"

A hint of disappointment came to Anna's eyes, and Henrietta felt a stab of guilt. She knew Anna did not deserve to be treated like the enemy, and yet, Henrietta could not help herself. Her world was black and white; either someone was with her or against her. There was no in-between.

"I heard your news," Anna began, a compassionate smile on her face before she shrugged her shoulders. "I couldn't just let you leave without seeing you again."

Taking a deep breath, Henrietta nodded. "Now, you've seen me."

A frown came to Anna's face, and she sighed, exasperation giving volume to her voice. "Henrietta, please! Do not act as though this does not affect you. I am your friend. Whether you believe it or not, I am your friend. And I know you better than anyone." Anna came forward, her gaze drilling into Henrietta's. "Talk to me."

Feeling tears threaten, Henrietta straightened her posture, reminding herself not to falter. "There is nothing to say."

"Do you love him?" Anna asked without preamble.

Henrietta's eyes went wide, and her insides twisted as though she had received a punch to the stomach. "If you know me as well as you say, then you know that I did not choose this."

Anna nodded. "I thought so, but I had to know." Again, she searched her friend's face. "Then how did this happen?"

"Does it matter?"

Rolling her eyes, Anna rested her hands on her sides. "Henrietta, you either tell me what happened or I'll find out from your uncle!"

Henrietta drew in a sharp breath, and her eyes narrowed.

"Aha!" Anna exclaimed. "He is threatening you, isn't he? How?"

Sighing, Henrietta closed her eyes. Then she walked around her friend and sat down on the settee, her legs trembling with the burden she carried. "He says he will send me from his house if I do not marry the marquis."

Coming to sit beside her, Anna gasped, "What? He wouldn't!"

"Yes, he would."

Observing her closely, Anna sighed. "You will not fight him on this, will you?"

Henrietta shook her head.

"Why?"

Even if she could have put into words what ached in her heart, Henrietta would never have shown weakness so openly. Not even to a friend. For only the strong survive.

"Who is he?" Anna asked.

Lifting her head, Henrietta met her eyes. "I thought you knew."

"I know his name, but who is he? Did he ask for your hand? Or did your uncle sell you off?"

Henrietta scoffed. "I thought you didn't believe him capable of such a thing."

"I do." Anna shrugged. "I just didn't want to believe it. So?"

Licking her lips, Henrietta said, "I met him once. Actually, he found me," she shook her head, "out in the woods. I was...practising." For a second, Anna seemed confused before her eyes went wide and she nodded. "Although I was disguised as a man, somehow he knew I was a woman. I don't know how."

"And?" Anna urged.

"And nothing," Henrietta said, shrugging her shoulders. "He suggested that he would find out who I was and betray my secret. I didn't think he could or even would, not until the day he came to see my uncle." She shook her head. "I don't know why though." She scoffed, meeting Anna's gaze. "Isn't it strange how similar our lives suddenly are? You received a proposal from a man you hardly knew for a reason you didn't know, and although you wouldn't have accepted him, you, too, had your reasons to do so. I suppose my time has come after all."

"What did you think of him?" Anna asked.

"What does it matter?" Henrietta snorted. "He is a brute, a far cry from a gentleman."

Anna smiled. "Gentlemen have many faces. If anything, my marriage taught me not to judge people too quickly. If you keep an open mind, you might even like him."

Henrietta laughed. "I thought you knew me. So, how likely do you believe that to be?"

Although Anna tried her best to convince Henrietta that her future was not lost, Henrietta knew that her personality and the events that had formed it and made her the woman she was today would not allow her to enter into this marriage with a hopeful heart. She would not change, could not, and just like her uncle, her husband would come to think of her as disrespectful and antagonistic, and he would hate her for it. Who knew what he would do once that happened?

Again, Henrietta saw her mother's lifeless body on the floor of the hunting cottage, a bruise darkening her left eye, a bruise that hadn't even had the chance to heal.

Despite a sense of regret that settled in her chest, Henrietta bade Anna farewell without even trying to mend the relationship that had meant so much to both of them. The time had not yet come. If it ever would, Henrietta didn't know.

Walking through the house, the only home she had ever known, Henrietta whispered her goodbyes, certain she would never return. When she came by the library, her uncle's voice drifted to her ears, and she stopped before stepping into view, listening.

"He is a marquis. I do not understand your objections," her uncle hissed, a hint of anger hardening his voice.

Her aunt drew a deep breath. "He is a foreigner. His ways are not like ours. What if he hurts her?"

"As long as she acts the dutiful wife, I doubt that will happen," her uncle replied, sounding distracted as though he was only listening with half an ear.

Henrietta was not surprised.

"You know her," Aunt Clara pointed out, a tinge of worry clouding her voice.

Her uncle chuckled. "Then maybe she'll learn the lessons I failed to teach her."

"But-"

"No!" Her uncle's voice had lost all patience. "Do not question my decision! If he is fool enough to ask for her hand, do not expect me to be the fool who denies it to him. The matter is settled. We leave for Scotland in two days."

Exhausted, Henrietta leaned against the wall and closed her eyes.

A dutiful wife?

That, she would never be.

Chapter Six

AN ENGLISH LASS COME TO SCOTLAND

Pacing the downstairs parlour of Castle Greyston, Connor stopped at the window again and again, gazing out at the lush, green hills that stretched toward the horizon. He squinted his eyes; however, all the movement he could detect belonged to a group of deer flying across the fields and vanishing in the thick underbrush of the forest.

"What are ye doing here?"

Growling under his breath, Connor turned to face his cousin.

Eyes narrowed, Alastair watched him with a hint of calculation, his gaze sweeping Connor's face and posture as though to determine whether or not it would be wise to say more. "Ye look troubled, Chief."

Connor drew in a deep breath as he detected a touch of displeasure in his cousin's voice at the formal address. He had hoped that his journey to England would allow Alastair to settle into the new situation. After all, neither one of them had had a choice in the matter. "Naw, not troubled," he replied, doing his best to sound unaffected by the sudden tension between them. "Excited. D'ye not remember the day before yer wedding? As I recall, ye were quite unlike yer usual self."

A quick smile lit up Alastair's face before he forced the corners of his mouth back down. "I do recall, aye." He swallowed, and his eyes grew serious as he stepped forward. "Why did ye not speak to me about yer plan to choose an English lass though? I do not understand. As the chief of Clan Brunwood, ye need to consider yer position. Many do not approve. Are ye aware of that?"

Connor sighed. He knew his decision had been a spur of the moment, one made without considering the effects it would have on his position in the clan. It had been quite unlike him, and he could not question his cousin's doubts. However, Connor did not regret his decision, could not, for the mere thought of that lass in his arms sent his heart into an uproar. Whatever the consequences, he would handle them!

Placing a hand on his cousin's shoulder, Connor leaned down and met his eyes openly. "Would ye have married Deirdre if she had been English?"

Alastair's eyes grew round for a moment before a deep frown drew down his brows. "Are ye saying ye chose her for love, Cousin?"

Connor chuckled, shaking his head. "D'ye not believe me? D'ye think me a spy of the English then?"

Laughing, Alastair stared at him. "Not a spy, no! Maybe a bit addled in the head!" He sobered as his eyes met Connor's once more. "Even if ye chose her for love, ye must know that her being English will make life difficult, no? Ye canna ignore the history we share. Despite the years that have passed, not all wounds are healed yet."

Connor nodded. "I am aware, Cousin. However, I do believe that the wounds of the past can only be healed by maintaining an open mind. What happened happened. We canna change that. But we can do our best to ensure that it willna happen again in the future. We're not enemies."

"I can only hope ye're right," Alastair said, the look on his face, though, held doubt. "Despite our differences in the past, I hope ye can believe that I want only yer best."

Clasping a hand on his cousin's shoulder, Connor nodded. "Aye, I do believe ye, and I thank ye for yer open words. Will ye promise me to always speak yer mind openly?"

Alastair nodded. "Aye, I will." His features softened, and a grin came to his lips. "Then tell me, Cousin, what kind of lass have ye chosen for yer bride?"

Connor laughed. "Frankly, I do believe she will claw my eyes out the first chance she'll get."

"Truly?" Alastair eyed him suspiciously. "Why exactly did ye choose her then, Cousin?"

Connor shrugged. "I'll be dammed if I know."

As her hands continued to tremble, Henrietta curled her fingers into the fabric of her skirts.

Ever since they had set out that morning, she had felt sick to the stomach. Knowing that it was the last day of their journey north, Henrietta experienced a sense of doom fall over her. She had not only been ripped from her home, but also the world she knew, and the future that lay ahead seemed darker with each turn of the carriage's wheels.

"Do not worry, my dear," her aunt said, a strained smile on her face as she glanced at the empty lands through which they travelled. "I'm certain you will find your new home to your liking."

"I'm certain you are right," Henrietta mumbled before returning her gaze out the window. As much as the empty land reminded her of the distance slowly increasing between herself and the only home she had ever known, she could not meet her uncle's eyes. Triumph gave a glow to his face that chilled her to her bones. He had always seemed cold, unaffected by her pain, but now, something else rested in his eyes that would haunt her for the rest of her life; she was sure of it.

Lost in her misery, Henrietta blinked when the sun touched a structure appearing on the horizon.

Greyston Castle. She thought and swallowed.

Taking a deep breath, Henrietta watched the imposing castle grow in size, its strong walls speaking of a prison she would never escape.

A village surrounded the walls, and smoke rose from many chimneys as the air still had a chill to it. People moved and animals stirred, their voices echoing to her ears. A mild breeze touched her cheeks as

Henrietta opened the carriage's window, and a hint of salt travelled on it, speaking of the ocean nearby.

"Finally," her uncle moaned, and the word sliced through Henrietta's soul like the axe of an executioner.

"They're here," Connor said as though to himself. Staring out the window, his eyes followed the carriage as it drew near. Surrounded by villagers, it soon passed through the open gate into the courtyard.

"Then let's welcome yer bride," Alastair replied, and together they hurried along the corridor and down the few steps to the front hall where his family stood waiting.

Alastair reached for his wife, Deirdre, who slipped her hand through the crook of his arm, a warm smile on her face as she met his eyes.

"Thank ye for arranging everything, Moira," Connor said to Alastair's younger sister. Her light-blond curls framed a strong face with piercing blue eyes, not unlike her brother's. As he stepped forward, she held out her hand to him, and he took it, giving it a quick squeeze. "I would be lost without ye."

Determined eyes looked into his as she nodded, a knowing smirk on her bold features. "As long as ye know it, Connor Brunwood. As long as ye know it."

The doors swung open then, and Connor stepped forward as Mr. Turner and his wife, followed by his future bride, climbed the few steps and entered the front hall, escaping the light drizzle that hung in the air. While her uncle's face spoke of victory, her aunt eyed her surroundings with suspicion.

As Connor glanced behind them at his future wife, he was not certain how she felt as her face was trained into a disinterested mask. Connor could only guess what emotions rested beneath.

"Welcome to Castle Greyston," he said, his voice echoing through the grand hall. "I hope yer journey was not too arduous."

"Not at all," Mr. Turner assured him as his eyes swept the assembly.

His nose crinkled ever so slightly, and Connor found his initial impression of the man confirmed.

Although polite in his manners and generous towards strangers, Mr. Turner had a calculated air about him that reminded Connor of a fanatic, someone willing to do whatever necessary to achieve a set goal no matter who would suffer for it.

Connor sighed as a stab of guilt pierced his heart. Had he not done the same? Had he not used Mr. Turner's obvious desire to rid himself of his niece in order to gain what he wanted?

His eyes shifted to his future bride, and he inhaled deeply as he saw the tension in her posture as she forced her features not to betray the emotions that surely raged in her heart. Her hands clasped together, fingernails almost digging into her skin, she stood rigid, her shoulders squared and chin raised, a proud and unyielding spark in her eyes, and yet, the slight tremble in her arms spoke of the chains that had brought her there.

Looking at her, Connor had to admit that she was a far cry from the fiery woman he had first met. Certainly, she had been distrustful of him, possibly even frightened, but he had seen the will to fight in her eyes that day in the clearing. Now, however, resignation rested heavily on her shoulders, threatening to crush her.

In order to have what he wanted, Connor had ignored her wishes and forced her hand, and in that moment as she stood before him, defiantly keeping her eyes from meeting his, Connor felt disgusted with himself.

All he could do now was make amends and hope that he hadn't destroyed the spark that had drawn him to her to begin with.

As the curious whispers behind him grew louder, Connor cleared his throat, glancing at his family, who was eyeing his future bride with open perusal while she herself pretended they did not exist.

Sighing, Connor bowed his head to her. "Allow me to introduce ye to my family," he began, and for the first time, Henrietta raised her eyes and met his.

A jolt went through Connor at the flicker that seemed to span the distance between them, reminding him why he had felt compelled to have her for his wife. Never before had a woman affected him quite like this. It went beyond physical attraction and desire. Whenever their eyes met, it was as though something flowed over him, weakening and strengthening him at the same time.

Connor knew that giving his heart to another would make him more vulnerable in many ways, and yet, it also made him feel as though he had not lived before, as though now that he had met her, his life was only just beginning. His senses seemed more alert as though he was seeing the world for the very first time.

Connor swallowed, and she averted her eyes as quickly as she had raised them.

Continuing with his introductions, Connor presented his mother, his great-uncle, various aunts and cousins, some more distant than others, but all living in Greyston and surroundings. The words flowed from his lips of their own accord for his eyes only saw her as she stood in the large hall, a hint of loss in her pale, blue gaze. Was she disheartened to be so far away from her family? Although she did not seem overly attached to her aunt and uncle, Connor knew from his enquiries that she had a brother, and he wondered why he hadn't accompanied them.

Once all introductions had been made, he had Greyston's butler escort them to their chambers in order to get some well-deserved rest after their long journey. For that very night, a festive celebration was planned in order to welcome Greyston's new mistress and present her to its people.

As she walked away, Connor felt a sense of loss, and his feet moved forward as though an invisible bond drew him to her side.

"Give her some time," his mother counselled as she came to stand beside him, a soft smile on her sharp features. As the rest of his family returned to their own activities, she placed her hand on his arm, her watchful eyes searching his face. "I did not ask before because it seemed ye wished not to be bothered with this," she said, and her eyes narrowed, "but why did ye choose the lass? She didna agree to this union, did she?"

Connor cleared his throat, holding his mother's gaze. "She didna," he admitted, shrugging his shoulders. "I can only hope that she will forgive me."

His mother nodded, and for a moment her gaze shifted to the large staircase that had carried his future bride to her chamber. She sighed, and her eyes became distant as though she was looking at something no one else could see before she opened her mouth and said, "She is a strong woman, and a proud one, but there is pain in her past, pain that echoes in her heart even today, pain that has her living in fear." Her eyes met his again. "Do not forget that."

Connor nodded, somewhat relieved that his mother's assessment of the woman he would marry the next day matched his own impression of her for he knew that his mother, like no other, possessed the ability to look into a person's soul. Never had he been able to keep anything from her if she wished to know.

However, he knew that it was a burden to his mother to know what others felt and still be unable to help them. More than once, she had told him that simply knowing something did not also set it right.

Chapter Seven
IN THE ROSE GARDEN

"Rest, my dear," her aunt encouraged her after they had retreated to their chambers. "We will see you tonight at the banquet." A strained smile on her face, her aunt closed the door behind her, her small footsteps softly echoing along the corridor as she returned to her own chamber.

Standing on the soft carpet in the middle of the room, Henrietta stared at the large four-poster bed before her eyes shifted to the vanity with the large mirror, the armoire in the corner and the small table under one of the windows with a bouquet of wildflowers on top.

Small windows opened the room to the outside. However, only dim light streamed in as the sky hung heavy with dark clouds, faint raindrops drumming on the windowpanes.

Henrietta sighed, her mind numb with the new impressions that had assaulted her that day. As much as she tried not to, she could still feel the stares that had washed over her upon her introduction. While some had held merely curious interest, others had burned with disapproval, hostility even, and Henrietta knew that she was not welcome in Greyston.

As much as her uncle wanted to rid himself of her, the people of

Greyston felt just as strongly about returning her home. Only they didn't have a choice for their chief had chosen her for his bride.

Shaking her head, Henrietta closed her eyes, sinking onto the soft mattress as her limbs grew heavy. Why had he chosen her? The question echoed through her mind. What did he want? Surely, he could have found a wife more suitable to his position.

Remembering the day in the clearing, Henrietta shivered. Although he had not been unkind or hostile, the way his sharp eyes had looked into hers and swept over her body had made her skin crawl. She had felt naked under his scrutinising gaze as though he could see through her defences and to her core.

Moreover, his physical presence had been intimidating. Although he was merely a head taller than her, he seemed to tower over her, his strong build able to crush her in the blink of an eye. Despite the foil in her hand, its sharp tip gleaming in the sun, she had felt defenceless against him.

Henrietta shivered at the thought. It reminded her too much of the night her parents had died.

What had she not done to keep that feeling at bay? To banish it from her heart and feel strong and in control? And now, here was this... this man who merely looked at her, and she felt like cowering in a hole in the ground. Was that how her mother had felt every time her father had looked at her?

Although exhaustion rested heavily on her, Henrietta could not lie down. Too much did her heart ache with the need to move, to voice her resentment about being forced into this situation, to rebel against the fate decided for her. Her courage, however, was currently lying dead at her feet.

Stepping up to the window, Henrietta glanced down into the courtyard where a loud bustle of people went about their business. Garlands were hung on the walls and in doorways. Torches were lit to replace the sun's dim light as it slowly sank below the horizon, and before long, music drifted to her ears, music like she had never heard it before. Eerie and mournful, and yet, strangely affecting.

With her eyes glued to the sight below, Henrietta wondered what her life would be like at Greyston. These people down there would be her people come the morrow. Would they come to accept her? Would she ever feel as though she belonged?

Henrietta shook her head and closed her eyes as resignation claimed her once more. Her limbs felt heavy, and she stepped toward the bed when a jolt of defiance went through her. Lifting her head and narrowing her eyes, pride swelled in her chest, and she drew in a deep breath.

No! She would not lie down and surrender. She would go out there and meet her fate with open eyes and a fierce heart. For only the strong survived.

Slipping on a cloak, Henrietta cracked open the door and eyed the corridor. When all remained still, she slipped out, carefully placing her feet on the rough floor. Passing by her aunt's and uncle's chamber, she swallowed, knowing that they would disapprove of her leaving her room and wandering the castle unchaperoned. However, what could her uncle do to her that he hadn't already done?

I will send you from this house.

As the thought echoed in her mind, Henrietta smiled. His threat held no sway over her anymore. So long as she did not offend her betrothed, her uncle's anger could not hurt her.

As she tiptoed down the staircase, Henrietta wondered if there was a way to break her betrothal. Of course, she could not do so herself. On the contrary, she would have to find a way to force her betrothed to do it for her. Would he disapprove of her wandering the castle on her own on the eve of their wedding? Would it be enough? Henrietta doubted it. What if she were to allow herself to be compromised somehow? Although she had no idea how to go about it, the idea had merit.

Reaching the grand hall, Henrietta looked around, her eyes sweeping over the tall columns supporting the next floor, the large doorways opening into parlours, a library, a music room as well as the large dining hall. Peeking inside, she found servants rushing to and fro, carrying place settings, chairs, linen, flowers and candles. A large table was set, three chandeliers dangling from the vaulted ceiling, casting their lights over the room.

When the music outside grew louder, Henrietta turned her head.

Later, she would spend enough time in the dining hall as it was. Now, she wanted to see the more casual festivities that had already begun outside. Tiptoeing across the hall, she reached a side door that opened into a large garden. Tall hedges framed a long stretch of lawn, a small fountain in the middle. Rose bushes grew near the walls, their arms climbing into the dark sky.

Following the small cobblestone path, Henrietta stepped up to the fountain, gazing at the water as it spilled out the top and fell in soft waves into the small basin. With the moon shining overhead, it glowed silver, and Henrietta reached out to touch it, its cool wetness running over her fingers.

A smile came to her face, and she wished she could simply remain in this garden forever as its peaceful tranquillity soothed her aching heart. The gurgling water and the soft tunes of the festivities mingled around her, and her trembling hands began to calm as her breathing evened. The night air smelled of conifers and wet earth, their strong aroma almost masking a faint touch of salt.

Henrietta closed her eyes, her fingertips resting on the rim of the small granite basin, its waters spilling over her fingers and chilling her skin.

Breathing in deeply, she savoured the fresh air that engulfed her as she stood silently in the night, and for the first time in a long while she felt strangely at peace. How unexpected!

A soft breeze touched her cheek, and goose bumps rose on her arms as a shiver went over her. Her eyes snapped open, and her senses reached out, exploring her surroundings. Holding her breath, Henrietta froze, her eyes darting left and right.

She was not alone.

Swallowing, Henrietta took a deep breath before she turned on her heel and came face to face with her betrothed.

A soft gasp escaped her, and she instinctively shrank back from his overpowering presence, almost losing her footing.

Quick as lightning, his hands reached for her, slipping under her cloak and settling on her slim waist, steadying her.

Henrietta's breath caught in her throat at the feel of his hands, and her eyes snapped up to meet his.

Without saying a word, he gazed at her, his eyes dark in the night as they ran over her face with such intensity that Henrietta could almost feel their touch on her skin.

As his hands slid from her sides onto her back, pulling her closer, her heart began to hammer in her chest, and fear washed over her as she found herself craving more. She wanted to know what it would feel like to be in his arms, to feel his body pressed against hers, to taste his lips on her own.

Shocked at these thoughts, Henrietta swallowed. She could not surrender. Losing a fight was one thing, but she would never willingly surrender. She could not.

A small part of her hoped that he wouldn't ask, that he would simply take what she couldn't give.

A soft smile curled up the corners of his mouth before his eyes dipped lower, tracing the curve of her lips. "Would ye grant me a kiss?"

Cursing him silently, Henrietta steeled herself. She lifted her chin and shook her head, her lips pressed into a thin line.

Watching her, his eyes became serious as he observed the delicate changes in her posture. "Because ye do not *want* my kiss? Or because ye canna *admit* that ye want it?"

A frown came to her face at his correct interpretation of her dilemma while anger surged through her at his taunting words. How dare he presume to know her?

Meeting his scrutinising gaze, she spat, "Because I do not care for it."

He chuckled, "Liar."

Henrietta's eyes widened before she glanced down at the arms that still held her. "I'd appreciate it if you'd unhand me immediately."

A soft smile came to his face as his hands remained where they were. Leaning down, he whispered, "Ye consider it a misfortune that ye were born a woman, do ye not, *Henry*?" A twinkle came to his eyes as he reminded her of their first encounter. "Ye dress like a man, ye fight like a man, and yet, everyone treats ye as a woman."

Henrietta swallowed, wondering how he knew. "I do, yes. While men are perfectly free to do as they wish, women are always at a disadvantage, always limited in their behaviour, in their choices." Averting her eyes, she tried to free herself from his embrace.

At her efforts, though, his arms tightened possessively around her. "What choice was not yers to make?" he whispered softly.

Meeting his gaze once again, Henrietta forced herself to remain calm. Somehow he already knew her too well. She would be at a disadvantage should he ever choose to...

"Ye were not free to refuse my proposal, were ye, Lass?" he asked straight-forward, and yet, a hint of disappointment clung to his voice.

"I was not," Henrietta admitted, and a delicate strength settled in her heart at having spoken the words out loud. She may not have had the choice to refuse him, but at least she had voiced her objections.

"And on what grounds would ye have refused me?"

Henrietta's eyes narrowed as she looked up at him.

"Because ye do not consider being mistress of Greyston a desirable position?" he asked, his eyes holding hers captive as he waited for her reaction. "Because ye did not wish to live so far from yer family?" He inhaled slowly before he lowered his head toward hers. "Or because ye do not want me?" he whispered, and his breath brushed over her cheek like a caress.

A tantalising shiver went down her back, and Henrietta found herself unable to withstand his penetrating gaze. Averting her eyes, she willed her hammering heart to calm down. He was so close. Too close. All she had to do was lift her head and...

Instead, she shook her head and shoved against him, trying to free herself from the powerful hold he had on her. Her strength was no match for his, though.

At her resistance, his hands slid further onto her back, pulling her closer until she stood firmly pressed against him. "Would ye have refused any man?" he demanded, his lips whispering in her ear. "Or is there someone ye would have accepted?"

At his words, the hands resting on her back tensed, and Henrietta could not keep herself from lifting her head. Looking into his face, she saw a hint of fear under the calm confidence that radiated off him with every word, every look, every motion. Did he truly fear her heart belonged to another? Did he care?

Holding his gaze, Henrietta said, "No, there is not."

Relief washed over his face, and a soft smile touched his lips before he nodded his head and his hands slowly released their hold on her.

Regret filled Henrietta when his hands dropped to his sides, and he stepped back. Pulling her cloak around her, she kept her eyes on the ground, the rose bushes or the glowing moon on the horizon, anywhere but on his face.

"I shall see ye at supper," he said in a soft voice that spoke of honest emotions.

Glancing up, Henrietta nodded her head, trying to hide how much his touch had affected her. However, when their eyes met, she could see on his face that he knew. Cursing herself, Henrietta fixed him with an icy stare, willing herself to fight the pull he had on her.

A soft smile touched his face before he inclined his head to her and then turned and walked away, the night swallowing him as though he had never been there.

As Henrietta finally released the hold on her strained muscles, she felt weak, her knees shaking as though they were pudding. Staring into the dark, she shook her head, unable to understand how he could have weakened her resolve so easily. She would have to be more careful around him.

Chapter Eight
ALONE AMONG STRANGERS

His hands still tingled with the feel of her when he made his way down into the dining hall.

When Connor had seen her step out into the rose garden, he had felt compelled to follow her, and he was glad that he had. She was the only woman who got his blood pumping with a single, defiant look.

He chuckled under his breath.

Despite her feigned disgust with the situation she found herself in, Connor had sensed her desire. It had taken all his willpower not to kiss her as she had shuddered in his arms. However, the steely resistance that she forced on her desire had stopped him. For some reason, she could not allow herself to care for him, to admit that she felt something at his touch.

But she would.

As the great hall began to fill with people in evening attire, Connor stood in a circle of cousins, their curious questions echoing in his ears. It seemed that there was not a single person in Greyston Castle who was not taken aback with his choice for a wife. Some openly spoke their minds while others merely hinted at their confusion or even disapproval of the situation, and Connor realised that a part of him had been naive to hope that they would not care that his bride was English.

The moment Henrietta followed her aunt and uncle down the large staircase, her eyes expressionless and unseeing as they swept over the assembly at her feet, a strained silence momentarily settled over the hall. Her hair pinned up with only a few tendrils dancing at her temples, she reminded Connor of the day they'd met, and he smiled as his eyes swept over her graceful neck. The emerald dress, however, was less to his liking. Not that it wasn't strikingly beautiful, accentuating her feminine attributes. Nevertheless, for a reason he could not name, it seemed like a costume on her, a far cry from the person underneath.

Greeting his guests at the bottom of the stairs, Connor held out his hand to his future bride, and after a moment of hesitation, she took it, her eyes barely meeting his. A soft tremble radiated from her hand into his own, and he noticed the tension in her shoulders.

Trying to meet her eyes, Connor gently squeezed her gloved hand, his thumb stroking her fingers.

After taking a deep breath, she looked up and met his gaze, her own betraying her discomfort with the situation.

Connor nodded his understanding and guided her toward the dining hall, inviting the rest of the assembly to follow. He led her to her chair and reluctantly released her hand before seating himself at the head of the large table.

After a multitude of toasts, most of which sounded not necessarily insincere but neither completely heart-felt, servants brought in the opulent food the kitchen staff had slaved over all day. Connor, however, barely tasted the various dishes, be they aromatic venison or fried fish, spiced vegetables or sweet fruits. His attention was irrevocably tied to the stoic woman at his side.

Silently, she ate her food like a bird, her eyes focused on her plate. No one addressed her, and neither did she speak to her aunt and uncle. Connor thought that it rather suited her and refrained from addressing her at the table as everyone within earshot would probably drop their own conversation and eavesdrop on theirs.

However, when supper came to an end, he led her away into the ballroom, and as the music began to play, the general atmosphere seemed to relax. People began to enjoy themselves as they stood up to dance, and Connor immediately guided his bride onto the dance floor, wishing for a moment of something resembling privacy.

As they began to move to the rhythm of the music, Connor watched her closely, again trying to catch her eye. When she refused to acknowledge his presence, he said, "Ye're an accomplished dancer. I'm not surprised."

At the daring tone in his voice, her gaze flew up, and a delicate frown settled on her face as she looked at him through slightly narrowed eyes.

A smile on his face, Connor waited until the music carried him closer to her before he whispered, "Would ye rather be sparing with a foil in yer hand?"

Her eyes met his, and he detected the hint of a curl to the left corner of her mouth. Encouraged, Connor asked, "I hope ye did not forget to pack it."

Again, her eyes narrowed as they slid over him, a hint of suspicion in them.

Connor laughed, enjoying himself. Although she was still a long way from putting her trust in him, they had found a way to communicate, and Connor had to admit he was looking forward to many more days spent with his wife and her sharp tongue.

***

A warm flush burned in her cheeks as Henrietta walked down the corridor toward her bedchamber. It had been a long night, and yet, she had to admit that it had not been the dancing that had put the colour in her cheeks.

Despite her best efforts to discourage his behaviour, her betrothed had rarely missed an opportunity to touch her. Whenever her hand had rested in his, his nimble fingers had massaged her skin, stroking her wrist and sending shivers down her back. More than once his hand had brushed over her back or down her arm as his breath had caressed her neck when he had leaned close to whisper in her ear. Had anyone noticed?

"Good night, my dear," her aunt said, giving her a quick hug. "It has been a long night indeed." As her uncle stood by the open door to their bedchamber, her aunt looked at her, a sad look in her eyes. "Do get some rest, will you? Tomorrow is an important day."

Henrietta nodded, a lump in her throat. "How long will you be staying?"

Her aunt sighed. "Noon."

"Noon?" Henrietta echoed in disbelief as her eyes drifted from her aunt to her uncle's disinterested face.

"I'm needed in London," he explained, his voice void of comfort or understanding, "and once you're married, there is no need for us to be here. Good night."

Retiring to her own chamber, Henrietta closed her eyes and leaned against the door.

For a short moment that night, she had been able to forget the purpose of their journey. However, now, it came rushing back, and her stomach began to twist and turn. She could not deny that she felt drawn to her betrothed. He had a physical presence that made her want to swoon into his arms. However, it was that new and unexpected desire that scared Henrietta more than spending her future in this unknown place with people who switched into the Gaelic tongue whenever she was near so that she could not understand a word they were saying.

Around him, Henrietta felt as though she could not trust herself. His presence compromised her own common sense, and she feared to lose herself, her own principles and understanding of the world. What would become of her if she allowed him to break through her defences? What would happen if he ever turned against her? Had her father always been the way she remembered him? Or had he once been a kind and caring man, a man her mother had fallen in love with?

Henrietta didn't know, and that thought scared her. If there was one thing she was certain of, it was that placing one's love and trust in someone would only lead to pain, betrayal and ultimately death.

No matter what, she could not risk it.

That night, Henrietta slept fitfully, her dreams assaulted by memories of a past long ago. When the morning came, she rose and dressed and followed her aunt and uncle down to the small chapel that sat to the side of the east wing of Castle Greyston. Her mind, however, remained focused on one thing: her mother's dead body, beaten and bruised.

As she walked down the aisle, the same disapproving faces met her that she had already seen the night before. Her future husband's second-in-command, Alastair, eyed her through slits as though she were an approaching enemy and he was taking aim to stop her. His wife, Deirdre, seemed to cower by his side while his sister, Moira, averted her gaze, her lips pressed into a thin line, anger radiating off her. Rhona, her groom's mother, watched her closely, her eyes sweeping over her as though taking stock.

Never had Henrietta felt this small and unwanted. The only one who had ever made her feel like this was her uncle.

Coming to stand by the altar, Henrietta kept her eyes cast down, unable to look at the tall stranger to whom she would be bound from now on. The priest rattled down his monologue, they mumbled their consent and then she was married.

The realisation hit her with such force that Henrietta felt as though she would sink to her knees, unable to carry the heavy weight resting on her heart and soul any longer. How could she have let this happen? All her life, she had wondered about her mother's choice to stay by her father's side. Deep down, she had always blamed her for what had happened because she had stayed, because she had not left. And deep down, Henrietta had always been certain that she herself would rather make her own way than be forced into a marriage with a man she did not trust.

And yet, here she was -- married.

How had this happened? Why had she not forced her uncle to make good on his word and allow him to send her from his house? Maybe Tristan would have stood by her after all? And even if he had not, had she not chosen a worse fate?

With a sigh, Henrietta remembered the unfinished letter she had written to Tristan before coming to Scotland. All night, she had sat over it, writing a few lines and then crumpling up the paper and tossing it aside to begin again. Words had eluded her, and in the end, she had given up. She had never finished the letter and, therefore, never sent it to her brother. If she had, would he now be standing beside her? Or would he have come for her? Would he have stood up to their uncle and protected her the way she had protected him when he had been a mere baby? Now, she would never know, and she cursed the coward that lived in her heart for robbing her of an answer.

Locked in her own doubts, Henrietta barely noticed what was happening around her. Occasionally, she caught a glimpse of her husband's face, his brows drawn down in concern as he looked into her eyes. However, Henrietta was unable to focus, and he quickly slipped from her mind.

Only when her aunt and uncle took their leave did Henrietta wake from her trance, and her eyes brimmed with tears as she watched their carriage draw out of the courtyard and head south, home.

Now, she was alone among strangers.

"Would ye like to take a stroll with us?" a soft voice asked beside her, and Henrietta turned her head, her gaze coming to rest on Deirdre. A gentle smile on her lips, the slender, young woman looked at her with compassionate eyes, and Henrietta's heart ached for the comfort she offered.

Nodding, she blinked back tears as her eyes shifted from Deirdre to Moira. The anger had vanished from the woman's face, replaced by a slightly strained smile.

"Come with us," Moira whispered as they drew Henrietta away from the festivities and toward the tranquillity of the rose garden. Passing through the main gate, they found themselves in a small oasis of peace and quiet, the sounds of the festivities only a distant echo.

"Ye must be sad to see yer aunt and uncle leave," Deirdre observed, her gentle hand guiding Henrietta to the stone bench in the shade of the outer wall. "Are ye fairly close to them?"

Sitting down between Deirdre and Moira, Henrietta sighed, "No, I'm not." Their brows drew down as they regarded her. "But they're all the family I have left."

Except for Tristan, her mind whispered.

"I canna imagine being that far from home," Moira admitted, her light hair blowing in the soft breeze. While Moira's skin tone and hair colour resembled Henrietta's, it was Deirdre's slim built that had Henrietta wonder about her own attributes. She knew she wasn't beautiful, and yet, she couldn't help but wonder what it was that had generally driven away her suitors. Why had her husband chosen her? What was it about her that appealed to him?

Deirdre gently squeezed her hand. "Do not worry. I know it must seem strange, but we are a friendly people." She smiled at Henrietta encouragingly. "And Connor seems fairly taken with ye. He is a kind man, and he will be a good husband to ye."

Feeling a blush heat her cheeks, Henrietta averted her gaze. "Thank you for your kind words," she said, meeting Deirdre's eyes again. "But..."

"Ye need a moment to yerself?" Moira asked, her bright blue eyes smiling at Henrietta as she patted her knee. "We will see ye to yer room and tell Connor not to bother ye for now."

"Thank you," Henrietta replied, grateful beyond words for their understanding. She could not have explained herself had they asked for details.

As Henrietta climbed the stairs to her bedchamber, Moira's words echoed in her mind.

For now.

Chapter Nine
AN HONEST LIAR

As the sun set over the horizon, Connor decided it was time to seek out his wife.

The wedding celebration was still in full swing when he excused himself and headed upstairs. After Deirdre and Moira had drawn her aside, she had not returned to the main hall but retreated to her bedchamber instead. Although he had missed her presence more than he would have expected, his cousins had suggested he give her some time alone.

Grudgingly, Connor had complied, seeing the wisdom in their words.

For a moment, he hesitated outside her bedchamber, arm lifted to knock, before he changed his mind and silently slid open the door.

Her bedchamber was dark; only a single candle burned on the small table in the corner.

His wife stood before the windows like a dark silhouette, staring out at the last rays of the setting sun. The far window was open, allowing in a cold breeze that played with the soft tendrils on her temple, and momentarily, she shivered, wrapping her arms about her.

Had she sensed his approach?

When he had come upon her in the rose garden, she had not been aware of him until he had come to stand behind her, and Connor had to admit he had been rather pleased with her unguarded reaction.

Stealthy as a feline circling its prey, he moved closer until the back hem of her dress carried by the soft breeze touched his legs. Gazing down at her as she stood quietly before him, Connor wanted nothing more than to reach out and draw her into his arms.

However, he knew that she would object, and so he remained quiet, savouring a rare peaceful moment.

She sighed then before her whispered voice echoed through the dark. "I know you're there."

Surprised, Connor frowned. "Did ye hear my approach?" he marvelled, thinking that he should hone his skills if a city lass had noticed him.

"I did not," she said, and a deep breath lifted her shoulders.

"Then how did ye know I was here?"

"I don't know," she whispered, then turned to face him, her bright blue eyes meeting his in the dimly lit room. "I just knew. I sensed that I was not alone, like before in the rose garden. Only now, I knew what it was."

Mesmerised, Connor stared at her. She had sensed him?

"What are you doing here?" she asked. "The music is still playing."

"I came to find ye." Unable to help himself, he reached out, cupping his hand to her cheek.

Immediately, she shrank back, her eyes widening before they grew hard.

Regretting the change in her mood, Connor smiled at her. "Ye're waiting in the wrong bedchamber, Lass," he said, his tone light.

Her eyes never wavered from his as she shook her head, taking a step backwards.

"Ye needna be scared," he whispered, keeping his distance so as not to alarm her.

"I am not scared!" she snapped, and a hint of the fight he had seen there before returned to her eyes.

Connor chuckled. "Are ye not? Ye look frightened though."

"I am not!"

Holding her gaze, Connor shot forward, pushing her back and trapping her between the wall and his body. "Liar!" he snarled, his head bent down to hers.

Gasping at his sudden attack, she stared up at him, a mixture of defiance and anger in her eyes. Her body, however, trembled in his arms, her pulse hammering in her neck proved him right. "Release me!" she demanded, her voice sounded almost pleading.

"Are ye scared?" Connor asked once more as his arms encircled her waist, pulling her against him. "Tell me, and I swear the truth will set ye free."

With her lips pressed into a thin line, she stared at him, and he could see that she was in two minds about how to reply. He knew that she was scared, and yet, she could not admit that, could not admit to a weakness. Instead, she glared at him. "Do not forget that I possess the skills to kill you," she hissed. "Nor do I lack the determination to do so."

Holding her gaze, Connor could see the desperation in her eyes. "Why would ye threaten me? Have I ever harmed ye?"

She remained still.

"Tell me, why do ye feel the need to attack me?" he asked, doing his best not to appear too threatening while neither allowing her to escape the confrontation. "Are ye scared I will force myself on ye?"

At his words, a shiver went over her, and she swallowed. "Isn't that what men do? They take what they want because they can."

Wondering about the reason for her negative outlook on men, Connor nodded his head. "Some men do," he said, looking at her imploringly, "as do some women. Let me assure ye though that I have no intention of taking something ye're unwilling to give, Lass, and I promise ye that I shall respect yer wishes," a soft smile curled up his lips, "if ye're willing to grant me a request."

At his open words, she had relaxed. Now, however, her eyes narrowed, and suspicion returned to them. "What request?"

Holding her gaze for a moment, Connor's eyes dipped down to her lips, and she drew in a sharp breath. "I would ask ye to grant me a kiss, one every day."

She exhaled slowly, and he could see that his request was not unwelcome. "I thought you would not take what I am unwilling to give?" she asked stubbornly, unable to meet his eyes.

While his right arm held on to her, his left moved upward, tilting up her face and forcing her to look at him. "Ye're not willing?" he whispered against her lips. "Ye could've fooled me, Lass."

As his mouth hovered above hers, Henrietta thought she would go mad. While her own desire urged her on, begging her to surrender, her fears screamed at her in warning.

She wanted him. Desperately. And she wanted more than just a kiss.

However, fear lived in her heart, reminding her of the price she would pay for love and trust. A kiss was not merely a kiss, but a sign of submission. If she gave herself to him, he would dominate her life from then on, and she would be caught in a web that would force her to submit to everything he demanded because she had relinquished every sense of self-worth in order to be with him.

Had her mother once had the courage to fight her father? Had she ever denied him anything?

As her fear triumphed over her desires, Henrietta met his eyes, her own hardened by the memory of her mother's fate. Knowing that she did not have the strength to fight him on a physical level, Henrietta allowed her tense muscles to relax and forced them to cease their resistance. Instead, she put all her strength and determination into her voice. "Believe what you wish," she said, her voice quiet and yet sharp as a blade. "But know that it won't change what is."

He sighed, regret marking his face. "D'ye always expect people to betray ye? To hurt ye? Or is there anyone on this earth whom ye trust, Lass?"

For a moment, Tristan's face flashed before her eyes before she shook her head and it disappeared. "There is not."

"It must be a lonesome existence," he whispered before taking a step back, his arms loosening their hold on her. "I'm certain ye have yer reasons to only expect the worst of people, and while I do not wish to prove ye right," his eyes, although soft, drilled into hers, and a fierce determination came to them that had her breath catch in her throat, "I canna sit idly by and watch ye spend yer life in fear."

"I am not-" Henrietta swallowed. "I do not understand."

"I am yer husband, and as such I am responsible for yer health, yer well-being and yer happiness," he stated, his eyes tracing the frown lines on her face, "as ye are for mine." He nodded, holding her gaze, before he stepped back, his arms releasing her. "I promise I shall always keep ye safe and protect ye even if it is from yerself."

Frowning, Henrietta stared at him. Although his words soothed the ache in her heart, she could not trust them. Men always made promises they would forget the next day, and she would be a fool to believe him. "I have always taken care of myself. I do not need your protection."

A rather indulgent smile came to his face. "That's where ye're wrong, Lass. I know that ye canna believe me now, but I shall prove it to ye." Taking a step forward, he took her hands in his and held on as she instinctively tried to yank them back. "Ye will share my room and my bed."

As his words washed over her, panic spread through her heart, and Henrietta stared at him in shock.

Softly, he squeezed her hands, his eyes gentle. "However, I promise to respect yer wishes. All I ask is that ye grant me a kiss, one for each day." For a long moment, he held her gaze openly, allowing her to see the sincerity with which he spoke, and despite her best efforts, Henrietta could not help but believe his words. "I shall always be truthful, and I would ask ye to do the same. Speak yer mind. Allow me to see who ye are. And do not fear me." A soft smile came to his lips. "I may not always like what ye say, but I shall never deny ye yer right to voice yer thoughts or punish ye for them. Again, I would ask ye to grant me the same right. Are we in agreement?"

Did she have a choice? Henrietta wondered. If she did not agree, would he still feel bound to honour her wishes? She could not be certain, and so she nodded her head, hoping against hope that he would not make her regret her decision.

"Good," he said, taking her by the hand, and escorted her out the door and down the corridor. "I've already had yer trunks brought to our chamber."

As she walked toward an uncertain future, a shiver went down her back, and his hand tightened on hers before pulling it through the crook of his arm.

When they had reached the end of the corridor, he opened the door to a large bedchamber.

A four-poster bed rested in its centre by the back wall, framed by two large windows on either side. In the corner stood a massive armoire, beside which Henrietta spotted her trunks. A circular rug occupied the left side of the room, an armchair as well as a chaise were situated along its shape.

"It is late," her husband stated, and a mischievous twinkle came to his eyes as he turned to look at her. "We should go to bed." At the evident shock on her face, he chuckled and then pointed to her trunks in the corner. "Change into yer nightclothes, and I shall do the same."

Henrietta's eyes darted around the room. "Here?"

A smile on his lips, he nodded. "I promise I shall keep my back turned...as long as ye do the same." His eyes became serious as they looked into hers. "Trust me."

Henrietta hesitated, narrowed eyes exploring his face before she snapped, "Fine."

He nodded and turned to the armoire. "Tomorrow, I shall have a wardrobe brought in for ye."

As he started to unbutton his jacket, Henrietta spun around as heat crept up her cheeks. Although she could not help but doubt his word, there was nothing she could do. If she were to turn around in order to assure herself that he was keeping his back turned and he noticed...

However, he could only notice if he were to break his word himself.

Shaking her head, Henrietta felt exhaustion wash over her. Never before had she been forced to be this alert, always aware of her surroundings, never, not for a moment, allowed to let down her guard.

As the sounds of clothes dropping to the floor echoed to her ears, Henrietta took a deep breath, and for a second was tempted to glance over her shoulder, curious what she would see. She bit her lip then as improper thoughts entered her mind and quickly turned to gather her nightgown from the open trunk at her feet.

As soon as she had untied the laces in the back, relieved to have been able to reach them on her own, Henrietta quickly allowed her dress to drop to the floor before pulling her nightgown over her head.

"Are ye decent?" her new husband asked, a touch of laughter to his voice.

Smoothing down her nightgown, Henrietta quickly tied the lace at the top. "I am," she answered, keeping her back to him. Although she was curious, she did not dare turn around as her heart hammered in her chest and her hands trembled. Would he kiss her now?

"Allow me to help ye with yer pins," he whispered beside her ear, and his breath tickled the soft skin on her neck.

Drawing in a deep breath, Henrietta stood still as his hands gently pulled the pins from her hair, dropping them on the floor, and strand after strand tumbled down. As he worked, the tips of his fingers brushed over her skin, sending her senses into an uproar. Then his hands came to rest on her shoulders, and Henrietta braced herself for what was to come.

"Look at me," he whispered, urging her to turn around. His hands again resting on her shoulders, he lowered his head and looked deep into her eyes. "I willna bite ye," he said, and for once his voice did not sound teasing.

Still, Henrietta swallowed before she raised her head. As much as he unsettled her, she would not cower before him.

A soft smile came to his lips, and his hands slid down her arms, gently grazing her skin as though no fabric separated them. Then his hands circled around her waist, once more pulling her to him, and his eyes held hers captive before they dipped lower, touching her lips.

As the imminent threat to her resolve towered above her, Henrietta averted her eyes, knowing they would reveal her innermost desires to him.

Instantly, his left hand came up to cup her cheek, once more tilting her head upward, forcing her to meet his gaze.

And so Henrietta closed her eyes instead and waited.

Suddenly blind, she could only sense him as he bent his head farther down to hers, his breath brushing over her lips. A shiver went over her, weakening her knees, and she lifted her arms, placing them on his, her fingers almost digging into his flesh as she desperately tried to remain standing.

His hand slid from her cheek to the back of her neck, holding her steady, before his lips lightly brushed hers.

A jolt went through Henrietta at his touch, and her fingers dug even deeper into his flesh.

As anticipation made her shiver, his hand nudged her head to the side before he planted a soft kiss on her cheek, his beard tickling her delicate skin.

Confused, Henrietta frowned.

"Open yer eyes," he demanded, a teasing note to his voice. "I've claimed my kiss."

Meeting his gaze, Henrietta felt a surge of disappointment sweep through her as her lips still tingled with unfulfilled desire. However, seeing the mischievous twinkle in his eyes, she cleared her throat and stepped back. "Good."

A knowing grin spread over his face, and feigned sincerity tinged his voice as he said, "I apologise if I took more than ye were willing to give."

A deep blush came to Henrietta's face, and she turned away. His hand, however, reached for hers, pulling her back.

Lifting her chin, he met her gaze. "If ye want more...," he whispered, and his voice trailed off. The look in his eyes told her everything she needed to know.

Unlike her, he did not hide his desire, and Henrietta wondered what it would be like to be free of the fears that bound her. Although she was well-aware of their influence on her, she could not in all honesty deny that they kept her safe. Had kept her safe all her life.

She could not say who she would be without them.

"I am tired," she whispered, withdrawing her chin from his grasp. Averting her eyes, she found the floor strewn with their clothes as well as her hair pins. As she knelt down to pick them up though, he stopped her once more.

"The servants will take care of them in the morning."

Henrietta's eyes swept over the room. "But..." Again, her cheeks began to burn with embarrassment. "What will they think if they find them like this?"

A low chuckle rose from his throat. "Surely, they will think we were dying to be in each other's arms and have spent a night of passionate love-making."

Gritting her teeth, Henrietta forced the rising colour in her cheeks back down. He was baiting her, and she was gullible enough to respond the way he wanted her to. When her pulse began to slow, Henrietta took a deep breath. "I bid you good night," she said in passing as she brushed by him and pulled back the covers, slipping into bed. The soft sheets welcomed her tired limbs, and she had to stifle a yawn.

"Good night," he said, a faint touch of surprise on his face as he rounded the bed and slipped in the other side. "Today was quite memorable," he whispered into the dark after extinguishing the candle. "I shall remember it fondly."

For a moment, Henrietta lay completely still, listening to the sound of his breathing and the soft rustles of the sheets as he moved, trying to get comfortable. Then the dark began to soothe her tense nerves, and as her muscles relaxed, an unexpected peacefulness spread through her. Sighing, Henrietta closed her eyes.

"I'd be much obliged if ye'd keep yer cold feet to yerself," he stated into the dark, an amused chuckle in his voice.

Instantly, Henrietta's eyes flew open, and she yanked her legs back, unaware that the warmth she had felt had come from him. Would this humiliation never end?

"However, I could think of a better way to keep ye warm."

Drawing in a deep breath, Henrietta rolled onto her side, turning her back to him, and closed her eyes. Moments later, she was fast asleep, for a few hours escaping the temptations so unexpectedly presented to her.

Chapter Ten
A FIERCE SPIRIT

When Henrietta woke up the next morning, the sun stood high in the sky, its rays reaching inside their bedchamber and bathing her face in a warm glow. As her eyes focused on her surroundings, Henrietta shot up, remembering where she was.

With her heart still hammering in her chest, her eyes searched the other side of the bed, and relief flooded her when she found it to be empty.

And yet, a frown settled on her face. Where was her husband?

Sliding from the bed, Henrietta tiptoed toward her trunk in search of a new dress when she realised that someone had picked up the clothes that had so carelessly been dropped on the floor the night before. A hint of colour rose to her cheeks, but she pushed it away determinedly.

Selecting one of her favourite gowns with a wide skirt, which allowed her legs to move more freely, Henrietta was about to pull her nightgown over her head when footsteps echoed from outside in the hallway.

A moment later, the door swung open, and her husband marched in. "Ah, ye're awake after all," he observed as his eyes slid over her in an intimate caress that raised goose bumps on her skin. Setting down the tray he had been carrying, he strode toward her. "Ye had me worried, Lass. Ye slept like the dead. I was tempted to dump a bucket of cold water on ye."

Staring at him, Henrietta didn't know how to reply. This man was impossible!

"Get dressed," he said, nodding at the gown she had chosen, "and eat something. Ye'll need yer strength for what I've planned." He winked at her then, and a devilish smile came to his lips before he turned around and marched toward the door. "I shall wait for ye in the courtyard," he said over his shoulder before turning back to look at her, "unless ye need help with yer gown."

"No," Henrietta replied, finally finding her voice.

Chuckling, he left.

After pulling on her dress, Henrietta sat down to eat. The hot tea and warm bread with butter and jam filled her belly in a most delicious way, and she realised how famished she had been. When had she last eaten?

Finally heading down the stairs in search of her husband, Henrietta felt as though she was walking through a hazy dream. How everything had changed in such a short time! Nothing seemed real, and yet, she felt the rough stone wall under her fingers and heard the faint echo of her footsteps resonate in the large hall. Stares followed her, and hushed voices reached her ears. Henrietta sighed at the realisation that this was her life now. Surrounded by people, and yet, completely alone.

"There ye are." Striding toward her across the courtyard, her husband led two horses behind him, neither one of which had a side-saddle. One was the black beast she had seen before at their first encounter while the other appeared a little more even-tempered, but no less tall. "This is Kerr. She's a kind soul with a fierce spirit," he said, handing her the reins. "I thought ye might suit each other."

Stroking the mare's nose, Henrietta eyed her husband questioningly.

"Ye didna truly expect a side-saddle?" he whispered, stepping closer, his eyes holding a challenge. "However, I could always have one brought out, if ye-"

"No," Henrietta interrupted him, running her hand over the mare's chestnut coat. "You forget I am used to riding like this." Then she pulled her skirts back, freeing her left foot, set it in the stirrup and pushed herself into the saddle with the ease of an accomplished rider.

A pleased smile on his face, her husband looked up at her. "I didna forget."

Averting her eyes lest she return his smile, Henrietta kicked her mare's flanks, urging her onward.

The wind caught in her loose hair, whipping it in her face, as Kerr carried her through the gate and onto the open plains, stretching all the way to the forest in the east and sloped back on the other side of the castle. The warm sun touched her skin, and she leaned forward, almost flattening herself to the mare's back, increasing their speed.

Racing toward the horizon, Henrietta marvelled at the sense of freedom that swept through her. If only she could ride on like this forever!

The thundering beats of her mare's hooves echoed in her ears, and only when the black beast pulled up beside her did she remember that she was not alone.

Glancing at her husband, Henrietta was surprised to see neither annoyance nor displeasure on his face, but rather the opposite. Smiling, he met her eyes, pointing to his left and the nearing tree line.

Begrudgingly, Henrietta followed his lead, and before long, they slowed down, their horses picking their way through the denser growing forest. The smell of pine and fir trees reached her nose mingling with the earthy smell of wet soil. They proceeded until they reached a small clearing, not unlike the one she had sought solace in at home.

A frown on her face, Henrietta turned to look at him, wondering why he had brought her there.

"Do not look so suspicious," he chided, rolling his eyes at her. Jumping off his horse, he tethered the beast to a low-hanging branch, then held out his hand to assist her down.

Ignoring him, Henrietta slid off her mare, landing sure-footed in the grass beside him.

Her husband laughed, "If I offer ye my assistance, it doesna mean I believe ye incapable of doing it on yer own."

"If that is indeed the case," Henrietta stated, "then you surely won't mind if I assist you out of the saddle upon our return to the castle." A challenge in her eyes, she looked at him, wondering if he would finally drop his mask and lash out at her.

He did not.

Instead, an amused chuckle rose from his throat as he stepped toward her. Skimming his thumb over her cheek, he held her gaze as his fingers travelled downward until they came to rest on her chin, tilting her head upward. Leaning closer, he whispered, "Are ye trying to anger me, Lass?"

"What if I was?" Henrietta asked, feeling her skin tingle with delight at his touch. "What would you do?"

Breathing in deeply, he searched her face, the desire to understand clouding his features. "D'ye not find it exhausting?" he asked. "To be distrustful of everyone all the time?"

"Even if that is the case," Henrietta said, not wavering under his gaze, "it does not change the fact that it is necessary. Would you let down your guard if an enemy lay in hiding, intent on doing you harm?"

"An enemy?" he whispered. "D'ye believe I would harm ye, Lass?"

"I cannot know that," Henrietta replied, "and since I do not know, I need to be on my guard. Would you consider that foolish?"

"Not in general," he admitted. "However, not everyone is an enemy. By thinking them to be, ye do them wrong."

Henrietta shrugged. "Better them than me."

A frown came to his face, laced with a hint of anger resting in his dark eyes. "Who hurt ye, Lass?"

Clearing her throat, Henrietta stepped back, leading her mare over to the trees where she tied her reins to a branch. All the while, she kept her head down, forcing the memories that had rushed to the surface of her mind back down. She did not have the strength to deal with her husband while her heart ached with the pain of the past. She needed to keep a clear head, or he would see her weaknesses.

"I am not yer enemy," he spoke out from behind her, and she spun around, her eyes taking in the two foils he was holding, one in each hand, "but at least for today, I wish to be yer opponent." Flipping one foil, he held it out to her hilt-first. "Will ye do me the honour of crossing swords with me?"

Reaching out her hand, Henrietta took the foil, unable to tear her eyes from her husband. What was he doing? Dimly, she remembered that Anna's husband had challenged her to a fencing match as well, and he had demanded spoils. Back then, Henrietta had counselled her friend not to allow herself to be fooled, that her husband was merely trying to endear himself to her in order to hide his true motives.

"Do not look so suspicious," her husband chided for the second time that day.

"Why then?"

"Because ye enjoy it, d'ye not?"

Torn, Henrietta glanced at the gleaming weapon in her hand, then back at her husband. "What are the rules?"

A smile spread over his face. "Considering that this is a training match, I hope we can agree not to injure each other."

"And should you win?"

"D'ye believe that to be possible, Lass?" he asked, his gaze searching her face before he stepped toward her and understanding lit up his eyes. "Or are ye afraid of the demands I might bestow on ye should ye lose?"

Henrietta drew in a deep breath.

His eyes narrowed. "Have ye been challenged to a fencing match before?" he asked, and his voice sounded tense as though he was afraid of the answer.

"Not me." Unwilling to elaborate, Henrietta stepped forward, foil pointing at his chest. "Shall we?"

Tying her hair in the back, she stood before him, strong-willed and relentless, and Connor wondered about the wounds of her past that had made it necessary for her to learn how to fight. Then she picked up her foil and stepped into position, her form impeccable and graceful, and unexpected pride surged through him.

Assuming the en garde position opposite her, he watched her

closely and noticed her eyes resting on his, taking account of every twitching or tensing muscle, trying to see his attack before it happened.

Grinning, he pondered how to charge her when she suddenly lunged forward, the tip of her blossomed foil coming dangerously close to his chest.

Side-stepping her attack, he stared at her, temporarily stunned with her expertise.

Pride lit up her face, and the honest smile that lifted the corners of her mouth took his breath away. She was radiant!

Back and forth, they went across the clearing, attacking and retreating, and Connor revelled in the joy that came to her face. "Who taught ye how to fight?"

"My brother," she said, forcing him down the clearing once again.

Her brother? He wondered. What kind of a man would teach his sister how to fight and then not even appear at her wedding? "Has he passed on?"

At his words, she froze, staring at him wide-eyed. Then she swallowed and shook her head. "No. Why would you ask that?"

Seeing the emotions raging within her, Connor lowered his foil and stepped forward. "I couldna help but wonder why he didna come to our wedding."

"You would not understand." Momentarily, her eyes sank to the ground before she once more raised her foil to his chest.

"And yer parents?"

A low growl rose from her throat, and she charged him.

More prepared this time, Connor side-stepped her attack and grabbed her sword hand, twisting the foil out of her grasp. Then he dropped his own and grabbed her by the arms. "Anger willna serve ye," he said as she fought against him. "Yer strength is nothing against mine. Yer only advantage is yer speed, yer flexibility." He lowered his head to hers, and she stilled. "If I get my hands on ye, ye're finished."

"You're wrong!" she snarled, and he saw a spark of pain lurking out from somewhere under the anger that controlled her.

"Is it?" he demanded. "Then free yerself!"

Holding his gaze, she remained still. Her eyes, however, shot daggers at him. "Release me!"

"What will ye do if I refuse?"

With her lips pressed into a thin line, she glared at him. "You cannot intimidate me!" she growled. "I'd rather die than bow my head to you!"

Seeing the determination clearly edged in her face, Connor took a deep breath, wondering what had made her so fearful of submitting defeat in a friendly match, of admitting a weakness to a companion-at-arms. From the raging anger he had witnessed, he thought it quite likely that her parents' marriage lay at its core.

From his enquiries, Connor knew that her parents had passed away when she had been a little girl, but for the life of him, he could not imagine what had happened to make her so distrustful of everyone around her. Whatever it had been, it had forced her out of reality and into a world where she could be strong and no one could harm her as long as she did not surrender.

Only, she was wrong, and she needed to know that.

Considering his options, he spun her around and forced her backwards until her back collided with the large trunk of a tree. A hint of fear in her eyes, she looked up at him, her hands still clawing at his arms. Only when his body pressed into hers and his head bent down to her lips did she still, a tremble shaking her delicate frame. "Admit defeat," he whispered, and her head snapped up, staring at him as though he had just struck her.

She swallowed, and her features hardened. "No! Never!"

Growling under his breath, he held her tighter until she gasped. "Surrender now or I swear I will take what ye're unwilling to give." Her lower lip trembled as she continued to stare at him. Then, however, her gaze travelled downward to touch his lips, and a slight shiver shook her.

Connor frowned. "Maybe ye're not unwilling at all," he whispered, and her eyes returned to his, "just afraid to admit what ye want."

As Connor searched her face, her features hardened once again as though she had just made up her mind. Defiance burning in her eyes, she snarled at him, "You asked me to trust you. You gave me your word only last night, and this morning, you are already willing to break it." She snorted. "Do you truly wonder why I am distrustful of the people around me?" She shook her head, sadness falling over her features. "Because they cannot be trusted. It is that simple."

Reminded of his promise, Connor hesitated. Although he wanted her badly, he had no intention of forcing himself on her. However, he needed her to understand her limits. With this overbearing attitude, she would only put herself in danger.

Swallowing his pride, he tightened his hold on her, his features hardening to match hers. "I have no intention of breaking my word," he growled, "merely of proving my point."

"What point?" she hissed. "That men are barbarians, slaves to their primal urges?"

A vile laugh echoed from his throat. "That yer strength is no match for mine."

As though by reflex, her eyes narrowed. "How dare you?"

"Surrender, and I shall release ye!"

Glaring at him, she shook her head.

Determined to make his point, his hand abandoned its place on her arm and slid lower. All the while, his eyes observed her face, seeing the delicate changes as she began to understand his intention.

She held her breath as his hand moved down her thigh, gathering a fistful of her skirts. "I could just lift yer skirts," he threatened, his gaze holding hers, "and take ye right here, right now. Could ye stop me?"

Her lower lip trembled, and he could see her struggle between the desire she clearly felt but couldn't admit to and the need to defy him and stand her ground.

"Could ye stop me?" he demanded once more, his hand moving upwards, dragging her skirts with it.

Instantly, her own hand fell from his chest and gripped his, stilling its progress. Her eyes met his before she dropped them, and her jaw tightened as she clenched her teeth. "No."

For a second, Connor wasn't sure he could believe his ears. However, the pained look on her face spoke volumes, and so he released her, reluctantly stepping back. "I do not mean to belittle yer abilities," he said, compassion ringing in his voice. "I simply mean for ye to see the truth. Ye do not possess the strength to stop me, and the sooner ye accept that the better. Ye are more capable of defending yerself than most women."

Her eyes left the ground and met his.

"Ye are." A reassuring smile on his face, he nodded. "And it makes me proud. But ye must not allow yerself to believe that ye're invincible. Ignoring yer limitations makes ye vulnerable. Embrace yer weaknesses, and they will make ye stronger."

Like the picture of misery, she stood with her head bowed, shoulders slumped, and so Connor did the one thing he knew would force her out of it. "En garde," he said, snatching his foil off the ground.

The flicker of a smile played on her lips as she bent down to retrieve her own, and Connor felt the tension of the last few minutes leave his body.

Chapter Eleven
A QUESTION OF RESPECT

When the sun finally began its descent, they mounted their horses and headed back to Greyston. Feeling the wind on her flushed cheeks, Henrietta smiled at the beautiful scene before her.

With the sun in its back, the ancient castle shone like a golden treasure. Hues of red and purple streaked across the dark blue sky, its brilliant colours trying to outshine the dark green of the earth, its meadows and woods vibrant with life.

Many years had passed since Henrietta had truly enjoyed herself, at least for the moment forgetting the battle she fought with the world day in and out. Although her fears had kept whispering warnings to her, the joy her body and mind had experienced at having a real opponent challenge her abilities, allowing her to explore herself, had soon overpowered the echo of her fears.

Now, racing across the plains toward the main gate, Henrietta felt reality slowly catching up with her as her eyes fell on the people of Greyston going about their business. As expected, the moment they entered the courtyard, all eyes were on them. Faces scrunched up with distrust and hostility stared at her, observing her carefully as though hoping to catch her at something unacceptable, proving them right.

How could her husband fault her for being distrustful herself? It was simply good sense.

"Were ye planning on helping me off this horse any time soon?"

Turning to look at her husband, Henrietta found him sitting atop his black beast, a challenging gleam in his eyes. "Are you mocking me?" she asked, her eyes taking in the many people in the courtyard.

Guiding his horse closer to hers, he met her eyes openly. "Not at all, my lady. However, ye challenged me, and like yourself, I wouldna run from a challenge."

"Why?" she frowned, wondering if he had an ulterior motive.

He sighed. "To prove my respect for ye, Lass. If this is important to ye, then I have no objections."

Shaking her head, she slid off her horse, the flicker of a smile touching her lips. Oh, why did he have to be so charming?

Stepping around her mare, her features back under control, Henrietta held out her hand to him. A smile on his face, he took it, his skin warm against hers, then swung over one leg and slid to the ground. "I thank ye kindly, my lady," he said, grinning at her before he bent forward and kissed her hand.

"Now, you are mocking me!"

A grin came to his face. "Maybe a little," he admitted, then took the reins from her. "Head on upstairs, Lass. Supper shall be served shortly. I suggest ye change."

Frowning, Henrietta glanced down at her dress, which was dirt-stained and dishevelled.

"Ye might wanna consider a bath." He grinned. "If ye need assistance..."

Henrietta swallowed. "Thank you, but no. I'll manage." Then she tore her gaze away from the mischievous twinkle in his eyes that sent shivers up and down her back and quickly walked away.

Soaking in the large tub, Henrietta wondered about everything that had happened that day. Despite his rather harsh lessons, she could not even hate him for the many times he had grabbed her with rough hands. On the contrary, his closeness excited her and made her forget the many lessons she had learnt throughout her life.

Henrietta knew her own reaction to him to be unwise, and she couldn't help but feel ashamed for allowing him to subdue her so easily. In the future, she would have to be more careful. But how could she when his mere presence sent delicious tingles into her belly?

Entering the dining hall on her husband's arm, Henrietta found herself the centre of attention once more. She could only hope that time would lessen their interest and prove to them that they had nothing to fear from her. However, that day had not yet come, and so she spent most of the meal with her eyes focused on her food, here and there exchanging a word with her husband.

Concern in his eyes, he seemed genuinely distressed about the situation. However, others also demanded his attention, and so Henrietta was relieved when Moira and Deirdre smiled at her from across the table. Returning their kind gesture, Henrietta's eyes were drawn to an older man sitting farther down the table. His dark eyes seemed to be burning a hole into her skull, his lips contorted into a snarl.

A cold shiver went down Henrietta's back. She had seen this man before. At her wedding, he had glared at her with the same hatred in his eyes, reminding her of the disgusted look her uncle occasionally bestowed on her as though she had no place in his world and wished he could remove her at the first possible opportunity.

After supper, Alastair demanded her husband's attention and excusing himself, Connor walked away, his cousin by his side.

Left to her own devices, Henrietta decided to return to her bedchamber when Deirdre and Moira came toward her.

"Don't mind them," Deirdre said, her eyes glancing around them at the questioning stares directed at Henrietta. "They're just curious. Ye're quite the curiosity in these parts."

Henrietta shrugged, trying her best to ignore the people around her. "They don't want me here," she said, drawing a deep breath as her eyes fell on the old man who had glared at her from down the table. Limping, he crossed the great hall, then disappeared through a side door.

"That's Angus," Moira explained. "Do not mind him. He hates the English."

"Why?"

For a moment, Moira looked at her as though unsure how to

answer the question directed at her. "'Tis history. Sixty years ago, it was the English who destroyed the Scottish clans. Angus was a young boy then." She met Henrietta's eyes, and below the sadness that clouded her own, there was a shimmer of something hidden. "The English executed his father before his verra eyes."

Henrietta gasped, "How awful! I'm so sorry."

Deirdre placed her hand on Henrietta's arm. "No one in their right mind would blame ye for what happened back then. However, some people have long memories, and the past still burdens them. It's a pain they canna let go of a pain that keeps their hatred alive." Shaking her head, she swallowed. "It saddens me to think of their suffering. It serves no purpose, for it only spreads misery."

Understanding only too well how the past could hold its sway over one, Henrietta swallowed, wondering if she would ever be accepted by the people of Greyston Castle. How could she expect them to abandon the pain learnt through lessons of their own past when she was unwilling to do so herself?

As Alastair returned to the great hall, his eyes searched the vaulted room until he found his wife. Starting toward her, he stopped as his gaze fell on Henrietta.

Seeing disapproval on his face, Henrietta excused herself, then quickly turned away and left in the opposite direction. She had no idea where she was going, but she did not have the strength to face another person holding a grudge against her because of something she had had no control over.

Walking on, Henrietta found herself in a part of the castle she hadn't seen before. Paintings of former clan chiefs decorated the walls, their eyes following her as though they, too, disapproved of her presence. Goosebumps rose on her arms as the last rays of the sun disappeared, dipping the world in black.

After a small eternity, Henrietta found a staircase that led up to the next floor. Heading upstairs, she proceeded down another long corridor until the echo of voices reached her ear, and before she knew it she found herself up on the gallery. Looking over the banister, she found the spot where she had stood with Deirdre and Moira not too long ago. Now, however, they were nowhere in sight.

Fortunately, realising where she was in reference to the great hall, Henrietta now knew how to find her bedchamber. She headed back toward the east wing, turned around a corner and then walked down the long corridor, wondering if she would ever be able to navigate this place with ease.

Not long after, her surroundings began to look familiar, and Henrietta was just about to turn the last corner when Alastair's angry voice hit her like a slap in the face. "I told ye. I do not want ye speaking to that woman!"

Henrietta stopped, ears alert and listening.

"But husband," Deirdre said, her voice soft, "how can ye speak so? She is all alone in a foreign land. She needs someone to speak to."

A smile came to Henrietta's face at Deirdre's compassion, and she leaned forward, peeking around the corner.

"She is not my concern," Alastair snarled, towering over his slender wife, his eyes ablaze with anger. "Ye are, and I do not wish for ye to be affected by her. Ye stay away from her. D'ye hear me?"

"But-"

"D'ye hear me?" he growled, grabbing his wife by the arms.

For a moment, she met his eyes, then lowered her gaze and sighed. "Aye."

"Good." Relaxing slightly, Alastair released her. "Connor is the one who married her. She's his responsibility. Let *him* deal with her."

As they returned to their bedchamber, Henrietta leaned back against the wall and closed her eyes as images of her parents flooded back into her mind. Her father's angry snarl, demanding her mother's submission, and her mother's whimpered sob, granting it without a fight.

The root of her fear still existed. Henrietta knew that. Once again, she had found proof that her fears were not unfounded. Not only her parents fit the picture of misery in a marriage, many others did as well, and she would do everything within her power not to follow in their footsteps.

Standing at the window of her bedchamber, Henrietta looked down at the soft lights of the village as it sat snug in the embrace of the large castle. The sun had finally abandoned its post, allowing the moon to bathe the world in a silvery glow. The sight was peaceful, and yet, Henrietta knew that anger stirred underneath.

"Are ye all right, Lass?"

At her husband's voice, Henrietta turned to face him. "I'm fine," she shrugged. "Just...thinking."

"About what?" he asked, coming toward her. His eyes met hers, and she saw the same hint of concern in them that she had noticed over supper.

Again, Henrietta could feel her defensive walls sink into the ground, and she cursed herself for her weakness. After everything she had been through, she had expected more from herself. Had life not hardened her? Taught her to protect herself?

Yes, it had. She realised. However, her heart and mind refused to walk hand in hand. While she knew to be careful, her heart refused to cooperate, solely focused on its own desire.

"They will come to see ye for who ye are," her husband said when she remained quiet, his dark eyes seeing the turmoil within her as though she were made of glass.

Henrietta shook her head. "And who am I?" she asked, lifting her eyes to his. "I thought I knew, and yet, ..."

Placing his large hands on her shoulders, he bent his head to hers. "Look at me, Lass." A soft smile came to his lips as she did. "We're not always the same. Ten years ago, I was not the same man I am today. People change. They learn and grow, and that's a good thing." He softly squeezed her shoulders. "I know that yer past taught ye to be distrustful of people, and it helped ye stay strong. It helped ye fight when ye needed to. Maybe now, 'tis time for ye to learn something new and change and grow." His arms slid from her shoulders down her arms and once more came to rest on her waist as though they belonged there. "But that doesna mean ye're not true to yerself."

As his arms held her, Henrietta wanted nothing more but to rest her head against his strong chest. Her fears, however, could not be so easily silenced or persuaded to abandon their post. His words rang true, and yet, she was helplessly drawn into the familiar abyss of the past that haunted her life. Would she ever escape it? Could she ever live unsheltered by her fears?

"Lass," he whispered, and she looked up at him, his dark eyes shining with a promise that warmed her heart. "Ye're not alone. Whoever abandoned ye in the past, canna touch ye anymore. Ye're safe here."

When her mind absorbed his words though, Henrietta stiffened. "No one abandoned me." Twisting out of his embrace, she pushed past him, ignoring the warmth his words had sparked in her heart. "You know nothing of what you speak. I have a family. I am not alone." Raising her head, she faced his questioning eyes. "And even if I was, I wouldn't mind. No one needs to protect me."

A hint of annoyance in his eyes, her husband scoffed, "No one wants to be alone, and every once in a while, we all need someone to protect us. If ye were not so mule-headed, ye would see that." As he inhaled slowly, she could see the muscles in his arms tremble with the effort to remain still. "I'm trying my best to be patient with ye, but yer antagonistic attitude thwarts my efforts at every turn. To be frank, 'tis verra frustrating." Raking his hands through his hair, he stared at her as though unsure what to do with her.

In Henrietta's mind though, a distant voice echoed with disgust and hatred as cold eyes looked at her with disdain. *Always arguing. Always disrespectful. Always antagonistic.*

Her uncle's words had stabbed her heart in a way she still could not understand. Somehow, they had shaken her confidence, and she had stumbled to her knees, her once unshakable belief to be acting with reason dead at her feet.

As she regarded her husband, her eyes hardened, and once more her defensive walls soared into the air, guarding the precious, little part of her soul that had survived the atrocities of her past. Why would he not leave? Could he not see that his words wounded her?

Swallowing the tears that threatened, Henrietta crossed her arms. "I never asked you for your opinion, and I'd appreciate it if you would keep it to yourself. You know nothing about my life as I know nothing about yours." She took a deep breath as her jaw clenched. "You made a mistake when you married me. I can only hope that you have finally come to realise that." Turning on her heel, she headed for the door without a clue where to go.

As Henrietta reached for the handle, a soul-stirring shiver went over her, and before she even felt his hands on her arms, she knew he was there.

Anger edged into his face, he spun her around, and her head snapped up, her eyes drawn to his as though by an unseen force. "I've made quite a few mistakes in my life," he growled, his voice heavy with emotion, "but marrying ye was not one of them. Of that I am certain." He lowered his head to hers, his penetrating gaze searching her face. "Go ahead, Lass, spit and bite, but ye will not drive me from yer side."

Henrietta took a deep breath, inwardly cursing his name. How was it that he always knew to tear down her walls with but a few words?

Pulling her into his arms, he swallowed, the anger leaving his face. "I believe ye still owe me a kiss, Lass."

Determined to keep him at a distance, Henrietta turned her head, offering her cheek. She felt drained and had no more strength left to fight him.

His left hand moved upward and cupped her cheek as he leaned forward, his warm breath caressing her skin.

Henrietta held her breath, willing her heart to still.

When his lips grazed her cheek though, moving sideways and farther down her neck, her knees grew weak and her hands curled into the fabric of his shirt, seeking to steady her. Ever so softly, his lips moved over her skin, nipping here and stroking there.

Chills ran up and down her body at his touch, so light and yet so intimate, that Henrietta gasped for air. Closing her eyes, she leaned against him, her body shuddering as his lips closed over the hammering pulse in her neck, sucking gently.

Then his lips moved upward and playfully nipped her earlobe before an amused chuckle drifted through the hazy fog clouding her mind. "Again, I apologise for taking what ye wouldna give."

As her eyes snapped open, Henrietta pushed herself off him, her face flushed as she stared at him in shock and humiliation. He grinned at her then, and her jaw clenched. "How dare you? You're doing this on purpose!"

His eyebrows went up. "Doing what on purpose?" Stepping forward, he held her gaze. "Are ye saying ye enjoyed my kiss, Lass?"

"No!" Henrietta spat. "Of course, not."

Again, he chuckled. "Liar!" As he shook his head at her, all mischief left his face and his eyes became serious. "Why can ye not admit that ye enjoy my touch? What are ye afraid of? That it will make ye look weak to admit that ye seek another's embrace?"

Clenching her teeth, Henrietta shook her head stubbornly. "I do not need anyone. I am not afraid to admit anything."

"Puh! Ye mule-headed woman! Can ye not see that this is the same as believing ye're invincible? Admitting to a weakness doesna make ye weak!" Raking his hands through his hair, he stared at her for a long time before his shoulders relaxed and he inhaled slowly. "Sleep on it, Lass, for I willna walk away from this." For a second, his eyes held hers before they dipped lower and touched her lips. "Tomorrow, ye'll owe me another kiss, and I swear I'll make ye feel something." Stepping forward, he leaned down to whisper in her ear. "Remember that, Lass."

Then he opened the door and left, his receding footsteps echoing to Henrietta's ears as she sank to the floor, shaking with his threat to challenge her once more as well as his promise to touch her heart.

Chapter Twelve
COMFORT & COUNSEL

My dearest Anna,

Sighing, Henrietta stopped, unsure how to put the confusion that raged in her heart and mind into words. However, if anyone could understand, it was Anna.

A hint of guilt washed over Henrietta as she remembered the harsh words she had spoken when her friend had come to her seeking comfort and counsel. Back then, Henrietta had been unable to give what she was now hoping for herself. Never before had her heart been touched by a man in such a way that she could have imagined Anna's predicament at finding herself wanting to believe that her husband cared for her. To Henrietta, it had been clear that that was not possible.

Now, she was not sure.

. . .

If you tear up this letter without reading it, I cannot blame you. However, if you read this, please know that I am deeply sorry for treating your heart's desire with such stubborn disregard. I assure you that I only acted the way I did because I truly believed my advice to be in your best interest.

As you know I never spoke about my parents and what happened to them. However, I wish to confide in you now in the hopes that it will allow you to understand the reasons behind my actions.

As far as I can remember, my mother had always submitted to my father's every wish. Without complaint, she always did as she was told, never standing tall, never demanding respect for herself. My father used her compliance, her powerlessness to exact his authority, and it cost her dearly.

I would have had a little sister had she not been stillborn after my father subjected my mother to another beating. I will never forget her little face, a shimmering bruise on her perfect little head.

Deep down, I thought losing her daughter would finally allow my mother to stand up for herself, for me. However, it did not. Nothing changed. I suppose her will had been broken before I was even born.

When I was five years old, my father killed himself, but not before taking my mother's life. That day, I swore to myself that I would never allow myself to be treated the way my father had treated my mother, that I would fight no matter what, and that I would never allow myself to be fooled into believing someone trustworthy.

Anyone.

And now, I cannot change. I am who I am, and I spoke to you the way I did because I feared you would one day wake up and find yourself trapped in the same hell. I never wanted that for you. I hope you can forgive me for not trusting your instincts.

Tears ran down her cheeks and dropped onto the letter. As the lines blurred before her eyes, Henrietta sat back and closed her eyes, remembering the hurt look on her friend's face. And yet, upon hearing of Henrietta's betrothal, Anna had come to see her, offering comfort and counsel.

. . .

Are you happy? I apologise for being so blunt, however, this is the question that plagues me. Is your husband the man you thought him to be? Has he ever made you regret that you put your trust in him?

Hesitating, Henrietta drew in a deep breath. She knew she ought to write more and speak about the questions that lived in her heart with regard to her own husband. Surely, Anna would counsel her wisely. However, she could not even admit the budding emotions in her heart to herself, let alone put them into words.

And so, she simply signed the letter and folded it up, handing it to her maid to be sent out immediately.

Feeling restless, Henrietta left her chamber and headed downstairs. However, when she crossed the great hall, all eyes came to rest on her, even if only for a moment, and Henrietta steeled herself against the disapproval pelting her soul from all sides. Her head high, eyes focused, she slipped out the side door to the courtyard.

Coming to a halt, she found her husband standing by the stables, discussing something with Ewan, the stable master. Not too far stood the old man, Angus, leaning on a cane, his pale eyes narrowed as he observed her husband, lips distorted into a sneer.

A shiver went over Henrietta at the sight, reminded once again of her uncle's snarl. How often had she seen him stare at her brother that way? She didn't know, and no matter what Tristan had done, it had never been enough. It had never pacified her uncle or changed his opinion.

Afraid her presence would only serve to anger the old man further, Henrietta turned and headed around the front entrance. In need of solitude, she entered the rose garden. However, as her eyes swept over the green oasis, dotted with brilliant reds here and there, she felt too restless to appreciate its calm beauty. Her heart thudded in her chest, and her feet forced her onward.

With a longing gaze at the water fountain, Henrietta walked down the cobblestone path until she reached the end of the small garden, her path barred by a tall-growing hedge. Reluctant to turn back, Henrietta followed a soft noise that echoed through the thick, green barrier, finding herself intrigued.

Someone was humming a melody.

Curious, Henrietta stepped up to the hedge, her eyes gliding over its leaves, seeking a hole in their midst that might allow her a glimpse at the other side. Unsuccessful at first, she soon came to the point where the hedge connected with the outer wall...leaving a small gap in-between.

Smiling, Henrietta stepped forward, pressing her back to the cold stone wall as she squeezed through. When leaves scratched her face, she closed her eyes until she had reached the other side, and the warm rays of the afternoon sun touched her face.

As her eyes swept over the sight before her, Henrietta sighed.

Scarcely the size of her bedchamber, the small garden seemed to be another world. Locked in by the inner and outer wall as well as tall-standing hedges, it harboured a number of carefully tended vegetable patches. The smell of wet earth and sunshine hung in the air, mingling with the aromatic scents drifting up from the small plants to her feet.

"So, ye've found my sanctuary."

Eyes snapping to her right, Henrietta found herself staring at the small, dirt-stained figure of Deirdre Brunwood.

A smile on her face, Deirdre stepped forward, brushing her hands on a large apron that did very little to protect her dress from the wet soil beneath her feet.

"I'm sorry," Henrietta said. "I didn't mean to intrude."

"Do not worry," Deirdre laughed, a warm glow on her face as she met her eyes. "I don't mind."

"What is this?" Henrietta asked as her eyes swept over the small space. "This does not look large enough to provide enough vegetables for the castle."

Deirdre laughed. "'Tis not. This is just...," she shrugged, "...my favourite place in the world." Taking Henrietta's hand, she drew her forward, and they walked the length of the garden with Deirdre pointing out the different kinds of vegetables she was growing.

"It's peaceful here," the young woman elaborated. "Sometimes the noise of the castle overwhelms me, and then I come here and I feel better."

Henrietta nodded. "I understand. However, I admit I was surprised to see you here. I suppose as Alastair's wife, you do not need to tend the gardens, do you?"

Deirdre laughed. "I do not, no. I am not here because I have to, but rather because I find it enjoyable. In fact, Alastair does not like it," she admitted, "but he would never deny me something that makes me happy."

Henrietta frowned, remembering the scene she had witnessed the day before. "Why would he mind?"

"He always worries about me," Deirdre said, a hint of sadness in her eyes.

Remembering her mother's expressionless face, Henrietta felt her hands ball into fists. "Does he ever...?" She swallowed, hoping she would not offend the young woman. "Does he ever get angry with you?"

Deirdre's eyes met hers, then narrowed for a second before she nodded. "Ye saw us, didn't ye? I thought I'd heard something."

"I'm sorry."

Deirdre shook her head. "Don't be. I have nothing to hide." Stepping forward, Deirdre met Henrietta's eyes. "Aye, he does get angry with me sometimes, but he wouldna lay a hand on me if that's what ye're thinking."

"I didn't mean to pry," Henrietta said, an apologetic smile on her face. However, deep down, she felt reminded of her mother and how she had always laughed at people's concerns whenever someone happened to spot a bruise and had provided a perfectly reasonable explanation. "I need to go," Henrietta said, determined to help Deirdre whether she wanted her help or not.

"Ye're welcome to come back anytime," the young woman said, a smile on her face as she turned back to her plants.

Uncertain as to how to proceed, Henrietta wandered the castle. What could she do? She needed to help Deirdre, but how? She was a foreigner. No one would believe her if it was her word against Alastair's, and Deirdre seemed unwilling to tell the truth, hiding behind lies. Did she have bruises on her arms from when her husband had grabbed her? Would that be enough to convince others? But who could she tell? Would her husband believe her? From what she had gathered, he and Alastair were good friends.

Moira. Henrietta thought. She and Deirdre were close; maybe she would listen. However, Moira was Alastair's sister, was she not?

Before Henrietta had made a conscious decision about what to do, she found herself outside Moira's chamber. Taking a deep breath, she raised her hand and knocked on the door.

Footsteps echoed from inside, and then the door was opened. "Henrietta," Moira greeted her, surprise evident in her large eyes. "Is something wrong? Ye look flustered?" Stepping back, she ushered her inside.

"Thank you," Henrietta said. "To tell you the truth, I am not certain." Seating herself in the armchair Moira had indicated, she folded her hands in her lap. "I am worried about Deirdre."

"Deirdre?" A confused frown on her face, Moira sat down across from her. "Has something happened?"

"I saw her last night," Henrietta began, entirely uncertain whether or not she was doing the right thing. "Alastair was angry with her for speaking to me." She swallowed. "Very angry."

Moira sighed. "Aye, he's been a bit irritable ever since Connor was named tanist, and when Connor brought home an English bride, I suppose he thought his own doubts justified." She shrugged. "'Tis difficult to explain, but everyone, including Alastair, has always assumed that he would be next in line. The title of clan chief is passed on by vote within the blood kin of a generation before it moves on to the next. After Uncle Hamish died, Alastair as the oldest ought to have been named," she explained. "It came as quite the surprise when Connor was chosen instead."

"Could Connor not have refused?" Henrietta asked, finding herself intrigued with the inner workings of clan life.

Moira shrugged. "'Tis a high honour. I don't think he wanted to offend anyone. So he accepted and named Alastair tanist in order to show good faith."

"But why was Alastair not named? Did something happen?"

Moira shrugged. Her eyes, however, wouldn't meet Henrietta's.

In that moment, the door flew open, and in walked no other than Alastair Brunwood, his face tense, his eyes burning with anger. "Moira, I-" As his gaze fell on his sister's visitor, they narrowed and the muscles in his jaw tensed. "What is she doing here?" he growled at his sister. "Did I not tell ye to keep yer distance?"

Jumping to her feet, Moira glared at him. "Ye canna tell me what to do, Alastair. I told ye that before."

Drawing in a slow breath, his eyes shifted to Henrietta.

Rising to her feet, Henrietta fought to keep her composure as the anger seeping off him hit her like a punch in the gut. Her head up, she met his glare, her own unflinching; her heart, however, was hammering in her chest, torn between alarm and outrage.

As he stepped closer, Alastair's calculating eyes swept over her face, and Henrietta swallowed. Then he took a deep breath and exhaled slowly, seeking to control the anger that burned within him. "I would ask ye to stay away from my wife," he hissed through clenched teeth.

A cold shiver went down Henrietta's back. "Why would you ask that? Because I'm English?"

A snort escaped him, and the left corner of his mouth curled up into a sneer. "Do not presume to know anything about me," he whispered, his voice low and threatening.

"Alastair, please!" Moira said and stepped forward, placing a calming hand on his shoulder.

Her brother shrugged her off though, his eyes not veering from Henrietta. "My wife is a gentle soul," he said, a hint of emotion echoing through his anger, "and I don't want her poisoned by yer anger." He leaned closer. "Stay away from her, d'ye hear me?"

"What is going on here?"

While Henrietta's eyes widened at the sound of her husband's irritated voice, Alastair's face betrayed no emotion at all.

Walking into the room, her husband eyed the situation before him with care. As their eyes met, Henrietta thought to see an unspoken question in them, and without thought, she nodded her head.

Instantly, his shoulders relaxed, and he came to stand beside her, his eyes fixed on Alastair. "Explain yerself, Cousin," he demanded.

Alastair shook his head. "I've nothing to say. Ye've made yer choices, and I've made mine."

Her husband drew in a slow breath. "Would ye excuse us?" he said into the room, then gestured for Alastair to follow him.

After the door closed behind the two men, Henrietta exhaled the breath she'd been holding. "What will happen now?"

Moira shrugged. "I can only hope Alastair will be able to accept the way things are now. If not..."

Chapter Thirteen
RUMOURS

"Why would ye speak to my wife in such a disrespectful way?" Connor demanded after slamming shut the door to his study. "Explain yerself."

"I have nothing to say," Alastair growled. With hands linked behind his back, he stood immobile like a stone column; only the muscles in his face seemed to twitch with the effort to control his emotions.

Connor took a deep breath. After all, Alastair was his friend and confidante. They had known each other all their lives, and he not only needed his support but he also wanted his respect. "D'ye see me as yer enemy?"

Alastair met his eyes, but remained silent.

Dread flooded Connor's heart. Although he had been aware that choosing an English woman for his bride would stir up emotions, he had not expected his friend to react the way he did. "Are ye angry because I chose an English lass or because I didna choose yer sister?"

Alastair's eyes narrowed. "Ye should know me better than to ask that question."

"I thought I did."

"Do not blame me for the problems ye've caused," Alastair snarled.

"Ye acted without consulting me. But ye never intended to, did ye? Now, that ye're the chief, ye can do as ye wish."

Shaking his head, Connor stared at his friend. "Ye know better than anyone that I had no desire to be chief. I, too, believed that it would be ye. Why do ye attack me? I've always stood by yer side."

Alastair scoffed. "Have ye?" His lips pressed into a thin line, he regarded him. "Not that anyone would tell me, but I've been keeping my eyes open, I've been listening, and I've heard rumours."

"Rumours?" Connor frowned. "What rumours?"

"D'ye truly deny it?" Alastair asked, disappointment clear in his voice. "I never believed ye to be a coward."

Gritting his teeth, Connor tried to remain calm. "If ye would kindly tell me what exactly ye're accusing me of!"

"Do not pretend ye don't know!" Alastair growled, his hands balled into fists. For a moment, he glared at Connor before he spun on his heel and strode out of the room, his angry footsteps echoing down the corridor.

Connor sighed. What was going on? If Alastair wouldn't tell him, then who?

Desperate to learn the truth, Connor spent all day roaming the castle, speaking to council members as well as close family and childhood friends. Since he did not know what kind of rumours Alastair had referred to, he tried his best not to give his enquiries a serious tone. However, most people seemed either unaware of what he was speaking or unwilling to share what they knew.

Standing outside in the courtyard close to the front doors, Connor was just speaking to one of his cousins, who like many others seemed unwilling to acknowledge that he had heard anything, when his wife slipped out through the side door and turned toward the rose garden. Connor immediately excused himself and hurried after her, calling her name.

At the sound of his voice, she turned her head, and her eyes swept the courtyard before they spotted him. However, once they had, an angry frown settled on her face, and she turned away, quickening her step.

Halting his own, Connor closed his eyes and took a deep breath.

This truly was a day to ignore. Secrecy, whispered rumours and hidden anger annoyed him more than loud shouting and open accusations. Oh, how he wished everyone would simply speak their minds!

Over supper, Connor managed to ignore the continued whispers and badly concealed stares. However, his blood boiled in his veins, and when they returned to their bedchamber that night, his patience was once more put to the test.

As she had all day, his wife continued to ignore him, her only acknowledgement of his presence coming in the form of hostile stares. When she did not answer him as he asked about her day, it was the final straw in a day that he wished he could erase.

Grabbing her arm, he pulled her back, forcing her to face him. "Why won't ye look at me?" he demanded as her eyes finally met his. "What happened today?"

Gritting her teeth, she glared at him. "Are you truly asking me?" Yanking away her arm, she stepped back.

"Ha!" Connor scoffed, raking his hands through his hair as frustration dug its claws into him. "I've spent all day asking what is going on. D'ye think anyone's giving me an answer?" Taking a deep breath, he tried his best to still his rapidly beating pulse. "Tell me how I've offended ye, Lass?"

Sad eyes met his. "You have no regard for others, do you? You simply take what you want, and if you have no rightful claim, then you achieve your goal through disreputable means."

Staring at his wife, Connor swallowed. Then his eyes narrowed, a suspicion forming in his mind. "Ye do not speak of yourself, Lass, do ye?"

Shaking her head, she rolled her eyes. "I have nothing else to say."

Growling under his breath, Connor shot forward and grabbed her arms. He lowered his face to hers, his eyes openly displaying the frustration and anger that pulsed in his veins. "What have ye heard? Tell me now."

Frowning, she glared at him. "Why do you pretend to be ignorant-?"

"Because I am!" he snapped. "Now, tell me!"

"Moira told me," she began, her eyes, however, still held disbelief, "that Alastair was not named tanist because of his temper."

"His temper?"

His wife nodded. "Rumours began to circulate that he had uncontrolled fits of anger and was prone to making irrational decisions. Some even witnessed how he lashed out at Moira for no reason."

Shaking his head, Connor released her. "That is not possible. Alastair is a good man. He may get angry at times, but everyone does. That is no reason..." Contemplating the rumours, he met his wife's calculating gaze. "But why does he blame me for...?" His eyes opened wide as realisation dawned. "He believes I circulated these rumours so that he would be considered unfit to become chief and I could take his place."

"Is he wrong to think so?" she asked, a clear challenge in her voice.

"Why do ye believe him over me?" he asked, disappointed that she would think him capable of such treachery. Had he only imagined the delicate bond that had formed between them over the last few days?

"Why would I believe you?" she asked, and her eyes flashed with anger. "I know from personal experience that you do not care for the opinion of others. Why should you treat your cousin differently?"

"I would never betray him," Connor snarled, "or you."

His wife scoffed. "I'd be a fool to believe anything you say! You speak of trust, and yet, you conspire even against family. Your cousin put his trust in you, and you betrayed him."

Stepping closer, Connor felt the blood rush into his head. "And what about ye? How did I betray ye?"

As she fixed him with an angry stare, her chest rose and fell with rapid breaths. "You spoke to my uncle behind my back. You knew that I would never have agreed to marry you, but you didn't care. And of course, he didn't, either."

Hurt that she would compare him to her devious uncle, Connor closed his eyes. "Would ye truly have preferred to remain in yer uncle's house? He would have married ye off eventually."

Laughing, she shook her head. "He would have tried, yes. However, I knew how to make certain that would never happen."

"Don't fool yerself, Lass. At some point, yer uncle would have found a man willing to endure yer hostile manner because of the offered incentive."

"You are mistaken if you believe my uncle would have offered much of his precious money in order to see me married."

Stepping closer, Connor met her eyes. "But he did, Lass. He did." Swallowing, she stared at him, shock evident in her eyes. "I am certain had I not made it clear that I wanted ye, he would have offered even more." Reaching out a hand, he gently placed it on her shoulder, and she blinked. "I refused to take it, Lass."

A frown came to her face. "Why?"

"Because I knew ye'd fight me, and I hoped it'd help convince ye that my intentions were honourable."

"Honourable," she spat, her eyes blazing with renewed anger. "You've made a mistake, Connor Brunwood. You should have chosen a Scottish wife for I will never be what you want." Nostrils flaring, she darted toward the bed, her hand sliding in-between pillow and mattress.

A moment later, she straightened, pulling out her hand and with it a dagger, its sharp tip gleaming in the candle light.

Connor drew in a sharp breath as fear flooded his heart. "Do not hurt yerself, Lass. I implore ye."

Shaking her head, she glanced at the dagger. "I wouldn't," she stated, then met his eyes. "However, you need to understand that...we will never be." Then she swept her long tresses over her shoulder, gathered them in one hand and settled the dagger just above her curled fist. "I am not the woman you want. Believe me." And with a single, forceful movement, the dagger cut through her golden hair.

For a long moment, they stared at each other, waiting, observing.

Then Connor's gaze moved from the challenge in her eyes down to her shoulders where the tips of her soft hair rested, and a memory struck a spark.

Not too long ago, he had come upon her in a meadow. Hair tugged away, hidden under a large hat, her face flushed with the excitement of her fencing practises, she had met his eyes. Despite the fear that had lurked under her portrayed courage and pride, she had stood her ground, and it had been that unwillingness to bend her will to anyone that had captured his heart.

Meeting her eyes once more, Connor smiled, and a soft frown creased her forehead as she regarded him with curiosity. "Do not for a second believe that this is the way to drive me away, Lass?" he said, coming toward her. Then, before she could reply, his hand shot out and twisted the dagger from hers.

Henrietta gasped, her eyes snapping up to his.

Again, Connor moved fast, and a moment later, more of her hair tumbled to the ground. "There," he whispered, skimming a finger along her jawline and down her exposed neck.

A shiver went through her at his touch, and she took a deep breath, the hint of a blush colouring her cheeks.

Holding her gaze, Connor lowered his head to hers. "Long hair or short," he whispered, "only a fool would ever mistake ye for a man, Lass, and I may be many things, but I am no fool. I know what I want." He took a deep breath and held her gaze for a moment longer, hoping that his words would find their way into her heart. "And what I want is ye. Don't ever doubt that." Then he stepped back and nodded. "I'll give ye some space, Lass, for I can see that ye're quite rattled, but know that I will return."

Turning the dagger in his hand, he glanced from the bed to her wardrobe in the corner. "D'ye have other weapons here?"

His wife swallowed, then took a deep breath. "No," she whispered, and her gaze shifted to the small dagger. "You cannot take that from me."

"Only for tonight. I promise," he said. "I'll return it to ye on the morrow when ye've calmed down." Then he turned and strode from the room.

Chapter Fourteen
IN A DREAM

As the door closed behind her husband, all strength left Henrietta's body, and she sank to the floor. Large tears formed in her eyes, blurring her sight, before they spilled over and ran down her cheeks, tearing heart-wrenching sobs from her throat.

Disgusted with her own weakness, Henrietta wrapped her arms around her knees, her fingers digging into her flesh as her body shook with the hopelessness that engulfed her.

After a while the storm in her heart calmed, and her muscles began to ache. Releasing her hold, Henrietta slumped to the side, saved from colliding with the floor by the large bed. As the side of the soft mattress touched her cheek, her eyes closed and she stilled.

Silence hung about the room, and Henrietta's eyelids grew heavy. However, a moment later, a soft knock sounded on the door, and they flew open.

Lifting her head, Henrietta waited. Had her husband returned? Embarrassed, she brushed the tears from her face, her eyes swollen and red, and scrambled to her feet.

Before she could say anything though, the door opened, and instead of her husband, her mother-in-law walked in.

Gaping at the older woman, her hair pinned up meticulously, her dress smooth, a calm expression in her sharp eyes, Henrietta felt the air knocked from her lungs. She could only imagine what her husband's mother thought of her in that moment. Never had they shared a kind word. On the contrary, her mother-in-law's eyes had always seemed to follow her, watching, judging. Her mere presence made Henrietta's skin crawl.

Stepping into the room, Lady Brunwood closed the door, then met Henrietta's eyes before her gaze swept over her face and down to the ends of her tresses before glancing at the long cut-off strands on the floor.

Self-consciously, Henrietta reached up, her fingers playing with the short ends of her hair.

A soft curl came to Lady Brunwood's lips before she shook her head, a hint of amusement in her eyes. "I see my son has made his point."

Henrietta didn't know what to say; however, the need to be truthful suddenly seized her. "It was I who cut it first."

Stepping forward, Lady Brunwood reached out a hand, running a strand of Henrietta's hair through her fingers. Then she met her daughter-in-law's eyes. "Why?"

Fresh tears came to Henrietta's eyes, and she turned her head away.

"Do not be embarrassed, my dear," Lady Brunwood said as her hands gently settled on Henrietta's shoulders then ran down her arms before grasping her hands. "If ye knew only half the things I've done in my life, ye'd know I'd never judge ye for what happened here tonight."

Lifting her eyes to her mother-in-law's, Henrietta wondered at the soft glow she saw there. Had it been there before? How could she have missed it?

"Wives and husbands do not always agree," Lady Brunwood continued as she eased Henrietta down onto the bed and sat down beside her. "Quarrels are a part of life."

Henrietta sighed. "I'm not certain I'd call it a quarrel, my lady."

An amused smile curled up Lady Brunwood's lips. "Then what would ye call it, Dear?"

Henrietta shrugged. "I don't know. I..." For a moment, she closed her eyes, then lifted her head and met her mother-in-law's curious gaze. "Your son should never have married me for I cannot be the wife that he wants. I'm sorry to be so blunt. I know you must hate me for saying so, but I cannot be who I am not."

"I do not hate ye, Dear; however, I do think ye're wrong." A soft smile came to her lips as she reached out and patted Henrietta's hand. "Ye are his match, and he is yers. If I didna believe so, I wouldna have sent him to find ye."

Staring at her mother-in-law, Henrietta swallowed. "What? What do you speak of?"

For a long moment, Lady Brunwood regarded her with a hint of suspicion in her eyes before she nodded. "Sometimes I see things in my dreams. Things that were, things that are, and things that will be. 'Tis a gift I've had since I was a child. I didna always appreciate it for too much knowledge can easily change the course of someone's destiny. 'Tis a heavy burden, but it also comes with beautiful rewards." A warm smile curled up her lips. "When my son returned home from England, I knew that he had found ye."

As her heart thudded in her chest, Henrietta remembered her own thoughts. How had he found her? How had he come upon her in such a remote place? A place that she had chosen because no one ever ventured there? "He never said-"

Lady Brunwood shook her head. "He doesna know." A laugh escaped her. "He's quite thick-headed and likes to believe that he makes his own destiny. He wouldna have believed me, and everything would've been different. I couldna risk telling him what I'd seen. I could only set his feet on the path and hope that fate would guide him to ye."

Henrietta felt a strange kinship echo in her heart as she thought about her husband's desire to make his own way. Was anything ever truly destined? Were two people ever meant to meet? To be together? To share their life? Was everything meant to be and nothing up to free will?

Taking a deep breath, Henrietta closed her eyes, knowing that deep down she could never believe that. Had her mother been destined to die by her father's hands? Had she herself been destined to lead a life of struggle?

"Ye do not believe me," her mother-in-law stated, a hint of regret in her voice. "I can see it in yer eyes."

"I'm sorry I-"

A gentle hand curled around hers. "Do not worry for I know that fate has dealt ye harshly, Dear. I am only glad that ye were able to open yer heart to my son."

Henrietta's eyes went wide. "No, I-"

An indulgent smile on her face, Lady Brunwood nodded. "Ye did, Dear, and I can see that it scares ye, but I implore ye, do not run from it. Fear is a loyal but selfish master, and it will not serve ye to obey its commands whenever someone touches yer heart."

"I am not afraid," Henrietta whispered, feeling the lie on her tongue as she spoke.

Lady Brunwood squeezed her hand. "We all are, but we must not allow Fear to dictate our lives."

"I'm not afraid," Henrietta repeated stubbornly. "I do what I do because people cannot be trusted. If there is anything I've learnt in my life, it's that those who trust others blindly will suffer for it."

"The way yer mother trusted yer father?" Lady Brunwood asked, her knowing eyes meeting Henrietta's as hers widened in shock. "The way you trusted yer mother?"

As the blood drained from her face, Henrietta stared at the tall woman with the strong hands and sharp eyes. "How?" she gasped.

Another indulgent smile came to Lady Brunwood's face. "I told ye, Dear."

"You saw me...and my parents?" Unable to comprehend what was happening, Henrietta shook her head, feeling as though the ground had been yanked out from under her.

"Only glimpses and emotions."

Henrietta swallowed, trying to shake off the sense of dread that always settled over her at the memory of her parents. "Then you know why people cannot be trusted."

"That day, all those years ago," Lady Brunwood began, "ye lost more than yer parents. Ye learnt a lesson, a lesson so cruel that it crippled ye in the worst way. Ye didna lose trust in the people around ye, but in yerself." Thick tears came to Henrietta's eyes. "Ye do not trust yerself to judge people correctly, to see when someone is dishonest, when someone seeks to do ye harm, and so ye distrust everyone in order to keep yerself safe." Lady Brunwood softly squeezed Henrietta's hand, her eyes holding neither judgement nor disappointment but compassion and understanding instead. "My son seeks to gain yer trust. He believes that if he proves himself to ye again and again, ye will come to see that he is indeed true to his word and eventually place yer trust in him. But I know that willna happen unless ye learn to trust in yerself again."

A sob tore from her throat as tears ran down her cheeks, and Henrietta buried her face in her hands.

"Do not be ashamed," her mother-in-law sought to comfort her. "Ye're a strong woman, but the fears within ye were born that day and have ruled ye ever since." A wrinkled hand settled under her chin, and Henrietta looked up, meeting her mother-in-law's eyes. "Yer mother betrayed ye that day. She knew even better than ye did that yer father couldna be trusted, and yet, she didna act. She didna have it in her to fight. We're not all the same. Ye are not yer mother. Know that. Believe that. And should the need ever arise, trust yerself to act and do as she could not." A smile touched her lips. "I do. I trust ye."

"But you don't even know me," Henrietta sobbed, wiping away the tears that kept flowing.

"I can see the woman ye are," Lady Brunwood insisted, "and I trust myself to see what is and not what I fear or hope might be." Brushing a lock from Henrietta's face, the older woman smiled. "There. Now get yerself to bed and rest for ye've earned it like never before. Sleep, and if ye need to speak, come and find me, and I'll tell ye the truth."

"Thank you," Henrietta whispered as Lady Brunwood walked toward the door. "Thank you."

"Ye're welcome, my dear," her mother-in-law said, a devoted smile on her face. "After all, ye're family now. Ye'll never be alone again, and when the day comes that ye can truly believe that, ye'll know how strong ye truly are."

As the door closed behind her mother-in-law, Henrietta stared in amazement before her eyelids once more grew heavy, and she lay down on the bed.

Ye're not alone. Her husband had told her the same thing, but she had not believed him.

Maybe one day, she would.

Chapter Fifteen
A CALL TO ARMS

When Henrietta awoke the next morning, her head throbbed painfully, and yet, her heart felt a little lighter. Never before had she shared her pain with anyone, not the way she had shared it with her mother-in-law. Still surprised to have judged the seemingly reserved woman so wrongly, Henrietta recalled her counsel.

Had she truly lost trust in herself?

Closing her eyes, Henrietta shook her head. She could not be certain. The emotions that coursed through her chest had been with her all her life. Fear. Suspicion. Doubt. Had there ever been anything else?

Only when she slipped from the bed did Henrietta remember that her husband had not come to bed the night before, and she could not help but wonder if his mother's counsel had had anything to do with it or if he had acted of his own accord. Did he truly desire her trust? Did he deserve it? Or would she one day come to regret trusting him?

As Henrietta brushed out what remained of her hair, she cringed at the sight of her reddened eyes in the mirror. People would stare and wonder; she had no doubt. What would they think?

A slight tingle went over her as though a warm breeze had touched her skin before the sound of her husband's voice reached her ears. "I trust ye slept well."

Somehow she had known he was there. Although he moved stealthily like a wildcat, Henrietta often sensed his approach; at least, when she was not too caught up in her own emotions.

Turning to face him, she met his eyes. "I did. Thank you."

He nodded in acknowledgement, and she could see the questions that plagued him in his eyes. However, he did not ask them, but merely stepped forward, drawing her dagger from his overcoat. "I promised I'd return it to ye on the morrow," he reminded her, holding out the small blade.

When Henrietta reached out her hand to take it, his hand seemed to tighten around the hilt and he met her eyes. "Promise me that ye will never hurt yerself."

Holding his gaze, Henrietta was surprised at the sense of honest sincerity that rang in his voice. However, the very moment she felt herself respond, her inner demons spoke up, trying to convince her that he was lying, pretending, scheming. Of course, he had an ulterior motive; one day, he would reveal it, and then it would be too late for her to protect herself from him.

How often had she heard her demons whisper warnings like these? How often had they been able to persuade her to distrust someone?

Henrietta swallowed, then rose to her feet and stepped toward him, desperately trying to shut out the voices in her head that shouted at her to turn back. Holding his gaze, Henrietta took a deep breath and then nodded. "I promise."

A soft curl came to his lips as he gently placed the dagger in her hand. "Good." For a moment, his eyes remained on her face before he stepped back. "Would ye like to ride out again today, Lass? Or would ye rather I leave ye alone?"

A soft tremble seized Henrietta as her fears once more battled her desires. Had it always been like this? She wondered. Never before had she been so consciously aware of the war constantly raging within her. "I..." She swallowed, then took a deep breath...and averted her eyes. "I think I'd rather be alone."

"Very well," he said, a hint of disappointment in his voice. "Call for me if ye change yer mind, Lass."

When the door closed behind him, Henrietta sank back into the chair, feeling weaker than she had in a long time. Doubt swept through her, and not the kind of doubt of which she was accustomed. She knew what it felt like to doubt those around her: their motives, their agendas, the truth of their words. However, now she found herself doubting her own judgement. Had her mother-in-law been correct? Or had her kind words been a clever manipulation so that Henrietta would let down her guard and...? And what? What good would it do them to gain her trust? After all, she was in no position of power.

Quite the contrary.

Burying her face in her hands, Henrietta sighed. Was she losing her mind? Seeing enemies where in truth there were none?

As her world came crashing down around her, Henrietta retreated into herself. She spent day after day sitting in her chamber, remembering all the people she had met in her life and how she had judged them. Again and again, she recalled situations in all detail. Had the look in their eyes betrayed their actions? Had the ring in their voices matched their words? Had she been wrong to judge them so harshly? Or had she been wise to do so?

How often had her father apologised to her mother, swearing that he loved her and that only the liquor had made him beat her? Remembering his eyes, Henrietta knew that he had been lying. Although she did not believe in much, deep down, she knew with every fibre of her being that love had it resided in his heart would have stopped his hand, for it would have hurt him too much to witness his wife in pain. However, it had not; therefore, his proclamations of love had been lies.

Next, her uncle's face rose before her eyes, and although Henrietta had never witnessed any physical abuse towards her aunt, she had seen countless times with what disregard he had always looked at her, spoken to her. He valued neither her presence in his household nor her opinions and thoughts. At the same time, her aunt did her best to excuse and explain his behaviour, hoping that one day she would believe the lies she told herself.

Then, there was Tristan.

For a moment, Henrietta closed her eyes and took a deep breath, afraid what she would find if she looked closer. Was her brother too much like their father? Is that why she had not asked for his help when her uncle had forced this marriage on her? Had she been afraid he would turn from her? But would he have?

Tristan had always been impulsive, a bit of a hot-head. He made rash decisions; therefore, he often suffered unexpected consequences. Countless times, their uncle had berated him for being careless, for allowing his temper to get the better of him and circumvent his rational mind. Aware of his parents' past, Tristan had always flinched when compared to his late father. Had he feared his uncle's accusations to be true? Did he doubt himself as much as Henrietta doubted herself?

Rubbing her temples, Henrietta paced the room, picturing her brother through the years as he had grown from a helpless infant into a man. But what kind of a man was he? What did she truly think and not fear he had become?

Henrietta could not tell, and that thought scared her more than anything ever had.

He was her brother, and she loved him, and yet, she could not place her trust in him. She couldn't be certain he would stand by her no matter what.

After two weeks locked in her chamber, Henrietta felt the sudden need to breathe fresh air, and so she hesitantly walked down the corridor and proceeded downstairs. As expected, all eyes turned to her, and whispers rose into the sudden silence.

Keeping her head up, Henrietta crossed the great hall and slipped out the side entrance. She walked down the cobblestone path to the other side of the rose garden and squeezed herself through the minuscule gap in the hedge.

The small green oasis welcomed her with open arms. A soft breeze caressed her neck-now freed from the heavy burden of her long tresses-and the sweet fragrance that danced on the air tickled her nose as though trying to wake her from the nightmare that had held her trapped for so long.

Breathing in deeply, Henrietta slipped off her shoes and stockings and walked the small space, enjoying the soft, cooling earth under her feet. She felt the warmth of the sun's early rays on her chilled skin and marvelled at the clear, blue sky overhead.

All her senses picked up little wonders: they saw, tasted and smelled. Henrietta felt as though she was being born again. Her heart and head felt light, untroubled, and for a moment, she closed her eyes revelling in a sense of balance that washed over her.

"Ye look different."

Henrietta's eyes snapped open, and she spun around.

Grinning sheepishly, Deirdre shrugged her shoulders. "I'm sorry for startling ye." Rising from the small boulder resting in the far corner by the outer wall, Deirdre stepped toward her, her warm eyes searching Henrietta's face. "I was worried about ye. Ye've kept to yer room for a long time."

Taking a deep breath, Henrietta nodded. "I...I don't know how to explain," she finally admitted, wondering if she truly didn't or if she did not trust Deirdre to know the thoughts that plagued her.

"'Tis quite all right," the slender woman said, her eyes sweeping over Henrietta's short hair. "I rather like what ye did there. It is quite unusual, but it suits ye."

Reaching to touch the tips of her strands, Henrietta smiled self-consciously. "I did it to make him see that..." She shrugged as the thoughts began to hammer in her head.

"I know," Deirdre said. Then she stepped forward and took Henrietta's hand. "It didna work though, did it?"

Henrietta shook her head.

"He cares for ye," Deirdre said, a shimmer of recognition in her brilliant eyes. "I've known him all my life, and I've never seen him look at a woman the way he looks at ye."

Withdrawing her hands, Henrietta stepped back as shivers ran down her back and the ground under her feet felt like a block of ice. "I need to go," she whispered, and snatching her stockings and shoes from the grass, she turned and left, ignoring the look of disappointment on Deirdre's face.

Like a wave, the voices in her head returned. Gone was the peaceful silence that had engulfed her before.

Deirdre meant well, and yet, her words laced with her own hopes and wishes had only served to remind Henrietta that everyone had an agenda, that everyone wanted something, that no one was free from desire.

Her uncle wanted her out of his house. Her aunt wanted a comfortable life. Her brother wanted...Henrietta couldn't be certain what he wanted.

Her husband wanted...her trust. Her mother-in-law wanted her to trust herself. Deirdre wanted her to open her heart to her husband. Alastair wanted her to stay away from his wife. Moira wanted...Again, Henrietta couldn't be certain. However, what plagued her most were not the desires that ruled those in her life. What plagued her most was that she didn't know why.

Why had her uncle been so desperate to rid himself of her? Why had her husband chosen her for his bride? Why had Deirdre encouraged her to place her trust in Connor?

Again, Henrietta's demons raged within her heart and mind, and their deafening voices echoed through her body. Try as she might, she could not silence them, and so Henrietta slipped her stockings and shoes back on, ignoring the dirt that still clung to her feet, and rushed from the rose garden.

Crossing the courtyard, she did not see the stares that stalked her. Neither did she hear the whispers that followed as she kept her attention on the stable across the yard. Slipping inside, she quickly located Kerr, threw a bridle and saddle on her and then mounted the spirited mare.

As though sensing Henrietta's emotional state, Kerr danced nervously, her hooves moving to an innate rhythm that only she understood, and the second, Henrietta loosened the reins, she shot forward.

Startled, a stable boy jumped out of the way as they passed through the large door, and again, people stopped and stared as the tall mare raced across the courtyard toward the outer gate, Henrietta clinging to her back, her eyes fixed on the horizon in the distance.

Once free of the stone walls keeping her trapped in a life she had not chosen, Henrietta felt her body relax. Flattening herself to Kerr's neck, she allowed the mare to take her where she wished, for once surrendering control not because she was forced to but because she chose to.

The wind whipped in her face and tore at her dress, and Henrietta's heart soared. Again, she could feel the warm rays of the sun touching her skin, and the smell of the nearing forest, earthy and warm, tickled her nose. Slowly, the voices in her head began to quiet, and a warm silence returned to her heart.

Maybe she was not fit to live among people. Maybe she ought to keep riding and not return.

The scent in the air changed, and Henrietta tasted a hint of salt on it.

Urging Kerr on, she proceeded onward, guiding the mare toward the tree line and along a well-trodden path. The smell of pine and conifer hung in the air, momentarily blocking out the clean, salty tang of the sea. However, when Henrietta left the forest behind and continued on across the grassy plains, the scent of the ocean returned, guiding her onward.

The wind grew stronger, and Henrietta squinted her eyes, keeping them fixed on the horizon where sky met earth. As she flew onward, Henrietta glimpsed large boulders dotting the cliff as though an ancient castle had once stood there, its crumbled stones now overgrown with moss.

Kerr slowed, her flanks heaving with exertion, and Henrietta straightened in the saddle, stretching her own weary limbs as her eyes swept over the sight before her.

The ruins occupied the highest point on the cliff, after which the land fell away and the ocean rumbled in the deep. Seagulls circled in the sky, occasionally diving down to catch fish, and a strong wind carried with it the scents of the world.

Slipping her feet out of the stirrups, Henrietta dropped to the ground, her eyes fixed on the edge. She released Kerr's reins and walked on, rounding the ruins, until she approached the edge of the cliff, her heart hammering in her chest. A deafening roar reached her ears from down below as the waves crashed against the rock wall, and its force made Henrietta shiver. Never before had she felt as small and helpless as she did now in the presence of these natural forces.

Glancing over the edge, she watched the waves as they rolled in from the sea, their waters travelling the world, free and unconfined.

Although the height made her skin crawl, Henrietta sank to the ground a mere arm's length from the edge. Her eyes drank in the sight as the wind continued to tug at her hair and her dress, its strong breath chilling her skin and stinging her eyes.

And yet, Henrietta did not move, and for a long time, she simply sat there and felt the world around her while her demons slept, allowing her a moment of peace.

Chapter Sixteen
A WEAKNESS REVEALED

Hours had passed since his wife had left the castle in a frenzy as though the devil had been behind her. Hours since he had been alerted to her rushed departure. Hours since he had gone after her, afraid of what she might do if he did not find her in time.

Where could she have gone? She was not familiar with these parts. He had already searched the area around the castle as well as the clearing where they had fenced, however, without luck.

Entering the forest, Connor spotted hoof-prints in the soft ground and hurried onward. Judging from their depths, he guessed that she had not slowed down, but instead raced through the forest the same way she had left the castle. He could only hope that she had not been thrown at such a break-neck speed.

Allowing his gelding free reins, Connor scanned his surroundings, hoping to catch a glimpse of her. However, it wasn't until he had left the forest behind and proceeded toward the old castle ruins that he detected movement on the horizon.

Kerr. He thought and urged his gelding on.

Squinting his eyes, he could only make out the mare; however, there was no sign of his wife, and fear clawed at his heart. What had she done? He cursed as his eyes travelled to the cliff face.

Pulling up beside his wife's patiently grazing mare, Connor jumped off his horse, his eyes searching frantically as he rushed around the ruins. His heart hammered in his chest, and his muscles ached all over as the strained tension he felt held them in a tight grip.

As he came around the last boulder, his heart stopped.

Standing at the edge of the cliff was his wife, her arms spread like a bird, head thrown back, eyes closed.

A gust of wind caught in her skirts, and she began to sway on her feet.

Instinctively, Connor rushed forward, hands reaching for her, praying that he would not grasp at nothing.

The moment his arm closed around her waist and he flung her backward, relief flooded his heart in a way he had never experienced before. He did not feel the dull thud as he hit the ground or the soft ache in his shoulder. All he felt was her soft body in his arms, alive and safe.

Shrieking, she elbowed him in the ribs, and he rolled over, pinning her to the ground. "What on earth are ye doing, Lass?" he snapped, panting under his breath. "Are ye so desperate to rid yerself of this life?"

For a moment, she stared up at him as though he were an apparition. Then she blinked, and the expression in her eyes cleared before they narrowed into slits. "What are you doing here?" she spat, trying to free herself. "Get off me!"

After hours in fear for her life, anger rose to the surface at the sight of the rebellious expression in her eyes, and Connor's hands tightened on her wrists. "Ye promised ye wouldna hurt yerself!" he snarled into her face. "Ye promised!"

Shocked, her eyes widened before they searched his face. "I didn't... I..." She swallowed, meeting his eyes openly. "I wouldn't have."

"Then what were ye doing standing up on the cliff? Arms spread as though ye were about to dive into the sea?"

She took a deep breath, and her eyes strayed from his. "That is not of your concern."

"Ye're my wife!"

Instantly, her eyes narrowed, hatred burning in their core. "Get off me!" she snarled, and every muscle in her body tensed, resisting.

Taking a deep breath, Connor gritted his teeth before he relinquished his hold on her wrists and rose to his feet, holding out his hand to help her up.

"I do not need your assistance," she snapped, jumping to her feet. "Why did you follow me? I thought I was free to go where I pleased."

"Ye are," he said, his hands balling into fists to keep his own anger from boiling over. "I followed ye because I was worried."

"Worried?" Meeting his gaze, her eyes narrowed, and an angry snarl came to her lips. "For I am just a feeble woman in desperate need of a man's protection, am I not?"

Exhausted, Connor growled, "Ye mule-headed woman! Would ye come off that high horse of yers for a moment to see that I am not yer enemy!" Gritting his teeth, he fought down his anger. "I was worried because I know that something haunts ye, Lass, and the manner in which ye left made me fear ye'd reached the end of yer rope." He glanced at the edge behind her. "I couldna bear the thought of losing ye."

Staring at him, his wife swallowed, and for a moment, he thought to see a spark in her sad eyes. A spark of hope, of pleasure as though his words had touched something deep inside her. "I came here to... think," she whispered, her eyes barely meeting his. "I wouldn't have jumped. I promise."

Connor nodded. "Good." Then he stepped toward her, and her eyes rose up to meet his. "Ye're a proud woman," he began, "and I do not wish to insult ye, but I feel compelled to make ye understand." When she didn't lash out at him or run away, he took a deep breath, feeling encouraged. "I never said I doubted yer heart, yer courage or yer wit. Only the strength of yer arm." Instantly, her eyes narrowed. "Are ye truly so conceited that ye canna admit yer own limitations? Why would ye lie to yerself for I can see that ye know the truth?"

For a moment, her eyes closed, and she remained silent. Looking up though, she shook her head.

"Then fight me," Connor challenged, "hand to hand, and may the best fighter win."

"What?" Henrietta asked, uncertain whether or not to believe her ears. Had her husband just challenged her to a fist fight?

"Why do ye hesitate?" he asked, holding her gaze. "If we are truly equally matched, then there is no reason for ye to refuse my request." He stepped closer, and his eyes drilled into hers, an open challenge in them.

Henrietta swallowed as her demons readied themselves for battle. She could not allow him to intimidate her. She could not allow herself to be weak for only the strong survived. She had learnt that long ago.

Stepping back, Henrietta dug her heels into the ground, her muscles tense, ready for whatever lay ahead. Her eyes narrowed as she watched him, and her hands rose before her body.

"D'ye accept my challenge?"

"I do."

The words had barely left her lips when he lunged forward, his large hands reaching for her.

Henrietta spun to the side, rotating on one heel, and slipped from his grasp.

He came at her again and again; his attacks, however, were half-hearted and playful. He held back, and Henrietta's anger rose to new heights. He did not believe her a worthy opponent.

"Ye're so fixated on appearing strong, on not admitting a weakness," he said approaching her once more; "have ye never considered what it would mean for ye to lose a challenge, Lass? Have ye ever even been challenged to a real fight? Or have ye only ever fought yer brother in playful matches?"

The second she opened her mouth for a derisive retort, his right arm shot forward and his fist connected with her chin.

Henrietta's eyes flew open. However, there was no pain.

He had not struck her, but cushioned his attack and only touched his fist to her skin. Then he stepped forward and caught both her wrists in his large hands. "I have no intention of hurting ye, Lass, for I couldna bear to see ye in pain. However, I want ye to feel yer own limitations. 'Tis not enough to know them for it would be too easy for ye to convince yerself of the opposite."

Henrietta tried to free herself from his grasp but failed. Cursing under her breath, she glared up at him.

While she struggled against him, her arms trapped, her heart pounding with the indignity and shame of the position she had allowed herself to be manoeuvred into, her husband stood there like a stone pillar, calm, his eyes watching her, waiting for her to surrender.

"Release me!" Henrietta growled.

Holding her burning gaze, he shook his head and waited.

Once more, Henrietta yanked on her arms, and once more, he didn't budge, her wrists trapped in iron shackles.

However, when *he* gave *her* arms a soft tug, she flew against him, unable to maintain the distance between them. "There is no shame," he whispered, "in admitting one's weaknesses to a friend."

Meeting his eyes, Henrietta took a deep breath. A friend? Was he a friend? Could she trust him?

Again, her demons roared into life, and their deafening cries hammered in her head. However, somewhere underneath, a soft voice whispered of the longing she felt in her heart, a longing for someone to lean on, to confide in, to respect and trust. "If what you say is true," she said, holding his gaze as a soft tremble shook her, "then admit to a weakness of your own."

His lips thinned, and he breathed in deeply through his nose.

"It is easy to advise others," Henrietta whispered.

He nodded. "It is indeed." For a moment, he seemed to look inward as though contemplating the challenge she had issued before his eyes returned to hers. "Ye're right, Lass. I have no right to ask for yer trust if I am unwilling to give ye mine." He drew in a deep breath, and Henrietta felt a slight tremble roll from his hands into her arms. "I have never spoken to anyone about it," he began, "but I am trusting ye with this."

Henrietta nodded, a sense of pride swelling in her chest that he would share his darkest secret with her.

He swallowed. "I have trouble reading and writing."

Surprised, Henrietta watched him and saw the tension in his face as he waited for her reaction.

"I did learn," he explained when she did not react appalled by his admission. "However, I canna read as fast as others and understand what I've read. I need to read slowly, and still details often escape me." He shrugged. "It doesna matter how often I practise. I never seem to manage to read with the same ease as others. Spelling words is difficult as well."

For a long moment, they looked at each other as his words hung between them. It was as though they stood on opposite ends of a large ravine, and his revelation had begun to build a bridge from his side, its end dangling in the air, needing her to finish it.

Henrietta swallowed, then cleared her throat. "I...I don't know...if I can trust...myself."

"Trust yerself?" he whispered, and his hands released her wrists as he looked down at her, his forehead in a puzzled frown.

Rubbing her left wrist, Henrietta stepped back, her eyes sweeping over the ruins of the old castle. "To see others for whom they are." She hesitated, then turned back and met his gaze. "Your mother helped me see it."

A soft curl came to his lips. "Aye, she has her ways. I don't really understand how she knows the things she does. I never asked, and she never said." His eyes held hers before he nodded. "But she told ye, did she not?"

Henrietta nodded.

He stepped closer then, and his left hand came to rest on her shoulder before it ran down her arm and gently squeezed her hand. "Ye always expect people to betray ye. Why? What happened? Can ye not tell me? I swear I willna use it against ye."

Holding his gaze, Henrietta swallowed. Could she confide in him? Should she? His mother had simply known. There had been no need for Henrietta to explain. His mother had known, and it had made things easier.

"Who betrayed ye?" he asked, and his hand left hers to settled under her chin, making her look at him. "Was it yer parents? Or yer brother?"

Her jaw quivered as a single tear spilled over and ran down her cheek.

"What happened?"

Henrietta swallowed. "I was five," she began, remembering the night that had shaped her like no other, "when he killed her."

Her husband drew in a sharp breath, and a frown settled on his brows. "Yer father?"

"Yes." For a moment, Henrietta closed her eyes. "He had fits of anger especially when he was drunk. No matter what he had promised before, he would turn against her," opening her eyes, she met his gaze, "and she would take the beating. She would cry and weep, but she would not fight to protect herself...or us."

By then, tears were running freely down her cheeks, but she only noticed them when he took her face into his large hands, gently brushing them away. As she tried to avert her eyes, he held her gaze. "She surrendered," he whispered, "when she should have fought. She betrayed ye as did yer father." He swallowed. "Did ye see what happened?"

Henrietta shook her head. "No, I was upstairs when their screaming woke me. I slipped out of bed, got my little brother and hid in the pantry. I don't know for how long I sat there, trying not to listen. I heard footsteps, and then a shot rang out." Taking a deep breath, she shrugged. "I wanted to help her, but I couldn't. My little brother, he..."

"Ye did right, Lass," he said as he held her gaze, willing her to understand. "Ye did right. Ye saw him safe."

Closing her eyes, Henrietta sagged against him as all strength left her body, and her limbs simply wouldn't support her any longer.

He caught her though, his strong arms coming around her, and sitting down on a knee-high boulder, he pulled her onto his lap, holding her tight and murmuring words of comfort while Henrietta wept like never before. Years of unshed tears ran down her cheeks as she cried her heart out, all the pain and disappointment, all the fear and anger that had tortured her for so long.

"Ye did right," he said over and over as he stroked her back and brushed the hair out of her face.

Clinging to him, Henrietta allowed herself a moment of weakness and rested her head against his shoulder. Even if it would only last a moment, she clung to the sense of warmth and safety that engulfed her.

When her tears finally died down, Henrietta stilled, and embarrassment began to burn in her cheeks. She should never have allowed her husband to see her so vulnerable. Yes, he had promised not to use it against her, but so had her father. Over and over, he had pleaded with her mother to believe him, only to break his word the next time anger seized him.

Straightening, Henrietta slipped off her husband's lap and turned her back to him as she brushed away the last tears. She took a deep breath, and a shiver ran over her a moment before his hands settled on her shoulders and he pulled her toward him until her back rested against his chest.

"Ye do not fear the people around ye because ye do not trust them," he whispered in her ear as his breath tickled her neck, "but because ye canna tell whether or not ye should, and so ye look at everyone as a threat." Gently, his hands urged her to turn and face him. "It keeps ye safe, but it is lonely, is it not, Lass?"

Meeting his gaze, Henrietta felt her resolve weaken. She knew she shouldn't, and yet, she couldn't help it. She was so tired, tired of the constant struggle, tired of being on her guard all the time, tired of fighting alone.

"Will ye let me hold ye, Lass?"

Unable to deny herself the comfort he offered, Henrietta nodded, welcoming the strong arms that came around her. She closed her eyes, enjoying the feel of his hands as they slid over her back and up and down her arms. His warm breath caressed her skin, and she shivered as his lips brushed over her neck.

Pulling back, she stared at him, seeing an echo of the desire that had seized her so quickly reflected in his eyes. Her arms came up, pulling her closer against him, and her eyes lowered to trace the line of his lips.

A soft smile came to his mouth as he bent his head to hers. "Take what ye wish, Lass, for I am yers if ye'll have me."

Biting her lip, Henrietta held his gaze for a moment longer. Then in one fluid motion, her hands reached up and pulled him down to her, and the instant her mouth claimed his, it was as though the sun exploded overhead. Never in a million years would she have expected the emotions that ran through her body as his lips moved over hers. Gentle and teasing at first, then passionate and demanding.

Losing herself in the moment, Henrietta forgot the world around her until a soft nicker reached her ear, and the sound of thundering hoof-beats echoed across the plain.

An annoyed growl rose from her husband's throat as he lifted his head and his lips parted with hers. As he turned to the approaching rider, his arms remained firmly around her, holding her close. "Alastair," he mumbled as his tanist reined in his horse and then slid to the ground, his jaw tense as he gritted his teeth and regarded them through narrowed eyes.

"What troubles ye?" her husband asked, and the arm still holding her tensed.

Coming to stand before them, Alastair's eyes slid from Henrietta to her husband, open disapproval evident in them. "A messenger arrived sent by Brogan Brunwood," he said. "He says his daughter is missing. Probably taken."

Henrietta drew in a sharp breath while her husband's eyes narrowed. "By whom?"

Alastair shrugged. "That is unclear. He asks for yer assistance."

Her husband nodded. "Certainly. Ride ahead. We'll be along shortly." Then he turned to Henrietta and led her a few steps away as Alastair returned to his horse. "I'm sorry, Lass," he whispered, and a soft curl came to his lips as he glanced down at hers. "Very sorry, but this is an urgent matter. We need to return to Greyston."

Overwhelmed by everything that had happened within the last few minutes, Henrietta merely nodded, uncertain how to feel about all these new developments.

Chapter Seventeen
HEAVY BURDENS

Upon returning to Greyston, her husband immediately excused himself and headed in the direction of his study followed by Alastair and a few other men Henrietta could not name. A council was called, and the messenger would be heard.

To Henrietta's surprise, Rhona and Deirdre waited for her in the grand hall with smiling faces, welcoming her back as though she were a daughter of the clan.

"Do not ever scare me like that again," Deirdre chided while shaking her head. "When I saw ye come racing out of the stables like a mad woman, I was certain I'd never see ye again."

"I'm sorry," Henrietta whispered, touched beyond words at the honest emotions she saw on the young woman's face.

Rhona smiled as she wrapped a strong arm around Henrietta's shoulders, knowing eyes looking down at her. "It served its purpose though, didn't it?"

Henrietta frowned. "Its purpose?"

Rhona chuckled, and her eyebrows rose into arches before she glanced in the direction of her son's study. "Only this morning, defeat and hopelessness marked both of yer eyes. Now, I see something else in yers as well as in his."

Feeling heat burn in her cheeks, Henrietta averted her gaze but could not prevent the hint of a pleased smile from curling up the corners of her mouth.

Again, her mother-in-law chuckled, and Deirdre stepped forward with curious eyes. "What happened?"

Uncertain how to reply, Henrietta opened her mouth but was saved from having to explain what she could not even comprehend herself as hurried footsteps approached.

"Has Connor returned?" Moira asked. "Did Alastair find him? I-" As her eyes fell on Henrietta, she stopped in her tracks and for a brief moment, her face held disapproval. However, before Henrietta could wonder about Moira's reaction, a delighted smile came to the young woman's face and she rushed forward, flinging her arms around Henrietta. "I'm so glad ye're back. We're all so worried."

"I'm sorry," Henrietta mumbled once more, uncertain how to understand Moira's strange behaviour.

After a few more enquiring questions as to what had happened between her and Connor, Henrietta excused herself, stating that she had a chill in her bones from riding out all day without a coat. It was not a lie; however, what Henrietta needed more than anything in that moment was to get away from their questions and be alone as her thoughts and emotions tumbled through her body in a rather disorderly fashion.

Returning to their bedchamber, she changed and then sat down in front of her vanity to brush her entangled hair. Unlike before, the brush easily undid the knots, and Henrietta smiled at herself, her fingers brushing over a short strand that ended in line with her jaw. Although she had meant it as a challenge, her heart rather enjoyed her husband's reaction to her short hair, and she remembered how easily his lips had found her neck now that her hair was out of the way.

A shiver went over her at the memory, and Henrietta sighed, knowing she could not ignore forever what had happened that day.

Lost in the moment, she had let down her guard and allowed him closer than was wise, and Rhona was right. Something had changed. What would they do now?

Standing by the window, Henrietta stared out at the darkening sky when footsteps echoed from down the hall. A moment later, the door opened and Henrietta turned to face her husband. "What did the messenger say?" she asked, desperate to speak of anything but the kiss they had shared that afternoon.

Connor sighed. "At first, he insisted that Brogan had no knowledge of his daughter's whereabouts, claiming that she had been snatched from her room in the middle of the night."

"But that wasn't so," Henrietta concluded, intrigued with the situation laid before her.

"It seems not," her husband agreed, his face weary. "Apparently, not only Fiona is missing, but also the chieftain's lad, Liam, as well."

"Oh." Henrietta stepped closer, her arms wrapped around herself at the sudden chill that had seized her. "You believe they ran away together?"

Connor nodded.

"But why?"

Looking up, her husband met her eyes. "Because they're in love."

A shiver went over Henrietta at the intensity of his gaze, and she quickly averted her own, turning back to looking out the window. "If they are in love, why can't they simply...?"

"Because Brogan refuses his consent," her husband explained, a hint of annoyance in his voice.

"Why?"

"I do not know," he admitted. "Brogan and Reid are good men. From what my father once told me, they used to be friends when they were young."

"Then what happened?"

"They refuse to speak about it. However, my father believed that a woman came between them."

Taking a deep breath, Henrietta turned around. "What will you do when you find them?"

Holding her gaze, her husband stepped closer. "I do not know. If her father canna be convinced to give his consent-"

"You would do that?" Henrietta snapped as her eyes narrowed. "You would force them apart because of their fathers' misgivings?"

Taking a deep breath, Connor gritted his teeth. "I canna say. I need to hear all sides before making a decision."

"Why is it your decision?"

"Because I'm their chief."

Henrietta snorted, "And that gives you the right to decide their fate?"

"Believe me," her husband growled, "I'm as displeased with this situation as ye. However, my hands are tied. I have a duty to my clan to settle disputes-"

"Disputes? These are merely disputes to you?" Henrietta shook her head. "I doubt Fiona and Liam would see it that way, having the choice taken out of their hands. Is it not also your duty to help them? But all you are concerned with is their fathers' wishes."

"'Tis not," her husband snapped. "However, this is not a simple matter. All sides need to be considered."

"But ultimately, it will be your decision," she accused, and before he could answer added, "Is that why you spread rumours of Alastair's incompetence so that you would be named chief?"

At her words, the muscles in his jaw tensed and his eyes narrowed. For a brief moment, she thought he would storm toward her when his posture suddenly relaxed and he shook his head, a knowing smile curling up the corners of his mouth. "For a second there, Lass, I was ready to strangle ye," he said, a hint of amusement in his voice. Then the expression on his face sobered, and he stepped toward her, eyes dark with emotion. "Ye canna fool me, Lass. I know what drives ye to say these things."

Henrietta frowned.

"Ye seek to drive me away," he explained, his gaze holding hers. "Ye're trying to anger me because ye're afraid of what happened today."

Swallowing, Henrietta averted her eyes, knowing only too well that he was right.

"I am not one to deceive others," he said in hushed tones as though whispering a secret. "I never lied to ye about what I wanted or not. I have no desire to be chief, and I never did. However, I feel a duty to my people." Again, his hand settled under her chin, and reluctantly,

Henrietta raised her eyes to his. "But that is not what ye wish to know, is it, Lass?"

Holding his gaze, Henrietta took a deep breath. "Why did you marry me?"

A soft smile came to his face as he stepped forward and his arms came around her, pulling her closer. He lowered his head to hers until the tip of his nose almost touched hers. Then he whispered, "I married ye, Lass, because I love ye."

Trembling, Henrietta stared at her husband as the warmth in her heart grew, struggling to hold at bay the icy cold fingers that clawed at her soul. Did he speak the truth?

"Did ye not see that, Lass?" he whispered, and an amused smile touched his lips. "Ye might be the only one in Greyston who didna know." His eyes strayed from hers, tracing the curve of her mouth. "I still have a kiss to claim."

Although delicious tingles swept through Henrietta at the thought of his lips on hers, she almost opened her mouth to protest his reasoning. After all, they had already shared a kiss that day. However, when his dark eyes looked into hers and his warm breath tickled the side of her neck, all fight left her body. Her hands ran up his arms and curled into his shirt, pulling him closer.

A soft chuckle rose from his throat before he lowered his mouth to hers.

Closing her eyes, Henrietta felt her heart skip a beat as his lips brushed against hers, only to freeze a moment later when a loud knock sounded on the door.

Startled, Henrietta's eyes flew open, and she saw the angry tension in her husband's jaw before he spun around and strode toward the door.

Pulling it open, he growled, "What is it?"

A young man stood outside their chamber, unease clear on his face as he found himself at the other end of her husband's anger. "Eh...I... eh...another messenger has arrived, Chief. Sent by Reid Brunwood."

Taking a deep breath, Connor nodded, and the young man turned on his heel and fled back down the corridor. For a short moment, her husband closed his eyes and rested his head against the side of the door. Then he turned to her, regret clearly visible in his eyes. "I'm sorry, Lass. I need to go." However, he didn't move, and for a moment, he simply stood there, staring at her, and the muscles in his jaw tensed. Then as though having made a decision, he strode toward her.

Before having taken two steps though, he stopped, gritting his teeth. "If I kiss ye now, I'll never leave," he murmured to himself before his eyes met hers, a promise burning in them. "We'll finish this later."

Then the door closed behind him.

Chapter Eighteen
ONLY FOR TONIGHT

After pacing the length of her bedchamber for what seemed like hours, Henrietta finally changed into her nightgown and went to bed. Torn between desire and fear, she tossed and turned, hoping to hear her husband's footsteps approaching the door and at the same time fearing that she would.

I married ye, Lass, because I love ye.

His words echoed in her mind, and Henrietta couldn't deny the silent joy that danced in her heart. No one had ever loved her, and somewhere deep down, she thought that no one even could. After all, was she not an arguing, disrespectful and antagonistic woman? Who would love someone like that? How could he? Or had he not spoken the truth?

Rolling over, Henrietta raked her hands through her hair as Fear's cold fingers squeezed the joy from her heart. He couldn't have been sincere. He had only spoken of love because men always did when they sought to get their way. And yet, she couldn't help but wonder why he had married her if not for love.

As contradicting emotions wreaked havoc in her body, Henrietta alternately cried into her pillow and pummelled it with her fists. When exhaustion finally stilled her hands, she rolled onto her side and closed her eyes, hoping to escape the decision to refuse or accept him.

If she were asleep upon his return, surely he would not wake her; would he?

Silence fell over the room, and Henrietta's aching heart calmed as she tried her best to fall asleep. And yet, her mind raced with all the implications of that day and wouldn't allow her the sweet oblivion of slumber.

When footsteps finally echoed to her ear, her strained nerves almost snapped.

Forcing herself to lie still, she listened as the door opened, then closed. She heard her husband approach the bed. Awfully tempted to open her eyes, Henrietta squeezed them shut instead, her fingers curling into the blanket.

When his boots thudded onto the floor, she flinched, ready to bolt from the bed. However, her limbs were too exhausted, and she breathed in relief when they wouldn't move. Straining her ears, she heard the soft rustling of fabric as her husband changed into his nightshirt. His bare feet barely made a sound on the floor as he rounded the bed. He blew out the candle he had brought in, set it on the table in the corner and slid into bed.

Breathing a sigh of relief, Henrietta waited, listening for the sounds of him having fallen asleep.

Instead, however, he rolled over closer to her, and she could feel the warmth radiating off his body. "I know ye're not asleep, Lass," he whispered, and his warm breath tickling her skin rose goose bumps on her body.

Terrified, and yet, intrigued, Henrietta remained quiet.

An amused chuckle escaped his throat before he slid even closer, and she could feel his body moulding itself to hers. Then his arm reached over, and he brushed a strand of her hair behind her ear, his fingertips gently grazing her skin.

At his touch, Henrietta flinched, but she forced herself to ignore him, squeezing her eyes shut.

"Stubborn as a mule," he mumbled into her ear, a hint of delight lacing his voice. A moment later, his hand settled on her shoulder, urging her to face him. "I promise I willna bite ye."

At his words, an excited tremble went through her, and yet, her whole body ached for his touch. Taking a deep breath, she rolled onto her back and met his gaze.

Looking down at her, his eyes held hers for a moment, then ventured lower, tracing the line of her jaw, down her neck to the small lace thread that tied her nightgown in the front. "D'ye think it wise to retire to bed when ye still owe me a kiss?" he whispered, meeting her gaze once more. "'Tis dangerous to tempt a man in such a situation."

Her eyes narrowed at the veiled challenge in his words. "I am not afraid," she insisted stubbornly.

He grinned. "Liar."

Regarding him closely, Henrietta drew in a deep breath, then slid her hand backwards and under her pillow, her hand reaching for the small dagger she kept by her side at all times.

Seeing her intention, her husband's hand whipped out and like a striking cobra grabbed her wrist before she could reach the small blade. An amused smile curled up his lips as he shifted, and she felt his body pinning her to the mattress. "There is no need for ye to defend yerself, Lass. I promised ye I willna take more than ye're willing to give. And although I am tempted …" he glanced down at her lips, and his voice trailed off as he lowered his head to hers.

Feeling the cold steel of her dagger brush against her fingertips, Henrietta held his gaze, and for once in her life, she did not feel conflicted. As her demons slept, a soft smile curled up her lips, and seeing it, her husband's eyes lit up like two brilliant stars in the night sky.

"Ye're beautiful when ye smile, Lass," he whispered before his lips brushed against hers, gentle and patient, asking for permission.

Abandoning all thoughts of retrieving her dagger, Henrietta withdrew her hand from under the pillow, and her arms came around him as though they belonged there, pulling him closer. Her mouth opened, and she answered his kiss, asking for more.

Like a beast suddenly unleashed, his lips devoured hers as his hands moved up her body, over her arms to her shoulders, tracing the slender line of her neck until he buried them in her hair.

Feeling herself respond in ways she had never expected, Henrietta strained against him, wishing that this night would never end.

As his mouth left hers, a hint of disappointment came over her until his lips travelled over her chin, along her jawline and down her neck, kissing and nipping as they went.

Closing her eyes, Henrietta moaned as swirls of pleasure danced on her skin.

Gently, he bit her earlobe before he suddenly stilled. Resting his head in the crook of her neck, he took a deep breath. Then he lifted his head, and even in the dark, she could see the tension on his face as his eyes searched hers. "I want ye, Lass," he whispered, his voice choked with desire. "Tell me if ye want me as well."

Biting her lip, Henrietta stared up at him, feeling oddly reminded of the night before their wedding when he had come upon her in the rose garden. Then, too, he had asked her for permission, and she had refused to give it. Could she grant it now? Had she not already signalled her agreement? Did he truly need to hear her say the words?

Unable to speak her heart's desire, Henrietta reached up to pull him back down to her as her head lifted off the pillow, her lips straining to reclaim his.

However, a breath away from her mouth, he pulled back, a frown on his face. "Ye canna say it, can ye?"

As her head sank back into the pillow, Henrietta averted her gaze, her cheeks hot with embarrassment.

A frustrated growl rose from his throat, and his hands dug into the pillow beside her head. "Look at me, Lass," he commanded. "Look at me!"

Reluctantly, Henrietta met his gaze, surprised at what she saw there. It was not anger that drove him, but exhaustion.

"I want ye, Lass," he whispered, "and I've told ye so. More than that, I've given ye my heart openly and without restraint." He swallowed, and she could see that he, too, was afraid of how vulnerable his words made him. "Despite how strong and confident I might appear to ye, Lass, can ye not imagine that fear also holds a spot in my heart?

Can ye not see that I, too, am afraid to be rejected by the woman I love?" He took a deep breath, and she could feel his heart thudding in his chest. "I need ye to tell me if ye want me as well. If not," he closed his eyes and shook his head, "I willna bother ye again. I swear!"

Frozen in place, Henrietta stared at him, knowing that if she could not overcome her fears, she would lose him for good. Worse, she would hurt him, break his heart and make him regret that he had ever given it to her.

All her life Henrietta had been afraid to entrust her heart to someone, afraid to be vulnerable and at the mercy of another's whims. Never before had she held someone else's heart in her own hands. Never before had she felt the weight of that responsibility.

Only now, when her husband looked down at her with a longing so desperate that it nearly broke her heart did Henrietta understand that fear was a double-edge sword in more than one way for she was not the only one who would suffer. His heart, too, was at risk.

Inhaling deeply, she closed her eyes and opened her mind to the desires hidden deep in her heart. And despite her own fears, she had to admit that she had come to care for her husband. Deeply even.

No matter what she had done, she had not been able to sway him from her side. They had fought and argued, and yet, he had stayed, his words not always kind, but honest. He had always treated her kindly though and shown her the respect she so longed for.

Opening her eyes, Henrietta met his gaze, and a soft smile came to her lips. "I do want you," she whispered, ignoring the doubts that clawed at her heart. Right there in that moment, they could not hurt her for his love wrapped her in a protective shield they could not overcome.

He stared at her as though unsure whether or not to believe his ears before his eyes closed and relief washed over his face. When he looked at her once more, all uncertainty and exhaustion had vanished. Instead, his eyes spoke of things yet unexperienced, and as he lowered his head towards hers, he whispered, "Trust me, Lass, if only tonight."

Wrapping her arms around his shoulders, Henrietta closed her eyes, enjoying the sensations his touch stirred within her. "Tonight."

She could not promise more.

Chapter Nineteen
BROKEN

Feeling his heart hammering in his chest, Connor reached out and pulled his wife into his arms, cradling her head on his shoulder. He kissed the top of her head and sighed as the memories of what they had just shared floated into his mind.

Although hesitant at first, she had warmed to his touch quickly, her own hands growing bolder with each moment. She had smiled and sighed, moaned and gasped, and for once, her face had been devoid of fear, distrust and suspicion. Instead, pleasure and even a hint of love had shone in her eyes, and Connor had lost his heart to her all over again.

However, as they lay in the dark, their bodies gleaming with sweat and their hearts racing, he felt her body stiffen: her muscles tense and a slight shiver shake her.

Closing his eyes, Connor took a deep breath. Deep down he had known that all her fears and doubts could not be overcome in one night. It was progress, but it was not the end. He had not yet won her heart, and he was far from winning her trust.

If only he knew what to do. Never in his life had he felt so helpless. She was his wife, and he had sworn to protect her, and yet, he could only stand by and watch her battle the demons of her past alone.

"Are ye all right, Lass?" he whispered into the dark.

Again, the muscles in her shoulders tensed, and he felt her limbs straining to distance themselves from him, and so he reluctantly released his hold on her.

Immediately, she rolled away, turning her back to him, the blanket clutched in her hands as though it were a lifeline.

Propping himself up on one elbow, Connor looked at her as the dark reclaimed his own heart as well. It was as though they were one; whenever she suffered so did he. "Did I hurt ye?" he asked, afraid that he had done something to cause her pain.

Again, a shiver shook her slender frame before she abruptly sat up, pulling the blanket around her. In the dim light, her eyes were dark as they searched her surroundings. Then she bent forward and snatched her nightgown off the floor, hastily pulling it over her head as though trying to hide herself from him.

"Please talk to me, Lass."

Instead, she fled the bed, her trembling hands reaching for the night robe that hung on the peg by her wardrobe.

Concerned by the frantic look in her eyes, Connor slipped from the bed. Stepping towards her, he hesitated and then pulled his own nightshirt on as well.

Just as she was about to fling open the door, he grabbed her and spun her around.

Her eyes were round as plates, and she looked like a cornered animal as she stared up at him, her jaw trembling.

"I mean ye no harm, Lass," he tried to assure her. The thought that she would be so fearful of him pained him greatly.

"I know," she whispered to his surprise. Her body, however, continued to tremble as he urged her back toward the bed.

Sitting down on the mattress, she pulled up her legs and wrapped her arms around her knees, her teeth chattering.

Connor took a deep breath and then knelt down before her. "What frightens ye so, Lass? Can ye not tell me?" He swallowed as her eyes met his. "Let me help ye. There's nothing I wouldna do for ye."

The ghost of a smile touched her lips, and yet, she shook her head. "I know. I just..." As she shook all over, her fingers dug into her arms and her eyes held a desperate plea. "I c-cannot h-help it. I c-can't m-make it s-stop," she stammered.

Connor rose to his feet and then reached for her, feeling the need to hold her in his arms.

Seeing his intention, his wife shrank back, her eyes widening.

"I willna hurt ye," he pleaded as his heart twisted in his chest. Nothing had ever pained him so than seeing the all-consuming fear in her eyes in that moment.

Scrambling back to the other side of the bed, she pulled the blanket around herself, once more hugging her knees to her body. Wide eyes met his as big, round tears streamed down her face. "I know," she whispered again and again.

Not knowing what to do, Connor stared at her.

"I'm sorry," she whispered, her voice choked with the emotions running rampant in her heart. "I really thought I could..." She swallowed. "I wanted to believe that..." For a moment, her eyes closed. "I did not mean to hurt you," she whispered, "but I cannot give you what I don't have."

Frowning, Connor stepped toward her. "What? But I-"

Instantly, she backed away, shaking her head. "I am broken," she whimpered, sobs tearing from her throat. "You need to let me go. Y-you need to move on." Forcing back her tears, she pressed her lips together, trying to regain control. "Please hear me; I cannot give you what you seek."

As complete hopelessness washed over him, Connor finally understood how she felt. Despite her efforts, despite understanding the origins of her fears, she was helpless. Whenever they wished, her demons would seize her, and although she had fought them before she could not do so indefinitely. One day, they would win, and then she would be lost.

Lost to herself, and lost to him.

It was inevitable; was it not?

As she cowered on the bed, the picture of misery, Connor knew that he had to find a way to save her, to protect her from herself. If she could not fight her demons alone, then he would find a way to stand with her.

"All right," he finally said. "I will leave for the night so that ye can rest, but ye have to give me yer word that ye willna venture from this room, Lass." He held her gaze until she nodded. Then he stepped back and headed for the door. Turning back to look at her, he added, "Every wound can heal, Lass. It might leave a scar that will always remind ye of the injury ye once had-it might even pain ye-but it will only be an echo of what once was."

Closing the door behind him, Connor fervently hoped that he was right.

Chapter Twenty
MEANT TO BE

When the sun finally began its ascent, Henrietta still sat in bed, staring at the wall, her gaze unseeing to what was around her. Her sobs had quietened long ago; her throat, however, was raw. Swollen and red-rimmed, her eyes felt as though they were on fire, and every muscle in her body ached.

Her heart, though, was what pained her most. One moment, it would almost double-over in agony as though a searing-hot dagger had been plunged into it. A moment later, all emotions would vanish into thin air, leaving behind an emptiness that almost made her wish for the pain to return.

Her husband's face occasionally floated before her mind's eye, adding guilt to the pool of emotions that assaulted her. Her thoughts, however, remained unfocused, and she could not have voiced a single one had someone been there to hear it.

As the sun climbed higher, Henrietta closed her eyes, its brilliant sting a physical pain she had not expected. Lying back down, she curled up into a ball; her heart beat a faint echo of the night before.

Soft footsteps echoed to her ears then, and before her soul could even cry out in pain, the door opened, and her mother-in-law walked in.

Relieved, Henrietta sighed, knowing that Rhona would not ask for answers. Rhona simply knew.

Approaching the bed, the older woman placed a wooden tray on the mattress, and the scent of warm bread and tea drifted over. In answer, Henrietta's stomach growled in protest at having been so considerably neglected.

"Sit up, Child," Rhona said in her gentle voice as she stepped forward and fluffed up the pillow, helping Henrietta to settle back against the headboard. Then she placed the tray on her lap, pulled up a chair and sat down.

Slowly, Henrietta sipped her tea, her stomach welcoming the nourishment like never before. Although she did not taste the bread, its warmth felt wonderful, and the pain in her stomach subsided. All the while, her mother-in-law waited quietly.

Relieved not to be pounded with questions, Henrietta relaxed, and the ache in her sore muscles calmed. When she had finished eating, she lay back, her eyes suddenly heavy with fatigue.

"Sleep, Child," Rhona whispered. As though it had been a command, Henrietta's eyes closed, and she was soon lost to the world.

How long she slept, Henrietta did not know. However, when her eyes opened once more, she found Rhona still sitting by her side, a soft smile on her kind face.

"It was a deep sleep," the older woman observed as she leaned forward and took Henrietta's hand. "I trust ye feel better rested now."

Swallowing, Henrietta nodded as images of the previous night found their way back into her conscious mind.

"He feels helpless."

Henrietta peered at the older woman from under her eyelashes. "Who?"

An indulgent smile came to Rhona's lips. "He has never known a problem he couldna solve, and it frightens him."

Averting her eyes, Henrietta swallowed. "I did not mean to cause a problem."

Rhona chuckled. "It will do the boy good to test his limits. I love him dearly, but occasionally he is too full of himself."

Henrietta felt a smile tug at the corners of her mouth. She could not help but wonder about how strange her mother-in-law was; and yet, she did not wish her to be any different. "Did he tell you...about last night?"

Glancing at the older woman from under her eyelashes, Henrietta found her shaking her head. "He didna," Rhona said, "and he never would. Not without yer permission."

Henrietta took a deep breath as a gentle warmth touched her heart. "He is a good man," she whispered, wondering when she had come to believe that.

"He is," Rhona agreed, her sharp eyes watching, observing. "Ye opened yer heart to him last night, did ye not, Child?"

"I did not mean to," Henrietta admitted, her fingers playing with the corner of the blanket. "It simply happened."

"We rarely mean to. The great loves are the ones we don't see coming. They sweep us off our feet and knock the air from our lungs." Rhona chuckled. "I hated my late husband on sight."

Henrietta's eyes snapped up. "You did?"

Rhona nodded. "He was an overbearing, loud, mule-headed man, and when we first met, I wanted to claw his eyes out every time he opened his mouth. That's when I knew."

"Knew what?"

Rhona shrugged. "That I would one day lose my heart to him whether I wanted to or not."

"Did you never regret it?"

"I might have had he not also lost his to me," her mother-in-law said, a wistful smile on her face. "Despite all his faults, at his core he was a good man, and he loved me." Rhona reached out and took Henrietta's hand, her eyes meaningful as she spoke. "As my son loves ye. Has he told ye so?"

Averting her gaze, Henrietta nodded.

"Good boy," her mother-in-law said. "Life is too short to be hiding from the people we love. He can be overbearing, but deep down he knows his path." Gently, she squeezed Henrietta's hand. "And he knows that his path lies with ye."

Overwhelmed, Henrietta withdrew her hand. Pulling up her knees once more, she hugged them to her chest, gently rocking back and forth.

All the while, Rhona's watchful eyes followed her. "It scares ye. To hear that someone cares for ye feels like a curse to ye."

As tears streamed down her face, Henrietta's fingers dug painfully into her arms. "I don't know why. I know it is foolish, but I can't help it."

After rising from her chair, Rhona settled onto the bed, and her right hand gently took hold of Henrietta's chin, turning her head. "Ye're not yer mother, Child; nor is my son yer father. Not everyone is doomed to repeat what ye lived through."

"I know," Henrietta sobbed. "Please believe me. I know. But I can't…"

Rhona nodded. "Yer demons are strong," she observed, "and they refuse to show ye any mercy." Leaning forward, she looked deep into Henrietta's eyes. "Ye will have to fight them, or they will never release ye." Rhona took a deep breath, and a hint of sorrow came to her eyes. "Listen, Child, we all have regrets, moments in our past we wish we could alter, we wish we could have seen coming."

Sensing the pain in her mother-in-law's words, Henrietta found the ache in her own heart subsiding, and she took hold of Rhona's hand.

Closing her hand more tightly around Henrietta's, Rhona sighed. "I knew my husband would die," she whispered. "I saw it in my dreams."

"What?" Henrietta gasped.

"And yet, I couldna save him," the older woman went on as though she was alone in the room. "I only caught a glimpse of what would happen, and I misinterpreted the signs. He slipped through my fingers like so many before." She lifted her gaze to Henrietta. "That is why I rarely act upon my dreams now. A part of me feels that what is meant to happen will, and my dreams merely intend to prepare me for what is to come, not change the outcome. Too much knowledge about the future causes more harm than good."

"And yet, you sent Connor to England," Henrietta whispered, "to find me."

Rhona nodded, a soft smile on her face. "I'm only human, Child. My heart, too, beats for those I love. I do not regret trying to save my husband's life; nor do I regret sending my son to find his one true love." As a blush came to Henrietta's cheeks, Rhona squeezed her hand. "Whatever my dreams are meant to do, I believe that you two were meant for each other."

Fresh tears welled up, and Henrietta squeezed her eyes shut. "Your words sound wonderful," she whispered, then once again she met Rhona's eyes. "So wonderful that I do want to believe them." A smile came to her face that she couldn't suppress. "I want him. I do. I didn't realise it before but…" Swallowing, she shook her head. "I cannot change who I am. I am beyond hope. I cannot give him what he deserves."

"Ye think too much, Child," Rhona chided, her gentle eyes smiling. "My son loves ye. His heart is already yers, and ye do not have the power to return it even if ye wish ye could. If nothing else, believe that. Nothing ye do will sway him from yer side, and the sooner ye come to accept that, the sooner ye will find the strength to slay yer demons. We canna know what the future will bring," Rhona said, a mischievous twinkle in her eyes, "but what good is the present if we always live in fear of what might happen?"

Henrietta shook her head. "I don't want to be afraid anymore, but I don't think I can stop. It is who I am. My fears and doubts and suspicions are a part of me. I don't know who I am without them."

"Don't ye want to find out?" Rhona asked, her eyes holding a challenge that spoke to something deep in Henrietta's being. "Do not think too much, Child; for once in yer life, simply live. Go to my son, find out what kind of man he is, and allow him to find out who ye are." Again, she squeezed Henrietta's hand. "And when yer fears and doubts return, give them a voice. Do not hide them. Do not keep them to yerself. Share them with him, and with time, their voices will grow quieter. I promise."

Closing her eyes, Henrietta felt a strange sense of peace sweep through her, and although her doubts remained, she did not feel overwhelmed by them as she had before. If only Rhona was right! If only there was a way for her to live without fear, to love without restraint!

Her husband's face rose before her inner eye, and Henrietta wondered how she had not seen it before. Whenever he looked at her, love and devotion shone in his eyes. His words had always been truthful; never had he lied to her. And despite the animosity she had shown him, he had always been by her side, doing his utmost to protect her, even from herself. Never had he raised his hand to her. Never ignored her objections. Never punished her for speaking her mind. If anyone was worthy of her trust, it was him!

A soft smile tugged up the corners of her mouth as Henrietta opened her eyes and met Rhona's patient gaze. "I will try," she whispered as tears of joy rolled down her cheeks. "I promise I will try."

"Ye're a strong woman," Rhona said, her own eyes moist with emotion, "and I'm proud to call ye my daughter."

Chapter Twenty-One
A LOVE MATCH

After Rhona helped her into a new gown, Henrietta ventured downstairs. For a moment, she stopped outside her husband's study but then quickly walked past, knowing that she wasn't quite ready to face him yet. Instead, she stepped outside, welcoming the warm rays of the sun on her skin and crossing the rose garden. She then squeezed through the gap in the hedge.

As always Deirdre's little oasis welcomed her, and a sense of peace and warmth washed over her still frayed nerves.

"Good day," came Deirdre's voice, and Henrietta spun around, startled.

Catching her breath, she looked at the young woman, and a smile spread over her face. "It is as though you are a part of this garden, Deirdre, and it hides you from those around you, keeping you safe."

A radiant smile on her face, Deirdre stepped toward her, brushing her dirt-stained hands on her apron. "That's beautiful." Nodding her head, she gazed around her little haven. "I do feel at home here." Then she turned back to Henrietta, and her eyes became serious. "How are ye? Ye look as though ye've had a rough night."

Knowing how red her eyes still looked, Henrietta nodded. "I did," she admitted, "but I'm starting to feel better."

"I'm glad to hear it," Deirdre said, honest relief in her eyes as they continued to watch Henrietta.

Clearing her throat, Henrietta stepped around the young woman, trying to collect her thoughts. "May I ask you something? About your marriage?"

"Certainly."

Unsure how to begin, Henrietta heard Rhona's voice echo in her head. "How did you come to be married?" she asked straight-forward. "Was it a contract?"

A dreamy smile came to Deirdre's face, and in the blink of an eye, Henrietta understood the deep connection between the young woman and her husband. "No, it wasna. In fact, his parents encouraged him to choose a different bride." Her eyes shone as bright as stars. "But he loved me, and he wouldna hear of it."

"Why would they?" Henrietta asked, hoping her questions would not offend the young woman.

"Because I'm fragile." Meeting her gaze, Deirdre sighed, and sadness came to her eyes. "As was my mother. After miscarrying many times, she finally managed to carry me full-term, but then she died giving birth to me."

"I'm sorry," Henrietta whispered, remembering the little sister she could have had. "So, his parents were afraid that he would lose you as well."

A soft chuckle escaped Deirdre, and she shook her head. "I do not wish to speak ill of them, but they were never the sort of devoted, kind-hearted parents that Rhona and Ewan were. They had expectations, and they tried their best to instil them in their children." She shrugged, and a deep smile came to her face. "I suppose he would have married according to their wishes, had I not captured his heart. His parents never forgave me for that."

"But he married you," Henrietta said, feeling a warm glow swelling in her chest, "despite their objections."

"He did," Deirdre confirmed with love shining in her eyes. "He is my match in every way. Where he is loud, I am quiet. Where he is rash, I am cautious. Where he is strong, I am weak; and where he is weak, I am strong."

"I never thought of it like that," Henrietta admitted. "When I saw you that day, I thought..."

"I know," Deirdre said. "Some people do, but those who do always judge based on their own experiences, their own fears." Her eyes grew soft, a silent question resting in them.

Henrietta swallowed. "My parents' marriage was one of fear and pain until the day that my father took both of their lives."

Deirdre gasped.

"The memory of these few years haunts me still," Henrietta said. "I'm afraid to love because a part of me believes that love is inevitably followed by pain."

Stepping forward, Deirdre reached for Henrietta's hand. "Pain will find ye no matter how well ye believe ye can protect yerself." She swallowed. "I've miscarried three times, and the last was...it was a boy." Tears came to her eyes, and her hands tightened around Henrietta's. "He was so small. He had little fingers and toes and the most beautiful little face. Before, I'd miscarried early when the baby was still just a thought and a wish. But that last time, it broke my heart." Blinking, she forced back tears. "Pain will find ye. Ye canna help that. But when it does, 'tis good to have someone to help ye bear it."

Feeling tears of her own run down her face, Henrietta took a deep breath as she looked down at the fragile woman before her whose strength exceeded her own by far. "Do you not regret...?"

"No!" Deirdre shook her head vehemently, determination shining in her eyes. "Of course, I wanted my children to live, but I do not regret trying to bring them into this world. They are worth every tear I shed." She took a deep breath as more tears threatened. "Neither do I regret marrying the man I loved, the man I still love. All the pain and sorrow we've been through has made us even more certain that we've chosen the right path. An easy love that is never tried will just as easily fail when a storm approaches. But after everything we have been through, I know that nothing will ever be able to tear us apart, and that makes me feel safe."

"Safe," Henrietta whispered, wondering what it felt like to feel safe and if she would ever feel it herself. Meeting Deirdre's eyes, she nodded. "I'm sorry I thought...I can see now that he truly loves you, and I'm happy for you." Dimly, Henrietta recalled how Alastair had demanded she stay away from his wife because Deirdre was a gentle soul and he did not wish her poisoned by Henrietta's anger. At the time, Henrietta had not seen the reason for his outburst, but now she understood.

Alastair was a good man, and he loved his wife beyond hope.

"If ye can see that Alastair loves me," Deirdre said, "can ye not also see that Connor loves ye just the same?"

A soft smile came to Henrietta's face, and for a moment, she closed her eyes. "I can, yes. Now, I can." She took a deep breath. "However, I have only now come to understand that love is not what scares me, not love itself. I'm afraid it won't last, or that it will change, and I won't see it. I don't know if my mother ever loved my father. I was too young. But I wonder. Did she love him? Is that why she endured his anger? Did he ever love her? And if so, when did he stop and why?" Shaking her head, Henrietta rubbed her temples. "I cannot help these questions. They are an echo of the doubts that live in my heart, and whenever I am tempted to love and trust, they pull me back, make me see the danger I am putting myself in. No matter what I do, I cannot stop them. It's as though they have a life of their own, and I am not strong enough to silence them."

Feeling utterly defeated, Henrietta closed her eyes and raised her head to the sky, feeling the soft wind brush over her heated skin. Hopeful one second, and forlorn the next. All her life, the extreme emotions that rolled through her heart and mind, forcing her to do their bidding, had been so much a part of her that Henrietta was baffled by the idea that if she fought hard enough, she might be able to rid herself of them. A part of her doubted that it was even possible.

Should she try; she would surely fail.

"Are ye happy now?" Deirdre's soft voice asked beside her, her small hands coming to rest on Henrietta's shoulders. "D'ye wake up in the morning with a joyous heart?"

Opening her eyes, Henrietta met Deirdre's eyes. Was she happy? What was happy? Henrietta remembered moments not tormented by her demons. Moments she had shared with her brother or Anna, laughing and smiling. But had she been happy?

"If ye do not know," Deirdre said, her soft eyes clouded, "then ye're not." Her hands slid down Henrietta's arms and grasped her hands, her eyes searching Henrietta's face. "I know ye're scared of what might happen if ye open yer heart to someone. Ye're scared it will bring ye more pain and loss. But ye're already in such pain every day that I do not believe it to be such a great risk." A soft smile came to her face, and she looked at Henrietta imploringly. "Think of what ye have to gain. The risk is minimal, and I promise ye Connor willna disappoint ye. And neither will I."

Sniffling, Henrietta smiled through tears. "Thank you, Deirdre."

"Think about it," the young woman said before a mischievous smile tickled her lips. "But not too much."

Henrietta laughed. "I promise."

Chapter Twenty-Two
LOST IN THE WOODS

Returning to the front hall, Henrietta thought about the advice not only Rhona but now also Deirdre had given her. Naturally, her fears argued that she ought not to trust them. However, Henrietta's heart could not imagine either of those two women to cause her any intentional pain. On the contrary, for the first time in her life, Henrietta felt appreciated, welcomed, cared for and even loved. No one had ever before looked at her and seen the pain that lived in her heart. Not even Tristan and Anna.

However, maybe they couldn't have. Maybe it had been Connor's influence that had dragged it out of its hiding place and into the light of day. He had pushed her over the edge, forced her to feel and face her fears so that they were now etched into her face for all to see.

Climbing the stairs to her bedchamber, Henrietta stepped around a corner and collided with none other than Angus Brunwood.

Shocked, she stumbled backwards as did he. However, when his eyes met hers and recognition found him, a snarl came to his face. "English rat," he hissed, his eyes narrowed into slits.

Taken aback by the hatred that poured from him, Henrietta felt rooted to the spot, staring at the old man as though he was a ghost risen from his grave.

The muscles in his jaw tightened as his cold eyes slid over her. "He doomed us all when he brought ye here." Taking a step toward her, he whipped a carving knife from his coat. "I will slit yer throat before ye can curse us again."

Terrified, Henrietta stumbled backwards until her back hit the wall, her hand reaching inside her own coat...to find the secret pocket empty.

Her dagger still lay beneath the pillow in her chamber.

"Wait!" she called, backing away as he came after her. "I don't mean you any harm. I swear I-"

"Lies!"

"Please, I-"

"Angus!" Moira shouted, her voice harsh and final.

Glancing behind her, Henrietta saw the tall, young woman standing there with wide eyes. Then Moira shook off her initial shock and strode toward them. "Drop that knife, ye crazy, old fool!" Stepping between them, she snapped the carving knife from Angus' grasp before turning to Henrietta. "Are ye all right?" Her eyes slid over her, and relief came to her face when she found no injuries. "Go and rest. I will speak to him."

Nodding, Henrietta backed away. Her feet, however, would not carry her in the direction of her bedchamber. As though a predator was still after her, she felt the need for open space, not a confined room. And so she turned and hurried down the stairs, feeling the old man's hateful glare burning a hole into the back of her head.

Without conscious thought, Henrietta crossed the front hall and slid out through the side door. However, when she reached the rose garden, its usual tranquillity irritated her nerves and the walls around her felt like a trap. Turning on her heel, she returned to the courtyard and headed out the main gate, her eyes fixed on the open land stretching out before her.

Instantly, her heart beat calmed, and the air she drew into her lungs brought a sense of peace to her aching soul. Step by step, Henrietta marched out into the open, unwilling to even turn her head and glance back at the receding castle walls that slowly fell behind. She crossed the small stretch of grassland until she reached the tree line and proceeded down a well-trodden path. The soft rustle of leaves mingling with the gentle songs of birds and crickets pulled her forward.

Only when the sky slowly grew darker and the dim light fighting its way through the dense foliage overhead began to wane did Henrietta realise how far she had walked.

Stopping, she turned her head, but all she saw were trees growing amidst thick underbrush. The path she had walked had long since thinned and was now almost gone. Had she turned off the main path somewhere? Henrietta couldn't recall.

When a soft drizzle touched her face, Henrietta lifted her head to gaze up at the canopy overhead. It had started to rain, and here and there, raindrops found their way through the forest's roof. Sighing, Henrietta turned in a circle, eyes searching for the way back. However, in the dimmer-growing light, she saw nothing that sparked recognition. How would she get back?

"Ye seem lost, Dearie."

As a gasp tore from her throat, Henrietta spun around and found herself staring at an old woman. Wrapped in a cloak, she stood with a stoop, white hair peeking out of the woollen hood covering her head. A water bag was slung around one shoulder, and an old wicker basket filled with different kinds of plants and mushrooms hung on her left arm.

"You startled me," Henrietta wheezed, her hand clutched to her chest.

"That is quite evident," the old woman chuckled. "Would ye care for a spot of tea?"

Surprised, Henrietta smiled. "I certainly would," she said, glancing around but seeing nothing that promised the hospitality she had just been offered.

By the time she returned her gaze to the old woman, Henrietta only saw a receding back, slowly disappearing among the trees. Afraid to be left behind, Henrietta hurried after her. "Where are we going, Mrs...eh?"

"The name's Morag," the old woman said over her shoulder. "Simply Morag."

"I'm...Henrietta."

"I know, Dearie."

Frowning, Henrietta followed Morag deeper into the forest until they came upon a strange dwelling that looked as though it had risen from the earth, a large tree growing out of its roof on either side. The trees' roots ran across the small house and down its sides, disappearing into the ground. For all intents and purposes, it looked like a small hill with a door and a short chimney stack puffing soft, white smoke into the darkening night.

Henrietta shuddered as a sense of ancient heritage washed over her.

"'Tis been in my family for generations," Morag confirmed Henrietta's thoughts as she opened the small door with a soft creak and stepped inside. Carefully, she placed her basket on a short table before setting down the water bag beside what appeared to be a small stove, that emanated a soft glow and a welcoming warmth. "Sit down, Dearie."

Choosing one of the two rather wobbly looking chairs, Henrietta watched the old woman rummage through her little kitchen.

Pulling out several jars, Morag mixed dried leaves in a small mortar, then crushed them with a pestle. Although she moved with care, her hands worked without thought as her eyes frequently ventured to Henrietta, eyeing her with open perusal. Her eyes, however, were not unkind, merely curious.

Uncomfortable, Henrietta cleared her throat. "What are you doing?" she asked, indicating the crushed leaves.

"Tea," the old woman replied, a mischievous smile on her wrinkled face.

"What kind?"

Morag shrugged. "This and that. 'Tis a choice of the moment." Her eyes met Henrietta's. "Never the same, and yet, always right."

Uncertain how to reply, Henrietta remained quiet. Although the old woman's strange ways made her feel somewhat uncomfortable, Henrietta slowly felt herself relax. There was something soothing about this little dwelling as well as the woman's company that eased her turmoil.

"Why do you live out here?" Henrietta asked, curious about why anyone, let alone an old woman, would reside so far away from Greyston Castle.

Morag shrugged. "Although not silent, the forest is quiet compared to the castle and its village. Here, I can hear my own thoughts and know them to be mine." Glancing at the many jars aligned on the wall, Morag met Henrietta's eyes for but a moment. "Ye might have guessed that I've a way with herbs, Dearie. I learnt from my mother who learnt from hers. Healers of my family have lived in this verra dwelling for generations. It is here where we are closest to nature's own heartbeat, undisturbed by the troubles of the world." A smile came to her face. "'Tis peaceful here. Simple. Pure. New ways are not always better. We all come from here but we often forget. Despite all the achievements the world's made, we're still fragile as we have always been. I live here to not forget."

For a while each dwelt on her own thoughts, and a comfortable silence slowly settled about the room. Then Morag poured two cups of tea and walking over set down one in front of Henrietta before she settled into the other chair, her hands wrapped around her own cup. Closing her eyes, the old woman sniffed the steaming liquid, and a smile came to her lips.

Raising the cup to her own lips, Henrietta, too, closed her eyes and waited for the tea's aroma to engulf her. The scent was delicate at first, then grew stronger as it danced from one fragrance to the next, all mingling into a single one that never remained the same, but kept changing no matter how often Henrietta thought she had detected its flavour.

"Why are ye here, Dearie?"

Across the rim of her cup, Henrietta met the old woman's eyes. "I'm lost."

Morag nodded. "'Tis true, but why are ye here?"

Henrietta frowned. "I just walked. I didn't see where I was going, and now, I don't know how to return."

"D'ye wish to?"

Startled, Henrietta looked up.

"Ye can speak the truth here," Morag assured her, "and no harm will come to ye."

"The truth," Henrietta mumbled. Taking a deep breath, she shook her head.

"'Tis not easy to find."

"No, it's not," Henrietta agreed, meeting Morag's eyes openly. "The truth is, I don't know."

The old woman smiled. "Few things are certain, and those who claim to know what lives in their hearts merely ignore the doubts they don't wish to see. To admit that one doesna know speaks of a truly honest soul."

Touched, Henrietta smiled and took another sip from her tea.

"Yer eyes speak of great pain," Morag spoke into the dimly lit room, "of fear, and yet, also of hope." Squinting, she searched Henrietta's face as though reading the words she spoke from the pages of a book. "For a long time, ye lived in darkness, but only recently a spark was struck."

Her hands wrapped tightly around her cup, Henrietta froze as her husband's face appeared before her inner eye and a gentle warmth engulfed her.

Watching her, Morag smiled. "Whose face did ye see just now?"

Henrietta swallowed. "My husband's."

"Does it frighten ye?"

"It does."

"Does he?"

Henrietta frowned. "What do you mean?"

"Are ye frightened of him or of the love ye have for him?"

As her demons screamed in her ears, Henrietta shook her head, her hands closing more tightly around the hot cup. "I...I..."

"D'ye love him?"

Henrietta took a deep breath. "Yes."

"Does he love ye?"

"I don't..." His voice echoed in her ears. "He said he did."

"D'ye believe him?"

"Yes."

Morag smiled. "Is he kind to ye?"

"Yes."

"Does he protect ye?"

"Yes."

"Does he respect ye?"

"Yes." The answers flew out of her mouth without a conscious thought, and Henrietta realised with some surprise that she honestly believed them to be true.

"D'ye fear him?"

"No." Again, something spoke from deep inside her, and Henrietta met the old woman's eyes as a gentle smile played over her lips. "He is a good man."

Morag nodded. "Aye, he is." Setting her cup on the table, the old woman leaned forward. "But ye were never afraid of him, were ye? Of what *he* might do?"

At Morag's words, the warmth vanished from Henrietta's being, replaced by a dreadful cold that chilled her fingers despite the warm cup in her hands.

"Ye're afraid of what *ye* might do, are ye not?" The old woman held her gaze for a long moment. "Buried deep in yer soul, ye believe yerself to be of weak character, do ye not?"

Closing her eyes, Henrietta nodded.

"We're all weak sometimes," Morag whispered across the table, her sharp eyes unbending under the uncertainties of life. "Even a strong man like Connor Brunwood is not always strong. He, too, holds fear and doubt in his heart. He, too, depends on others for his own happiness."

Remembering the day on the cliff, Henrietta nodded. He had shared his deepest secret with her, one that made him feel inferior to others, one that had him doubt his own abilities, his own worth. Yes, even a bear of a man like Connor Brunwood knew the meaning of fear and doubt.

"None of us is isolated from those around us. We're all intertwined, dependent on each other." Morag nodded, her fingers brushing over the smooth wood of the old table. "There is no shame in that, no weakness," as she spoke, her sharp eyes slowly rose from the table until they met Henrietta's, the intensity in them spell-binding, "as long as ye stay true to yerself, as long as ye do not allow yer will to bend to another's, as long as ye don't betray yerself."

Henrietta shivered, her heart hammering in her chest as the core of her fear rose from the depth of her being. "How can I be certain I will not betray myself? How...?" Shaking her head, she closed her eyes, once more seeing her mother's bruised body, the rug underneath stained with her blood.

"There is nothing wrong in compromising," Morag continued, and her hands reached across the table, freeing the cup from Henrietta's iron grip. "There is nothing wrong in sacrificing something for another, in giving in every once in a while, especially when it is not demanded by the other, but a gift given freely." Pulling Henrietta's cold hands into her own, Morag smiled at her encouragingly. "Ye'll know the difference between giving something and having something taken from ye if ye only listen to yer own sense of right and wrong. Trust yerself that ye'll know."

Henrietta took a deep breath as her fingers slowly warmed in the old woman's grasp. "Trust myself," she echoed. "It's not easy."

Morag shook her head. "'Tis not, but neither is it impossible."

"How did you know what plagues me?" Henrietta asked, wondering if Morag, too, possessed a similar skill as Rhona.

The old woman chuckled. "Nay, the winds whispered it in my ear." Then she cleared her throat and poured Henrietta another cup of tea. "Ye better drink up, Dearie, for ye'll be going home soon."

"Home? Will you show me the way back?" Henrietta asked, uncertain whether or not it would be wise to venture out into the forest in the dark of night.

"There's no need," Morag said as a soft smile curled up the corners of her mouth. "Yer husband will come for ye."

Henrietta's eyes went wide. "He...?" Staring at the old woman, Henrietta was about to object when she saw the certainty in her deep blue eyes. "But how would he know where I am?"

"His mother will point him down the right path."

Chapter Twenty-Three
A RAY OF HOPE

The wind howled through the trees as Connor followed the barely visible path, his gelding prancing nervously, its ears twitching as eerie sounds drifted through the chilled night air. The slim moon overhead provided insufficient light, and Connor cursed under his breath for the forest not only proved treacherous at night but also hindered his progress. A distance that would have taken him a mere hour during the day now took him half the night.

When Morag's hill dwelling finally came in sight, Connor breathed a sigh of relief and slid off his horse. Tying the gelding to a tree, he approached the small door, his muscles tense from the ride as well as the emotional turmoil that had befallen him upon discovering that his wife had run off once again.

Connor bent forward to knock. The door, however, slid open before he could do so, revealing in its frame the woman who had helped deliver him into this world. A smirk curled her lips as her piercing eyes met his, and she nodded for him to enter.

Ducking his head, Connor stepped over the threshold into the dimly lit room, his eyes instantly drawn to his wife seated at the small table in the corner, her hands curled around a cup of steaming tea. Taking a deep breath, she raised her eyes to his, and for a moment,

Connor thought to see a shiver run down her back. "Are ye all right, Lass?"

Returning her gaze to the cup in her hands, his wife nodded.

"I would've expected ye sooner, dear lad," Morag chided as she shook her head at him. Her eyes, however, held amusement as they wandered from him to his wife and back. "The lass has been waiting up for ye all night."

"I would've been here sooner," Connor snapped, feeling the need to defend himself, "had I known where she was." Turning to look at his wife, he found her still staring into her cup, and he couldn't help but wonder what had happened. After all, his wife was not one to shy away from expressing her opinions nor one to hide from his anger.

And curse them all, he had a right to be angry!

As his hands balled into fists, Connor forced a slow breath down his lungs.

"Now, don't fret," Morag chided, clicking her tongue as though he were a disobedient child. "Ye're not a wee lad any more. If she could've told ye, she would've."

"Is that true?" Connor asked as his eyes shifted back to his wife.

Swallowing, she raised her eyes to his once more. "I'm sorry." Her voice was but a whisper. "I did not mean to walk this far. I was...." Shaking her head, she searched for the words to explain. "I was lost in thought, I guess. I myself was shocked to see how far I had walked."

"How did ye find yer way to Morag?" Connor asked. "I didn't know ye were acquainted."

"I didn't," his wife replied. "She found me." Her gaze ventured across the room to the healer, and a smile touched her lips. "I don't know what I would've done had she not found me."

Frown lines settled on his forehead as Connor observed the silent exchange between the two women. Something had happened there that night. He was certain of it, and he desperately wished he knew what it was. "Shall we return to the castle?" he asked instead of the many questions that coursed through his mind just then.

Hesitating, his wife glanced at Morag who stepped forward and held out her cloak. "Here, take this. The night air is quite nippy." His wife rose from her chair and allowed the healer to wrap her in the old, woollen cloak. "Yer place is with him, Dearie," Morag whispered. Then she glanced at him over her shoulder and said in a louder tone, "He might growl like a bear, but he has a gentle heart." Smiling, she nodded to his wife. "His anger rose from deep concern over yer safety, Lass."

Clearing his throat, Connor stepped toward the door. He had forgotten how much Morag's ability to read him like an open book unsettled him.

"Thank you," his wife whispered, then embraced the old healer before she turned to him.

Meeting her eyes, Connor smiled and then held out his hand to her, holding his breath as he waited for her to refuse or accept him. Would she lash out at him and tell him that she didn't need his assistance?

Instead, a slight flush came to her face. She didn't seem angry though, but rather bashful as she toyed with her lower lip and barely met his eyes.

An excited tingle went through Connor's middle, and for a moment, he felt reminded of his first infatuation with a village girl.

When his wife slipped her hand into his, her chilled skin touching his own, it was as though a shock wave went through him. Marvelling at the sudden onslaught of emotions, Connor stared down at her, and his heartbeat quickened when she averted her eyes, a tentative smile curling up the corners of her mouth.

Behind them, Morag chuckled.

What had happened? Connor wondered as he escorted his wife outside. After all, he was a grown man, and all of a sudden, he was mooning over his wife like a love-struck boy. However, what truly shook him to his core was that his wife, too, looked at him in much the same fashion. Had she come to care for him? Was that possible?

Glancing back at Morag, Connor wished he knew what the two women had talked about, for at this point he was ready to believe that Morag Brunwood was a witch after all.

"Will you help me up?" his wife asked as they stood by his gelding, and for a moment, Connor stared at her as though thunder-struck.

Then a smile came to his face when he saw the hint of shyness in her eyes as she looked up at him. "Of course," he whispered as though those two words held a deeper meaning meant for her ears alone.

Delighted with the change that had so unexpectedly occurred between them, he bent down to form a step with his hands. Quickly, she slipped her foot in and pushed herself up, swinging a leg over the gelding's back.

Sliding into the saddle behind her, Connor reached out a hesitant arm and pulled her against him, holding her tight. To his surprise and utter delight, she relaxed against him, one hand coming to rest on his forearm across her middle.

"Be good to each other," Morag said, a knowing smile on her face, before she stepped back into her dwelling and closed the door.

Enjoying the warmth of his wife's body pressed against his, Connor leaned forward and whispered in her ear, "Are ye ready to go home?"

A shiver went through her at his words, and he could see her closing her eyes, her neck bending further back, pressing her head against his shoulder as though she wished to be closer to him. Connor took an unsteady breath when she turned her head, her eyes open as he had never seen them. Without pretence, without a mask to hide her true feelings, she gazed up at him, and a shy smile came to her lips before she whispered, "Would you kiss me?"

Lifting his other hand, Connor traced a finger along her jawline as his eyes searched hers, desperately wishing to understand, but also afraid to lose the fragile connection that had so unexpectedly formed between them. As her eyes remained on his, her lips beckoning him forward, Connor bent his head to hers and placed a gentle kiss on her mouth.

With uncertainty in his heart, he pulled back and was delighted to find her smiling up at him, her teeth once more toying with her lower lip as though shyness had suddenly overcome her. Her eyes, however, held his, and she whispered, "Let's go home."

As she snuggled back against him, Connor's arm tightened around her before he urged his gelding back down the path they had come. Although they rode in silence, it was not the kind of silence that weighed heavily on his heart, but rather a silence that allowed his other senses to take over, and he became acutely aware of the wordless exchange between them.

In the thicket of the forest, they were forced to travel slowly, and so her back rested gently against his chest. Even through the thick fabric of her woollen cloak, he felt the soft beating of her heart, the way it quickened every time he turned his head from the road to gaze at her and his breath brushed over her skin. He felt her chest rise and fall against him with each breath as her hand continued to rest on his arm. Occasionally, a shiver would come over her and she would snuggle closer against him.

Smiling, Connor wondered if it had been the cold night air that had caused the shiver or rather her own awareness of him.

Once they reached the open plains, Connor urged his gelding on, sensing the exhaustion that rested in Henrietta's limbs. However, when they finally crossed through the main gate, Connor could not help but feel regret at the loss of closeness that was now inevitable.

To his delight, his wife was far from offended when he helped her out of the saddle, and she willingly slipped her arm through his as he escorted her up the stairs and to their bedchamber.

After he closed the door, he found her standing in the middle of the room, her eyes sweeping over the large bed. A slight blush came to her cheeks brought on by the memories of the previous night. Afraid that she would distance herself from him again, he strode toward her, reaching for her hands. "Don't be afraid, Lass. We don't have to-"

A shy smile came to her face then, and she placed a finger on his lips to stop him. "Would you just hold me tonight?"

Hoping that he had not imagined her words, Connor searched her eyes. "If ye wish to sleep alone, ..."

"No." She shook her head determinately, and Connor felt the strain of a long day fall from his shoulders.

Nodding his head, he stepped back. "I promise I'll keep my back turned," he grinned at her, "if ye promise to do the same."

A radiant smile on her face, she nodded, then stepped back toward her wardrobe, her eyes still holding his as though unable to tear herself away.

Forcing himself to turn around, Connor quickly changed. All the while, his senses were acutely aware of his wife only a few steps away from him. He heard every rustle of fabric, every quickened breath. He even thought to feel the soft warmth radiating from her body reaching across the room and touching his chilled skin. Keeping his back turned was like torture, and yet, the temptation to look coursing through his body excited him like never before.

When he finally heard her tiptoe toward the bed and slide under the covers, he glanced over his shoulder.

Buried under a thick blanket on the right side of the bed, she glanced over and met his eyes. Then her arm reached out and swung back the blanket from the other half of the bed, inviting him to join her.

As his heart beat in his chest with an excitement he had not known before, Connor slid between the covers. All the while, he searched her face, afraid to shatter the fragile bond between them. However, when she tentatively inched closer and then rested her head on his shoulder, his arm came around her shoulders with an ease as though they had spent twenty-odd years sleeping in each other's embrace.

At first, her breathing followed a slightly elevated rhythm, too intense for a good night's sleep while her heart beat against his chest, too fast as though they were still racing across the plains on horseback. However, after a while her breathing evened out, and her heart beat relaxed. Her muscles felt lax against his own, and the strain of that day fell away.

Holding her tightly against him, Connor closed his eyes, and a soft smile spread over his face. For a long time, he had imagined this very moment, and for a long time, he had feared it would never be. And now, here he was, holding his sleeping wife in his arms, her soft breath tickling his skin as she snuggled closer against him when a chilled draft touched her.

Never before had Connor felt at peace as he did in that moment, and he hoped with all his might that it would last, that somehow that night had changed things and set them on a path that led to a happy future.

He would give anything for that dream to come true.

Chapter Twenty-Four
TIME & PATIENCE

When the early morning sun tickled her nose and the bright daylight touched her eyes, Henrietta felt her dreams slipping away. Slowly, she returned from the land of slumber, and her senses began to register her surroundings. Before she even cracked open an eye, her tactile sense detected the warm body holding her. Her head rested on smooth skin, pulsing with the soft beating of her husband's heart. As she drew in a deep breath, his arm tightened around her, and to Henrietta's surprise, she did not feel trapped, but protected instead.

Lying still, she waited for her demons to awaken, her heart fearful of the sudden onslaught of distrust and suspicion. However, at least for the moment, all remained quiet, and Henrietta decided to enjoy her moment of peace for as long as it would last.

"Are ye awake, Lass?" Heavy with slumber, her husband's voice drifted to her ear. Shifting a little, he glanced down at her as she raised her head to meet his eyes. "'Tis been a long time since I've slept this well," he smiled, a captivated twinkle in his eyes as they slid over her.

Feeling herself blush, Henrietta bit her lip. "Neither have I. It is strange, is it not?"

"Very much so," he confirmed, and a rumble of laughter shook his chest as he sighed with contentment.

Pushing herself up into a sitting position, Henrietta glanced down at him and to her delight noticed the hint of disappointment on his face that she had extracted herself from his embrace. Her heart rejoiced at the open display of his emotions, and Henrietta wondered if Rhona and Morag were right. Could she leave her past behind and begin again?

"There is something I need to tell you," she said, feeling the need to put into words what lived in her heart. "I don't know if I can though. It is all still very confusing for me."

Propping himself up on his elbow, her husband nodded to her. "Say what is on yer mind, Lass, and I promise I'll try my best to understand."

"All right." Taking a deep breath, Henrietta searched her mind. "I've told you about my parents." He nodded, and a hint of sadness came to his face. "What happened all those years ago has...made me fearful," she admitted, "but not the way I always thought it had."

"What do ye mean?"

"I thought I distrusted people because I always feared they would turn against me. If not today, then someday. It was only a matter of time. After all, my father was the one who not only hurt my mother but ultimately killed her. Her own husband. If she could not trust him, trust in him to protect her, then no one else could be trusted either." Henrietta took a deep breath as her past surfaced, and yet, only a mild echo of her demons sounded in her mind and heart.

Listening, her husband's eyes had narrowed. "D'ye believe I would harm ye, Lass? I mean I canna blame ye for believing so. After all, we hardly know each other." His jaw clenched as he inhaled deeply. "However, I need to know. Please tell me honestly."

Shaking her head, Henrietta smiled at him. "No, I do not fear you. I never have. You're nothing like the man my father was."

An answering smile tugged up the corners of his mouth, and Henrietta could see that her answer pleased him greatly. "But d'ye fear that I will one day? D'ye fear that it is only a matter of time?"

"No." Reaching out, she took his hand in hers. "Of course, I do not know what the future will bring. However, this is not about you as it was not only about my father."

A soft frown settled on his brows once more, and Henrietta could see that he did not understand.

"I hated my father for what he did," she began, hoping that she would find the words she needed, "and I still do. However, it was my mother who taught me how to be truly afraid."

"Because she did not fight him?"

Henrietta nodded. Maybe her husband understood her better than she thought. "I simply cannot understand why one would not defend oneself if attacked, and yet, there had to have been a reason." Closing her eyes, Henrietta once more saw her mother's lifeless body on the blood-stained rug. "To fight an attacker and lose is...acceptable. As ridiculous as that sounds, it is all right because you've tried. You've tried your best, but you simply weren't strong enough." Remembering her frail mother, Henrietta shook her head. "I never expected her to triumph when he attacked her, but...why would she not defend herself? I'm not necessarily talking about a physical fight, but couldn't she have left him? Told someone?"

"Maybe she was afraid. Maybe she was afraid of what would happen."

"What could be worse than what my father did to her?"

Her husband shrugged. "Maybe she was afraid that no one would believe her."

"How could they not? The whole household knew!"

Holding on to her hand, her husband sat up. "'Tis not that easy for women to claim their own rights."

"Believe me, I know," Henrietta sighed. All her life she had fought to be accepted as a capable individual, one who could choose her own life. She had fought everyone around her on principle because she feared that if she gave in only once and lost a battle, she would lose the war. "I know it would not have been easy, and yet, I cannot imagine that her life was anywhere close to acceptable for her. How could it be?"

"Maybe it was simply familiar."

Henrietta shrugged. "What I'm trying to say is that what frightens me the most is not the thought of someone I care for turning against me. Yes, it would be awful and devastating, but what I truly am frightened of is," she took a deep breath, "that I will let it happen." Holding her husband's gaze, Henrietta waited, hoping to see that tiny spark of understanding that meant that he would listen.

"Ye mean out of love, Lass?" he asked, and Henrietta sighed in relief. "That ye allow someone to mistreat ye because ye love him?"

As tears streamed down her face, Henrietta nodded. It had taken her years to understand the root of her fears, and deep down, she had not expected him to understand. The fact that he did meant more to her than she could ever express. "It's what my mother did. Whether she truly loved my father or not, she rather deceived herself into believing that he didn't mean it, that it was an accident, that he would change one day and see the wrong of his ways rather than fight for herself and give up on a love to a man who-in all honesty-gave up on her a long time ago. That kind of love has lost all meaning. It is no love at all."

"So ye rather not love at all?" her husband asked, but his eyes held more than the question that left his lips. In his gaze, Henrietta read the need to know, and yet, also the fear to learn that they would never have a future together.

Henrietta smiled. "No."

The moment the words left her lips, such honest relief washed over his face that her heart opened to him a little more.

"I suppose I've never truly allowed myself to love," Henrietta admitted, feeling strangely liberated to be able to share her darkest secrets not only with herself but also with her husband. "Not completely at least. I've held my brother at arm's length and my friend as well." Anna. The name echoed in her head, and guilt flooded Henrietta's heart at the thought of what she had put her friend through. Hopefully, it was not too late to make amends. "I never told them how I felt. I never allowed myself to even admit it to myself. Whenever I used the word love, I didn't quite mean it." Lifting her gaze off the sheets, she met her husband's eyes. "But I want to. I really want to."

"I'm glad," he whispered and once again reached for her hand. "And

I am relieved that ye're willing to share this with me. To tell ye the truth, 'tis disheartening to fight a battle without knowing yer enemy."

"I suppose it is," Henrietta agreed. "I'm sorry for making this so difficult for you. However, simply because I want to change does not mean I can." Swallowing, she held his gaze. "It'll take time...and patience."

"I know." A deep smile came to his face. "But it will be worth it."

Chapter Twenty-Five
AN INSPIRING LOVE

After her husband had been called away, Henrietta ventured down to the rose garden and sat down on the granite bench by the small water fountain. In her hand, she held a letter from Anna. For the millionth time, she turned it from side to side, trying to glimpse the words written on the paper within. Of course, it was a futile attempt, and yet, Henrietta could not quite bring herself to open it.

Only last night, she had finally come to realise how her fears had affected not only her own life but also Anna's. The advice she had given her back when Anna had gotten married had been harsh and unrelenting, not taking into account that Anna and her husband were not the same people her parents had been. Back then, however, Henrietta had not been able to see that.

How had Anna reacted to her questions? Henrietta wondered, once more turning the envelope in her hand. Had she been furious? Or had she welcomed Henrietta's attempt at reconciliation?

Remembering how Anna had come to visit her before she had left for Scotland, Henrietta hoped that her friend was able to see past Henrietta's earlier attitude.

With her eyes fixed on the small envelope, Henrietta took a deep breath, then quickly opened it before her courage could fail her. Unfolding the sheet of paper, she glanced at the finely written words, her eyes sweeping over the letter as though trying to determine the tone of its message. Then Henrietta returned her gaze to the top and began to read, a slight tremble in the hands that held the paper.

My dearest Henrietta,

Allow me to set your mind at ease and assure you that I never believed you would intentionally ruin my happiness. I always knew that a dark secret lived in your past, and although I'd wished many times that you'd shared it with me, I understood that some secrets can haunt you in a way that prevent you from recognising the allies you have.

I assure you I've always been your friend, and I always will be. Of course, I was saddened by the course our friendship had taken, but I always reminded myself to be hopeful. I prayed that one day you'd find someone to confide in, someone who would stand beside you and face the darkness that threatened to chase even the last ray of sun from your life. Do I dare hope that you have found that someone in your husband?

From the questions you asked, I felt compelled to believe so, and it makes my heart soar. I always wished that you would find someone worthy of your love and trust, someone who would show you that love is not always followed by pain and loss.

My heart weeps for your baby sister and for you as well. Looking at my own daughter, I cannot understand how any mother could choose anyone else, even her husband, over her own child. Therefore, I cannot offer you an explanation for I have none. I can only assure you that not all mothers are like that, not even those deeply in love with their husbands.

To answer your question: no, my husband has never made me regret that I placed my trust in him. We are who we are. We love and we fight, but never without respect. As much as I desire his, he also burns for mine. Remember that. Whether we are men or women, we all want to be loved and respected, understood and accepted for who we are.

Yes, I am happy, deliriously so, and I consider myself very fortunate.

Please, write back and allow me to be a part of your life. I yearn to hear what kind of man your husband is and even more so how he found a way into your heart.

Today is truly a wonderful day filled with hope and promise, and yet, I miss you dearly.

Your friend always and forever,

Anna

As the lines blurred before her eyes, Henrietta pulled a handkerchief from her pocket. Dabbing away the tears, she stared at her friend's eloquent words, and for the first time since they had parted in anger, Henrietta did allow herself to admit that she missed Anna. Oh, what she wouldn't give to have her friend right here sitting on the bench beside her! If only-

"There she is."

Startled out of her thoughts, Henrietta lifted her head, surprised to see a young couple hurrying toward her. Although the delighted glow on their faces suggested a close acquaintance at the very least, Henrietta could not recall ever having met them.

Hand in hand, they walked toward her, their steps quickening as though impatient to reach her side.

Still confused, Henrietta folded up the letter and blinked back the tears that threatened. Then she lifted her head and waited, somewhat curious what this was about.

"Are ye her?" the young woman asked, hopeful eyes darting back and forth between Henrietta and the young man at her side. He, too, seemed excited, his hand clutching hers tightly as though afraid to be parted for even a short moment.

"Who?" Henrietta asked, raking her mind for a memory of these two radiant faces that looked at her as though she was the answer to their prayers.

"The chief's wife?" the man inquired while the woman appeared to be holding her breath.

"I am, yes."

At her words, a mixture of relief and unadulterated joy washed over their faces. The woman sighed with delight, and relinquishing the man's hand, she sat down on the bench beside Henrietta, her face glowing like the morning sun. "Ever since we heard, we wanted to meet ye. Ye're our inspiration," she said as her hands fluttered every which way as though unable to convey all she held in her heart. "Without yer courage, we wouldna have found our own. 'Tis because of ye that we're married today."

Completely at a loss, Henrietta stared at the young woman, certain that they were mistaking her for someone else. However, her last comment stirred something familiar in Henrietta, and squinting her eyes, she glanced from her to the man still standing beside them, excitedly wringing his hands. "You are Fiona and Liam, are you not?" she asked. "I heard that you'd run away. Your fathers are very worried." She stopped. "Wait, did you say you were married?"

"Aye," Liam confirmed, his eyes shining like Fiona's as they gazed at each other. Then he swallowed and returned his gaze to Henrietta. "We know that our decision will cause...misgivings," he admitted, then held out his hand to Fiona, who immediately rose from the bench to stand beside him, "but we're in love, and we refuse to bow our heads any longer."

Taking a deep breath, Henrietta felt as though she had suddenly been swept into a lovers' tragedy that she had no connection to whatsoever. "I'm sorry for the struggles you've faced," she said, her eyes shifting back and forth between them, trying to determine what it was they were asking, "but I'm afraid I do not understand."

"It was yer love," Fiona beamed, "yer courage that finally convinced us to fight for our love as well." A deep smile on her face, she looked up into Liam's eyes, his own a match to hers. "Our fathers sought to keep us apart since the day we were born." She turned her eyes back to Henrietta, wanting her to understand. "Some old feud stands between them. However, they refuse to talk about it. For a long time, we obeyed their ruling, hoping that time would change their minds." A grateful smile came to her lips. "But when we heard what ye did, ..."

"What do you mean, what I did?"

"...we knew we could no longer deny our hearts' desire," Fiona went on. "Knowing that our fathers would never give their consent, we ran away and got married before they could stop us."

Shaking her head, Henrietta tried to sort through the myriad of information she had just received. "Yes, my husband told me about your problem. However, I fail to see what that has to do with me."

As though she had just asked them what colour the sky was, the young couple stared at her. "Ye fought for yer love," Fiona said, admiration shining in her eyes. "Even though ye're English and he's a Scot, ye didna bow to obligation. Ye defied everyone and got married. Ye didna allow anyone to stop ye."

As it was now Henrietta's turn to stare at them, Liam nodded in agreement with his wife's words. "When we heard what ye did, we knew it was not only possible but worth it to fight for our love as well. Ye gave us the courage to stand up to our fathers, and we came to thank ye for it and to ask a favour."

Chapter Twenty-Six
FOR ALL INTENTS AND PURPOSES

Drawing a deep breath, Henrietta lifted her hand and knocked on the door. From inside, her husband's voice called for her to enter, and with trepidation in her heart, Henrietta stepped across the threshold to his study.

After everything that had happened between them in the last few days, Henrietta felt nervous around him. She had opened up her heart to him, and a part of her still lived in fear of what he might do with the knowledge she had entrusted to him. On top of that, she had only just now accepted a request addressed to her because of a misunderstanding, and yet, Henrietta had not had the heart to tell Fiona and Liam the truth about her own so called love story.

As the door opened, her husband turned toward it; the moment their eyes met, the strain fell from his face, and a soft smile tugged on his lips. In answer, Henrietta felt her own heart skip a beat as delighted tingles ran down her back, and she had to take a deep breath to steady her nerves.

Something had definitely changed between them.

Remembering that they were not alone in the room, Connor cleared his throat and turned back to Alastair, waiting rather impatiently in the armchair on this side of the desk. "Would ye give us a moment?"

"Certainly," Alastair grumbled as he rose from the chair. Walking past Henrietta, he glared down at her, and despite what she had learnt about him from Deirdre, she could not help but feel threatened by him.

When the door finally closed behind Alastair, Henrietta looked at her husband and not knowing how to begin said, "He does not like me, does he?"

For a moment, his eyes darted to the closed door before he shrugged. "Alastair is a complicated man. Do not take it personally."

Wringing her hands, Henrietta took a step forward, then stopped, her eyes glancing from her husband to his desk, to the window and the floor.

"We have to begin anew, do we not?" he asked into the silence, and when Henrietta lifted her eyes off the ground, a soft smile played on his lips. "Before, we knew how to talk to each other. Now, 'tis different."

Henrietta nodded. "It is, yes."

"Maybe ye could tell me why ye came to see me," her husband suggested before a mischievous twinkle came to his eyes. "I doubt ye came because ye couldna bear to be parted from me a moment longer."

A soft laugh escaped her, and Henrietta felt her muscles relax. "Frankly, no, that wasn't the reason."

Clutching his hands to his chest, his eyes widened in mock outrage. "Ye wound me, my lady."

"I had no intention of doing so," Henrietta said laughing, her words, however, sounded heart-felt, and the look on her husband's face told her that he had noticed as well. At his open smile, a hint of self-consciousness crept up her cheeks, and Henrietta quickly cleared her throat and said, "The reason I came is because I met Fiona and Liam in the rose garden."

"Ye did?" Connor asked in surprise. "I told them to keep their distance until their fathers arrive and we can sort this out."

"Well, they're determined to..." Henrietta frowned as a thought struck. Taking a step closer, she asked, "Did they tell you what inspired them to run off together?"

Connor chuckled, "To tell ye the truth, I rather growled at them when they were brought to see me this morning. Although I understand their plight, I am obligated to remain neutral. It would serve no one to encourage youngsters to run off whenever they disagree with their parents. That being said, I have every intention of convincing their fathers to give their consent." As he spoke, his eyes held hers, and Henrietta saw his need for her to understand his motivations and not mistake the duties he called his own for a cold heart.

"Thank you," she said, acknowledging his efforts, and the relief on his face told her that she had not misjudged him.

"Well then, what did they tell ye?" he asked, offering her the armchair that Alastair had vacated a few minutes ago. "Or were ye sworn to secrecy, Lass?"

"Not at all." Sitting down, Henrietta tried to find the courage to honour her promise. "On the contrary, they asked me to speak to you on their behalf."

"I see." Reclaiming his own chair, Connor folded his hands, his forearms resting on the table top. "I have to admit I am surprised that they sought ye out."

"As was I," Henrietta admitted, her eyes not quite meeting his. "However, from their point of view, I suppose it is a reasonable request."

Her husband's brows rose into arches. "And what is their point of view?"

Closing her eyes for but a moment, Henrietta felt an embarrassed smile tug up the corners of her mouth.

"Do not keep me in suspense, Lass," her husband demanded. "From the look on yer face, I have to assume something rather...indecent."

Biting her lower lip, Henrietta met his eyes. "Apparently, it was our love story that gave them the courage to fight for their own."

Her husband's mouth fell open, and his eyes went wide before laughter spilled from his mouth.

Surprised at his reaction, Henrietta shook her head, feeling a hint of displeasure. "Would you not consider ours a love story?" she tried to ask mockingly.

"Mine? Aye," he said, meeting her eyes openly. "Yers?" Holding her gaze, he remained quiet for a moment. "I do not presume to know. Does that offend ye, Lass?"

Averting her eyes, Henrietta took a deep breath, her fingers playing with the hem of her sleeve. No one had ever made her blush the way her husband did. Despite their short marriage, he seemed to know her better than anyone. Annoyingly so, she had to admit. "No," she finally said, lifting her head and meeting his eyes. "It does not offend me. After all, it is the truth."

Nodding, her husband's eyes searched hers. "Maybe it wasna a love match," he said, "but that doesna mean it won't be."

Henrietta swallowed as the intimacy of his words shook her to her core.

The physical act of love-making had always appeared as the most intimate connection between a man and a woman. However, now, seated, with the desk between them, they could not escape into an embrace or a kiss. Instead, they faced each other openly, their eyes revealing their innermost thoughts and desires, hopes and fears.

Never before in her life had Henrietta felt so vulnerable than in that moment when her husband sat across from her, more than an arm's length between them, his eyes resting on hers, reading in them what she could not say.

As strange as it was, when he embraced and kissed her, it was far less intimate a contact, and a part of Henrietta wished he would simply push the desk out of the way and pull her into his arms. Then, at least, she would be able to hide her emotions behind closed lids.

"So, they believe we went against obligations and expectations," her husband said, returning to their initial discussion, "when we got married, and that we did so because we were in love."

Swallowing, Henrietta nodded.

"I suppose it must seem like that to them," Connor mused, a soft smile in his eyes. "After all, there was no sensible reason for us to marry. For all intents and purposes, we should never have even met."

Hearing his words, Rhona's voice echoed in her head, reminding her that not all had objected to their marriage. After all, without Rhona's interference, they would never have met, and for a moment, Henrietta pictured her old life, the life she would have continued had it not been for the man sitting across from her, patiently waiting for her to reply. "I suppose so," she whispered, meeting his eyes, "but I cannot bring myself to regret what happened."

Holding her gaze, her husband took a slow breath before a deep smile spread over his face. "Neither can I, Lass, and I never have."

Chapter Twenty-Seven
'TIS WHAT FATHERS DO

Gone was the hostility that had marked their days before, replaced by a rather strange apprehension whenever they would cross paths. It was almost as though they had only just met, two people slowly getting to know each other. And yet, they lived the life of a married couple.

Smiling, Connor shook his head as he glanced across the covers at his sleeping wife. Curled up on her side, she slept peacefully, and Connor wondered if the day would ever come that he could simply reach out and pull her into his arms.

He didn't know, but he had hope. After all, had she not openly confessed to him only that afternoon that she did not regret having married him? Did that not mean that her heart had warmed to him? If only the demons of her past would release their hold on her.

Shifting onto his side as well, Connor gazed at her face, her eyelids closed in deep slumber. He breathed in her scent, and a strange fluttering sensation began in his stomach and then spread throughout his body. Once again, he felt like a boy falling in love for the very first time.

How did he feel? Excited? Nervous? Exhilarated? Euphoric? All of these applied, and yet, they were not enough to describe the emotions that tugged on his heart whenever he saw her.

Lying in bed with her now, barely an arm's length between them, Connor felt at peace. However, a part of him wished she would wake, open her eyes and look back at him with the same love he felt for her. Caught up in the moment, he reached out and gently brushed a strand of her short hair from her forehead.

She stirred.

As though struck, Connor snapped his hand back. Holding his breath, he waited, hoping she wouldn't wake and shrink back from him.

Minutes passed, but her eyelids remained closed, and Connor's heart beat began to slow down.

Then she rolled onto her back, her head snuggling deeper into the pillows.

For a moment, Connor thought she would simply sleep on when he noticed the changes about her.

Her chest began to rise and fall with increasing speed as her hands curled into the bed linens. Her head tossed from side to side, her eyes squeezed shut as though she was afraid to look. Behind her closed lids, Connor could see the movement of her eyes and finally understood that she was dreaming.

Unfortunately, her dream seemed to be far from pleasant, and Connor struggled with the decision to let her sleep on or to wake her instead.

"No! Mother! No!"

As the whimpers tore from her throat, Connor flinched. His limbs all but paralysed, he stared at her as heart-wrenching sobs filled the room.

Shaking off his trance, Connor sat up, then reached out and pulled her onto his lap. "Lass, wake up," he whispered in her ear, but she only continued her lamentations. Rubbing her arms and back, he spoke louder, and after a small eternity, her eyelids began to flutter. Relief filled him, and he held her closer, saying her name again and again, assuring her that she was safe.

At what point her sobs ceased, Connor couldn't say. He was still holding her, rocking from side to side, when her hand settled on his chest, its warmth seeping through the fabric of his nightshirt. Sitting back, he looked down at her, her eyes tear-rimmed and filled with such sadness as he had never seen it before.

"Are ye all right, Lass?" he whispered, knowing full-well that she was not, but not knowing what else to say.

Swallowing, she closed her eyes and snuggled closer against him.

Instantly, his arms tightened around her, and he was filled with the desperate need to protect her, to wipe away her tears and to ensure they would never return. Anger rose in his heart at the sight of her misery as well as his own helplessness. As much as he wanted to, he could not fight the demons that tormented her. Never in his life had he felt so powerless.

It had to be her. She was the only one who could fight her way out of the dark, out of the memories that haunted her. He could not do it for her, but maybe he could hold her hand.

"Ye called out in yer sleep," he whispered close to her ear, torn between the wish to distract her and knowing that such a distraction could only be temporary. "Ye called for yer mother."

For a long while, she remained still. He thought she had not heard him or simply pretended she had not. However, just when he was about to abandon his pursuit, she looked up, her eyes sad but determined.

"I saw it again," she whispered, and her hand curled around the front of his nightshirt, "the night my parents died."

Connor took a deep breath. "Tell me what ye saw."

"It was raining," she whispered, her eyes distant as she relived the moment her demons were born. "It had rained for over a week. We had been confined to the house, and my father was furious. He would yell; then he would drink, and then he would yell even louder." She swallowed, and a small shiver shook her frame. "My mother would try to keep us distracted, keep us quiet and out of his way, and it worked… for a week." She took a deep breath as though gathering the courage she needed to go on. "That night, though, he lost his temper. I could hear him yelling all the way up the stairs. I was afraid, more afraid than before. There was something in his voice that …" Closing her eyes, she shrugged. "Somehow I knew that that night it would be worse, so I went to get my brother."

Connor shuddered at the thought of two little children locked in a house with a madman, and as if that wasn't enough, it had been their own father. Anger rose in his heart, and he gritted his teeth against the desperate need to wrap his hands around the man's throat. After all, parents were supposed to protect their children, guard and guide them. All his life, his own parents had been there for him in every way, and he had taken it for granted, unaware of his own good fortune.

One day, he could not have been older than ten or eleven, he had been out hunting with his father, and a wild boar had suddenly rushed from the underbrush, charging in his direction. Terrified, Connor had simply stood and stared at the wild beast as it lunged toward him. He had thought his life forfeit when in the last second his father had pushed him out of the way, and the boar's sharp fangs had not pierced Connor's body but his father's instead.

His father had barely survived that day, and Connor had been riddled with guilt. At his apologies, his father had merely smiled, patted his head and said, "'Tis what fathers do."

What kind of a man would he have been if his own father had been like his wife's? Connor couldn't help but wonder. As he gazed down at her, he realised what a strong character she had to have for her father's atrocities had not turned her into a monster as well. Although she sought to hide it, she was a kind-hearted, compassionate woman, who-despite everything that had happened to her-still had hope.

"Tristan was only a few months old at the time, but I could barely hold him," his wife continued, allowing her memories to guide her through that one fateful night long ago.

Connor swallowed and reminded of her pain, the warmth that had flooded his heart at the thought of her inner strength and kindness slowly receded, replaced by a sense of dread.

"I sneaked down the stairs, afraid that my father would see us," she whispered, relived alarm in her voice. "I went into the kitchen and hid in the pantry." Shaking her head, a rueful smile came to her face. "I can still remember the smell of the old wooden box mingling with that of fresh potatoes. Isn't it strange what you remember after all those years?"

"'Tis true," Connor agreed, knowing only too well how easily the smell of charred wood and candle wax brought him back to the many nights of his childhood. Sitting in the parlour with his parents by his side, he had snuggled into their warmth as they had told him the ancient tales of their clan's history.

"I don't know for how long I sat there, but soon my arms grew heavy, and I was afraid I wouldn't be able to hold him any longer," she told him in a hushed voice as though afraid her father might hear her. "I was afraid he'd cry, and we'd be found out."

"But ye weren't," Connor prompted, knowing that she wanted nothing more but to shy away from the memories that still ached in her heart.

"No," she confirmed. "For a long time, nothing happened, and a part of me thought we could simply hide out in the pantry forever, and my father would never find us."

"What happened then?"

"My mother screamed, and I thought my heart would jump from my chest," she sobbed, tears streaming freely down her cheeks now. "It was so full of fear and pain. I..." She took a deep breath and tried to wipe away the wetness on her face. "I know I could not have saved her, but a part of me still blames me for not going to her, for not at least... trying." Again, she took a deep breath, and Connor could feel a new resolve strengthening her muscles. "But I had my brother to take care of. I could not risk his life, not even to save hers."

"Ye did right," Connor assured her once more, and as she looked up and met his eyes, he thought that she actually believed him. Even if only a little. "What happened then?"

"A shot rang out." Resting her head on his shoulder, she snuggled closer against him. "By the time I finally found the courage to leave the pantry, my parents were dead. I found them in the parlour." A tremble shook her, and her hands balled into fists. "He had slit my mother's throat and then shot himself. His hunting rifle was right there on the floor beside him."

Connor did his best not to picture the scene his wife had

described, and yet, he could not help but see a little, blond girl, her baby brother clutched in her small arms as she stared in disbelief at the lifeless bodies of her parents.

"That day changed everything," his wife whispered. "It changed me, and I don't know if I can ever go back, if I can ever get back what I lost."

Chapter Twenty-Eight
OLD HATRED

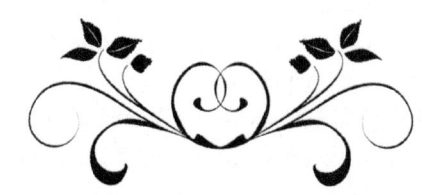

After a rather wakeful night, Henrietta felt strangely rested. Despite the lack of sleep, she did not curse the sun when it rose outside their windows. Reliving the night her parents had died and sharing it with her husband had eased her mind. Every time she confronted her demons, willingly facing the moment her fears were born, Henrietta felt their hold on her grow weaker. Maybe if she refused to hide from or ignore them, if she stopped pretending they did not exist, then she would slowly gain ground and step by step fight her way out, freeing herself of their influence.

That thought gave her strength and hope.

The only thing that bothered her that morning was a strange sense of obliviousness as though she had forgotten something important, as though the answer to her questions was right there before her eyes and she simply didn't see it.

"D'ye wish to join me today?"

Turning around, Henrietta fastened the lock of her necklace. "Join you?" she asked, meeting her husband's eyes. Ever since last night, he looked at her in a different way. Henrietta couldn't quite say what it was, but she liked it.

"Fiona's and Liam's fathers are to arrive this morning," he

explained. "As their chief, 'tis my duty to mediate their dispute." He grinned a little sheepishly as though embarrassed. "I thought considering their request ye might like to be there."

Taking a deep breath, Henrietta hesitated. So far she had lived in Greyston as though she did not belong, as though her stay was not permanent. However, things had changed. This was her home, and the only way it would ever truly feel like home was if she accepted reality.

With a smile on her face and a slight tremble in her hands, Henrietta nodded. "Yes, I would like that."

"I'm glad," her husband said, holding out his hand to her, and Henrietta could see that he meant it.

After a short breakfast of whispered words and meaningful glances in the company of the other residents of Greyston Castle, Henrietta walked down the corridor on her husband's arm, his other hand covering hers. While the gentle contact of their linked arms felt normal, they barely dared meet each other's eyes for a prolonged time. Henrietta was not ready to let her husband see what lived in her heart.

As they neared his study, angry voices drifted through the open door, and they were met by a rather pale-looking young man. Upon seeing them, he straightened, wringing his hands as he approached. "I escorted them to yer study...as instructed."

"I see," her husband mumbled, casting a weary glance at the door through which a heated argument could be heard. "How long has this been going on?"

The young man shrugged. "Since they've laid eyes on one another."

"Thank ye, Dougal," her husband said, and the young man eagerly took the opportunity to excuse himself from the scene of battle. "Well then, shall we?" Connor asked, looking down at her with a hint of mischief in his eyes. "Or have ye changed yer mind, Lass?"

Smiling, Henrietta shook her head. "Loud noises do not frighten me."

Her husband laughed. "I'm glad to hear it, for I'd much rather face them with ye by my side."

A feeling of warmth swept through Henrietta as her husband guided her to his study and through the open door. However, upon being met by two angry stares as soon as they stepped across the threshold, Henrietta swallowed, clinging more tightly to her husband's arm. Although these two men did not scare her, she regretted the change in atmosphere she experienced. Her husband's company had been such a delight while the two men radiated nothing but hatred. It felt like a slap in the face.

"Good morning," Connor greeted Brogan and Reid Brunwood cheerfully, ignoring the steam coming out of their ears. "Allow me to present my wife."

Upon his words, their eyes drifted to her and instantly narrowed.

Both men stood tall with broad shoulders and a prominent nose. However, while Reid Brunwood, Liam's father, appeared merely angered, Brogan Brunwood was the image of a raging bull, which had abandoned reason long ago.

"What is she doing here?" Brogan growled, and his eyes snapped back to Connor, open disapproval in them.

Squaring his shoulders, her husband took a deep breath, and Henrietta could tell from the tightening of his muscles how difficult it was for him to remain calm. "May I remind ye that ye're speaking about the mistress of Greyston Castle, yer hostess for the time ye decide to stay under its roof. I would ask ye to show her the same respect ye demand for yerself."

Gritting his teeth, Brogan mumbled something unintelligible that might have been an apology as well as a threat.

"Good," her husband said, then passed by the two men and gestured for her to sit on the settee. Turning back to the newly-weds' fathers, he pointed to the adjoining armchairs. "Please take a seat. Since we're all here now, I suggest we discuss the matter at hand. However," he raised his hand when both men opened their mouths, seemingly intent on releasing another tirade, "I ask that ye try to remain calm and only speak when addressed."

As their eyes opened wide, Connor nodded. "From what I'm told, ye've been in here yelling at each other for a good hour; have ye reached a satisfying conclusion?"

Both men took a deep breath, then scooted to the outside of their chairs as far away from the other as possible. Henrietta had to grit her teeth to keep from laughing. They were like stubborn school children!

"I didna think so," her husband concluded. "Now, from what I hear Liam and Fiona ran off and got married, a union of which ye two disapprove."

"My daughter didna run off," Brogan snapped, his face flushing red like a beet, "especially not with the likes of him. She's a good girl and was taken against her will."

"Puh!" Shaking his head, Reid glared at him. "My Liam would never have gone against her will. They're in love, as ill-advised as that is."

Henrietta frowned as she observed the two squabblers. Confirming her initial impression, Reid-while not delighted with his son's choice-seemed willing to accept the match. Brogan, however, appeared far from able to see the truth. For as far as Henrietta could tell, Liam and Fiona truly were in love. So, the question remained, why could Brogan not accept that?

"One at a time," Connor interfered before the two men would completely lose their tempers. "Brogan, did Fiona tell ye that she was taken against her will?"

"Of course not," Brogan huffed. "How could she have? Snatched from her bed in the middle of the night, how could she have left me a message? I'm certain she would've, had she been able to."

"I spoke to Liam and Fiona," Connor said before Reid could reply to the renewed insult against his son, "and I have to say that they both appear to be verra much in love. I didna get the impression that Fiona had been taken against her will."

"Of course, she couldna speak freely with the lad right beside her," Brogan countered. "Who knows what he threatened to do should she reveal the truth?"

"When I saw them," Henrietta said, remembering the promise she had given the two young people, "she seemed neither frightened nor intimidated."

For a moment, shocked silence fell over the room as all eyes turned to her. While her husband's face held an encouraging smile, the other two men stared at her as though she was the devil incarnate. Rarely had Henrietta seen such hostility in her life!

Lips pressed into a thin line, Brogan Brunwood glared at her. "With all due respect, *my lady*," he forced out through gritted teeth, "ye don't know my daughter and can, therefore, not rightly say whether she was frightened or not. As a stranger to these lands, ye'd be wise to keep yer counsel to yerself."

"Brogan!" Connor growled, his eyes narrowing into slits as he fixed the older man with an icy stare. "I believe an apology is due!"

Holding her breath, Henrietta glanced back and forth between the three men. Intrigued, she saw the bulging muscles in her husband's forearms as he forced his anger back under control, and she could not help but be impressed by the control he had over his temper.

Brogan looked torn between obeying his chief's request and the anger that coursed through his veins spurring him on. Clenching his teeth, he mumbled yet another unintelligible remark that could have been an apology. Henrietta, however, doubted it very much.

Meanwhile, Reid Brunwood observed the whole exchange with an interested as well as a shocked eye, his arms resting relatively calmly on the armrests of his chair.

"Yer father would never have stood for this," Brogan snapped, shifting his angry stare from Henrietta back to Connor. "He wouldna have allowed a foreigner to dictate-"

"She is my wife and, therefore, not a foreigner, but a Scot by marriage," Connor declared to Henrietta's surprise, "and she doesna dictate anything. She's merely observed as I have myself that yer daughter seems happily settled in her choice, a choice that seems to have been made freely."

Once again, steam seemed to puff out of Brogan's ears. "Ye should never have married her," he snapped, his ears deaf to the counsel offered. "Yer father wouldna have approved of an English lass as mistress of Greyston. 'Tis a disgrace, 'tis what it is."

"Brogan!"

Ignoring his chief's angry scowl, Brogan leaned forward, hands gripping the armrests of his chair. "'Tis yer fault, I say. Marrying an English lass gave that boy ideas," his eyes darted to Reid before returning to Connor, "that messed with his head. Ye should've kept with tradition and married yer cousin. Ye've betrayed yer people."

The moment Connor shot to his feet, the pulse in his neck

hammering rapidly, Henrietta knew that there was only one way to avoid a physical confrontation.

Rising from the settee, she stepped forward and placed a hand on her husband's arm. "I shall take my leave," she said, meeting his eyes. For a moment, he frowned at her but then nodded, the hint of a smile on his lips.

Turning to the other two men, Henrietta inclined her head. "I apologise for the trouble I caused," she said. "Please do not allow this issue to influence yer decision with regard to Liam and Fiona." Then she strode for the door and left.

Chapter Twenty-Nine
KEEPING WITH TRADITION

Walking down the corridor, Henrietta took a deep breath, glad to have escaped the heated argument, and yet, feeling oddly guilty for leaving her husband to deal with them alone. Her presence, however, would only have made things more difficult and not served any purpose. If she truly wanted to help, which Henrietta had to admit she did, then she needed to find out what had caused the rift between Brogan and Reid Brunwood. Maybe their children knew more than they thought, Henrietta hoped, and so she went in search of them.

After a few enquiries, she was not surprised to be pointed toward the rose garden where she found them sitting on the bench by the water fountain, hands entwined, their heads bent in trepidation.

When they heard her approach, they looked up, and a hopeful glow came to their eyes. Knowing that she had not done them any service, Henrietta felt herself cringe under their open admiration. If anything, her presence had made things worse, preventing Brogan from ever accepting that his daughter had chosen freely.

"Any news?" Liam asked as he rose to his feet, offering Henrietta his spot on the bench.

Taking the offered seat, Henrietta sighed, "I'm afraid not. Your father in particular," she looked at Fiona, "seems to be against the match. His idea is that you were kidnapped from your room and forced into this marriage."

"What?!" Fiona and Liam gasped as one, their faces almost ash-white with shock.

"Liam would never do such a thing," Fiona insisted. "He's the kindest, sweetest-"

"Your father seems to be blind to everything related to Reid Brunwood," Henrietta interjected before Fiona could go on, "which includes his son. Do you have any idea what happened between them?"

Looking defeated, Liam shrugged. "I couldna say. Ever since we were little, they never spoke to each other. Whenever my father would come upon hers, they would pretend the other wasna there. As children we thought it was wildly funny, and we often played the same game," his eyes travelled to Fiona, and a smile came to his face, "but never for verra long for it was more fun playing with her than without her. However, our fathers seemed to appreciate it when we shunned the other as well, and so we did whenever they were near. But only then."

"My husband told me," Henrietta began, remembering the day he had informed her of the two runaways, "that your fathers used to be friends. Long ago. Do you know anything about that?"

Fiona nodded. "Before she died, my grandmother told me that they grew up together like brothers, and it broke her heart to see them suffer. I could never understand what she meant. To me, they didn't seem sad, but angry, especially my father." Sighing, she shook her head. "But she never told me what happened between them."

My father believed that a woman came between them. Her husband's words echoed in Henrietta's ear, and she turned to the couple once more. "What about your mothers? Can they shed no light on the issue?"

With sadness in her eyes, Fiona shook her head. "Mine died giving birth to me. I never knew her."

"I'm sorry to hear that," Henrietta said, understanding only too well the loss of a mother. "And yours?" she asked Liam.

Liam shrugged. "My mother never said anything that would have explained their hatred for one another. However, she wouldn't."

"Why not?"

"Because my mother is...," he shrugged his shoulders as though searching for the right words, "determinedly cheerful. 'Tis as though she wills herself to see only the things that bring her joy, and whenever I asked her about the tension between our fathers, she only shrugged and said, 'What's meant to be will be.'" A frown on his face, Liam shook his head. "I never understood what she meant by that especially since my asking seemed to sadden her, and my mother is not sad on principle."

"I see," Henrietta mumbled, trying to picture the woman refusing to speak of something that obviously bothered her. "And how did your parents get married? Was it an arranged marriage or a love match?"

"It started as an arranged marriage," Liam said, "but they came to care deeply for one another. My mother once told me that she hoped I would one day find a woman who'd love me as much as she loves my father." A soft smile played on Liam's lips as he thought about his parents.

"What about your parents, Fiona?"

"It was a love match," the young woman beamed. "From what my grandmother told me, my mother was quite a beauty, and she had many suitors fighting over her hand."

"And she chose your father?"

Fiona nodded. "She did." Taking a deep breath, she looked at the softly gurgling water in the fountain. "He loved her dearly, and it still pains him to talk about her." She blinked, and her eyes returned to meet Henrietta's. "That's why I cannot understand how he can deny me my own love for he knows the weight of such pain."

"I am certain that your father is not wilfully denying you your happiness," Henrietta counselled, gently squeezing the young woman's hand. "Despite his anger, he does what he does to protect you. There must be a reason for his behaviour, something that allows him to believe that what he does is in your best interest."

Tears brimming in the corners of her eyes, Fiona nodded her head. "I know he loves me. He's always been there for me, counselled me, guided me with a gentle hand and pride shining in his eyes. And yet, sometimes I catch him looking at me in a way that…that almost breaks my heart as though the mere sight of me pains him."

"Do you know if you resemble your mother?" Henrietta asked.

Fiona nodded. "I'm afraid I do." Burying her face in her hands, the young woman sobbed.

Rising from the bench, Henrietta stepped away and made room for Liam. The young man pulled his wife into his arms and rocked her gently, whispering words of comfort in her ear.

For the second time that day, Henrietta decided that her presence was not needed and retreated into the castle.

From what Fiona and Liam had told her, Henrietta suspected that the woman who had come between Reid and Brogan had been Fiona's mother. After she had chosen Brogan, Reid had married a woman chosen by his parents, a woman who knew about her husband's love for another but chose to ignore it in order to find the happiness she sought.

However, why was Brogan the one determinedly set against the match? After all, it had been Reid who had lost the woman he loved to another. Shouldn't he be the one holding a grudge?

Henrietta frowned, certain that there was something else. Something that hadn't been revealed yet. Something only Brogan Brunwood was aware of.

Whether he wanted to or not, she would have to speak to him. For Fiona and Liam's sake.

Quietly, she proceeded down the corridor toward her husband's study, listening intently for loud yelling and angry voices. When all remained quiet, she pressed her ear against the door, wondering if the meeting had already come to an end or if they were conversing in more appropriate tones.

Only silence met her ear, and Henrietta was about to step back and knock when footsteps approached from the other side of the door. Before Henrietta could react, the door was flung open and she came face to face with her husband.

Finding her listening at his door, a grin spread over his face and a mischievous twinkle came to his eyes. "Curious, Lass?"

Feeling a slight blush heat her cheeks, Henrietta raised her chin and met his eyes with a smile on her lips. "Not in the least. What on earth gave you that idea?"

Her husband laughed. Then he beckoned her inside, and his face sobered. "I apologise for the way Brogan spoke to ye, Lass. He shouldna have."

Henrietta shook her head. "Do not worry yourself. I've been spoken to with even less regard."

Connor frowned as he searched her face. "Yer uncle?"

Henrietta nodded, feeling a familiar sting of regret at her uncle's disregard for her. However, now it was of little consequence, and Henrietta realised that she had come to cherish the new life that had been forced on her, and a smile came to her face that instantly wiped the frown from her husband's. "He cannot hurt me anymore," she said with a sigh, "and it feels good. Liberating."

"I am glad to hear it, Lass." Holding out his hands, her husband pulled her into his arms and planted a gentle kiss on her forehead. "Ye deserve to be happy, and I will do everything in my power to make certain ye are."

Stepping back, Henrietta searched his face, the expression in his eyes, the line of his lips to see whether or not he was truthful. It was an old habit, one that she could not quite shake yet.

But she would.

"Thank you," she whispered, a hint of embarrassment stinging her joy at having doubted his intentions. "I promise I shall do the same."

"Then we're both in good hands."

Henrietta nodded, surprised at how certain she felt all of a sudden. "Indeed." Remembering the reason why she had come to her husband's study, Henrietta cleared her throat. "May I ask what happened with Reid and Brogan? Were you able to make them see reason?"

Connor's face darkened. "Unfortunately, not." Taking an exasperated breath, he shook his head. "I have to say Reid doesna seem to be the problem here. 'Tis Brogan who canna forget his hatred for the sake of his daughter's happiness. He demands that the marriage be declared void on the grounds of forced consent. He argues that Liam coerced her into the marriage against her will. Naturally, Reid is outraged that his son is being accused of such a deed." Raking his hands through his hair, Connor sighed. "At present, I doubt that Brogan is willing to see reason. Every argument laid at his feet, he stubbornly disregards."

In a strange way, her husband's words echoed in Henrietta's chest as though they were her own. How often had she stubbornly insisted on her opinion despite every reasonable objection? Closing her eyes, Henrietta took a deep breath as emotions flooded her heart that she was still fighting to control. "He's afraid," she whispered and lifted her eyes to meet her husband's gaze.

"Afraid?" he frowned. "What makes ye say so?"

Henrietta shrugged, unable to explain what she knew in her heart. "It's the look in his eyes. He is driven, driven by something he has no control over. I think a part of me recognises that."

Watching her closely, Connor nodded. "What do ye suggest?"

"I need to speak with him. I need to find out what he fears so. Otherwise, he will never listen. It's what fear does. It makes you unreceptive to reason," Henrietta said, hoping that her own experience with fear would at least once serve her, "and besides, the arguments you've brought forth are not connected to what he fears. It must be something else. Something he is hiding from all of us. Something he might not even have admitted to himself."

"All right," Connor said, his eyes still watching her intently. "If ye believe it to be the right thing, I will send for him in the morning. For tonight, I think we all could use some rest." He held out his hand to her and waited patiently.

Henrietta nodded, then slipped her hand into his and allowed him to escort her from the room. However, as they walked down the corridor toward the dining hall, Henrietta's mind conjured something to the surface of her consciousness that she had only heard in passing. Something she hadn't paid any attention to.

Ye should have kept with tradition and married yer cousin.

Stopping in her tracks, Henrietta looked up at her husband and for a moment hesitated.

A frown on his face, Connor searched hers. "Is something wrong?"

"You should have kept with tradition and married your cousin,"

Henrietta repeated the words she had heard a few hours ago. "That's what Brogan said."

Her husband swallowed, then nodded. "It was," he confirmed before his eyes narrowed, and then swept over her face. "What are ye asking, Lass?"

Averting her gaze, Henrietta took a deep breath, feeling somewhat foolish. What right did she have to be hurt by the thought that another woman had been meant for her husband? After all, she had not wanted him.

A gentle hand settled under her chin and made her look up. "Ask what ye wish, and I promise I'll tell ye the truth." His eyes held hers, and she could see that he meant what he said. But did she want to know? On the other hand, didn't she already know? Or rather suspect?

Squaring her shoulders, Henrietta swallowed. "Which cousin?"

At her question, a hint of delight came to his eyes as though he cherished the thought that she might feel jealous at the idea of him married to another. Holding her gaze, he lowered his head slightly and said, "Moira."

Inhaling deeply, Henrietta nodded. "I suspected as much."

"How so?"

Henrietta shrugged. "I cannot say. There's always something slightly odd in the way she..." Again, she shrugged. "I really cannot say. It's just a feeling I had as though she didn't like me because I took you from her."

Connor frowned. "Has she been unkind to ye?"

"No," Henrietta hastened to clarify. "Not at all. It was more subtle than that. Maybe she herself is not even aware that she resents me for it. I think she's been trying to be my friend."

"I'm glad," Connor said, and his hands gently closed around hers, pulling her closer, his eyes even more intent than before. "Lass, I need ye to know that it was an arrangement. Even less than that. It was never even agreed upon." He swallowed and nodded for emphasis. "Although I care for her, I never wanted her, not the way I want ye, Lass." Pulling her closer, he wrapped his arms around her, and Henrietta felt the slight tremble in his voice as his words resonated from his chest into hers. "I never regretted the choice I made. Not for a second. I need ye to believe that."

As an excited quiver ran through her, Henrietta smiled. "I do believe you, and I have to admit I am glad to hear it."

Relief washed over his face, and he lowered his head down to hers, the tip of his nose gently touching hers. "As am I."

Chapter Thirty
A VOICE IN THE DARK

Sleeping peacefully, Connor frowned when a swift kick to his shin startled him. Instantly, the cocoon of slumber began to recede, and his consciousness resurfaced. His ears detected agonising moans; whereas, the rest of his body continued to register slight attacks, a hand slapping his shoulder, an arm landing across his midsection or a foot connecting with his already bruised shin.

When awareness finally seized him, Connor shot up, one hand roughly brushing the sleep from his face as he turned to look for an intruder. Instead, he found his wife thrashing on the bed as though in a fever fit, her body convulsing painfully. Her face spoke of agony, however, not physical but emotional, and he grabbed her by the shoulders. "Lass, wake up!"

Instantly, her eyes flew open, wide with terror as she glanced around, trying to determine her surroundings. "Connor?"

"Aye," he confirmed, his heart soaring at the sound of his name on her lips. "'Tis me, Lass. You're safe. You're home."

Slowly, her breathing evened, and she rested her head against his shoulder, her right hand reaching over and almost digging into his arm as though he were a lifeline, preventing her from sinking to the depths of the ocean.

"A bad dream?" he asked, knowing that it was so. "Was it yer parents?"

Not lifting her head off his shoulder, she nodded. "Only this time, I couldn't see. It was as though I was blind. Everything was dark."

Again and again, Connor stroked her back until he felt her muscles relax. "What frightened ye so, Lass?"

"I'm not sure," she whispered, her fingers digging deeper into his flesh. "It was as though someone was lying in wait, watching me." She shivered. "And I couldn't see."

"D'ye think it was yer father?"

Taking a deep breath, she shrugged her shoulders. "Everything seemed strange, somehow out of place. For a long time, all I could hear was my brother's soft breathing as well as the rain pelting the room. As strange as it sounds, it was rather peaceful. Then my mother screamed, and everything changed. Everything became dangerous and threatening."

For a moment, she remained quiet, searching for the remnants of her dream, and Connor wondered what had brought on these nightmares now of all times. Had they returned because she was finally willing to deal with the demons of her past instead of hiding from them? However, as though they had a life of their own, they seemed determined to keep her from slaying them once and for all.

"I heard the shot ring out as I have many times before," she continued in hushed whispers, "only it didn't stop then."

"What d'ye mean?"

"Usually I wake up when I find my parents dead," she explained, "but this time I didn't. I never left the pantry." Sitting up, she rubbed her hands over her face, her brows in a frown as she tried to make sense of what she remembered. "I was in the pantry, and I heard the shot, and then..." Squinting her eyes, she shook her head as though unwilling to believe what her mind told her. "It cannot be right."

"What?" Connor asked, feeling goose bumps crawl up his arms. "What did ye hear, Lass?"

The frown still on her face, she met his eyes. "I heard footsteps. Loud and stomping, they climbed the stairs and went from room to room before returning to the ground floor." Again, she shook her head, her eyes wide. "I heard a voice."

Reaching for her hands, Connor held her gaze. "Whose voice?"

"I don't know." Staring at him, she shook her head. "I don't know."

"What did it say?"

For a second, her eyes narrowed before frustration washed over her face. "I cannot remember. It sounded like a curse, like someone growling in anger, but I could not understand the words."

Holding on to her hands, Connor searched her eyes. "D'ye believe it to be a true memory or something yer mind conjured?"

Shaking her head, his wife shrugged. "I don't know. I don't remember ever dreaming this before." She looked up from her hands and met his eyes. "Why now?"

"I don't know," Connor whispered and pulled her into his arms, holding her tight, "but we will find out. Together."

Chapter Thirty-One
HELEN OF TROY

Wringing her hands, Henrietta walked the length of her husband's study as he sat on the corner of his desk watching her. Casting a glance in his direction, she asked, "How can you remain so calm? If he's unwilling to speak to me, I fear there'll be nothing we can do."

Connor cleared his throat, his eyes searching for hers. "Even if he doesna understand, even if he refuses his consent, he doesna have the power to declare the marriage void."

Stopping in her tracks, Henrietta stared at her husband. "Are you saying you would go against his wishes?"

"I would, aye." Rising from the desk, he came toward her and took her hands in his, a soft smile on his face as his eyes met hers. "I believe as ye do that Fiona and Liam are in love, and I canna deny them what I want for myself."

Although he had told her before, Henrietta only now realised how much she meant to him, and the breath caught in her throat as she found her husband looking down at her with love and devotion shining in his eyes. "You really do love me, don't you?" she whispered as her vision began to blur, and a single tear rolled down her cheek.

At her question, a gentle smile touched his lips, and he pulled her into his arms, his eyes never leaving hers. "Ye're the only woman I've ever loved, Lass, and the day that ye can truly believe that will be the happiest of my life."

"I-"

A knock sounded on the door, startling them.

Clearing his throat, her husband stepped back and then toward the door to open it while Henrietta quickly brushed the tear from her face and dabbed a handkerchief to her eyes. Never had she shed as many tears as in the last few weeks. This marriage had truly changed her.

"Good morning, Brogan," her husband said as he opened the door, and Fiona's father walked in.

The older man grumbled a greeting in return but instantly froze when his eyes fell on Henrietta. His lips thinned, and he took a deep breath before turning on his heel.

"Stay." Closing the door, Connor stepped in the man's way. "This is an urgent matter, and we need to discuss it."

"But not with her here," Brogan grumbled, glaring at Henrietta.

Trying to stay calm, her husband took a deep breath. "Brogan, I-"

"Connor?" Stepping forward, Henrietta placed a hand on his arm and whispered, "Would you excuse us?"

Holding her gaze, his eyes widened, and for a moment, he didn't say a word. Then his gaze shifted to the man standing behind her before it returned to hers. "Are ye certain, Lass?"

Henrietta nodded. "Please."

"I'll be right outside," he told her, his eyes holding hers for a moment longer, assuring her that he wouldn't be far. Then he reluctantly stepped back. "My wife wishes to speak to ye alone," he told Brogan whose mouth dropped open in surprise. "If ye do not treat her with the appropriate respect, ye may not live to regret it. Am I understood?"

Gritting his teeth, Brogan swallowed a reply and nodded.

"All right." Opening the door, Connor stepped outside. However, before he closed it, he looked at her imploringly and repeated, "I'll be right outside."

"Thank you," Henrietta whispered before the door closed, and she was alone with a man who hated the very sight of her.

Feeling her own hands tremble, Henrietta squared her shoulders and took a deep breath, then met Brogan's eyes, a gentle smile on her face. "I wished to speak to you alone because I know how difficult it is to reveal something personal of yourself to another," she said, noting the hint of surprise and suspicion that came to the man's face. "I need to ask you a few questions, and I am asking you to answer them for Fiona's sake."

Brogan snorted, "Do not pretend ye care about my daughter," he spat. "I willna tell ye anything for 'tis none of yer concern. Ye're an outsider, and married to the chief or not, ye'll never understand his people. Do not presume to know me!"

Seeing the stubborn determination on his face that Henrietta recognised only too well, she sighed, knowing that there was only one way for her to win his trust. "We all have our past, and it shapes us more than we like to admit," she began, linking her hands as her own demons reawakened. "Over time, we start to see Pain and Fear and Doubt as our allies, keeping us safe, protecting us," she shook her head, "but we're wrong because they keep us tied to our past as though the present had never come and the future is just a hollow dream."

Brogan swallowed, and for a short moment, his eyes dropped to the floor.

"I recognise such a past in you," Henrietta said, her eyes pleading with him to believe her, "because my own held me trapped for a long time as well. Only recently have I begun to see the truth of what made me the person I am, and although it is painful to confront the demons of your past, it is also worth it."

Brogan took a slow breath, and although the snarl had disappeared from his face, Henrietta could see that he was not convinced.

"When I was five years old," she began, feeling her fingernails dig into her skin, "my father killed my mother and then himself."

Staring at her, Brogan swallowed, his eyes wide with shock.

"He had always had a temper," Henrietta continued, "which was only intensified by his love for spirits. Hardly a day passed when he would not lash out at my mother and me. I cannot count how often bruises covered her face or how often I hid hoping he would not find me when anger overtook him once again." For a moment, Henrietta closed her eyes and took a deep breath, feeling a single tear roll down her cheek. "I did not see how it happened, and I am grateful for that. At the time, I was hiding in the pantry, holding my baby brother, praying he wouldn't wake up and cry. All night, we stayed in the pantry, and I listened to my father's shouts and my mother's sobs...until the house fell silent."

Brogan's face had gone pale at Henrietta's account of the night her parents had died, and the hatred had vanished from his eyes, replaced by sadness and empathy.

A soft smile came to Henrietta's face as she saw that he did not look at her as an enemy or a foreigner any longer, but someone he could relate to, someone he could understand instead, and hope grew in her heart. "What happened in my past made me distrustful of... everyone," she admitted, feeling a new strength in her heart. "I was certain that everyone, especially men, would eventually turn against me, and that the only way to protect myself was to not rely on them, to keep them at a distance," a sad smile came to her lips, "to keep myself from ever loving them. It is a lonely existence."

Clearing his throat, Brogan took a deep breath as his eyes searched her face.

"I know that you love your daughter," she said, and a gentle smile came to his lips, "and that you are a good father to her. Fiona loves you dearly, and it pains her to hurt you, but she cannot give up on the man she loves." Taking a step forward, Henrietta looked at him imploringly. "I know that you would not stand in the way of her happiness unless there was a good reason."

Brogan's jaw clenched as his hands balled into fists.

"I know you have a reason for what you do, and it is not because you believe her to have been forced into this marriage. That is an excuse so that no one will ask you for the real reason. Only, as you have seen, it is not enough of a reason. Considering the circumstances, no one can accept it as true; therefore, it is assumed that you merely object to the marriage out of anger." Shaking her head, Henrietta stepped forward. "Unless you share your true objections, no one, not even your daughter, will be able to understand."

Brogan sighed, his mouth opening and closing as though he wished to speak but could not find the courage or the words.

"Is it about your late wife?" Henrietta asked.

Instantly, Brogan's eyes flew up, and he stumbled a step backwards as though he had been punched in the gut. "What do ye know of my wife?"

"Only what Fiona told me," Henrietta said, now more convinced than ever that Fiona's late mother was the key. "She said that her mother had been a beautiful woman, much sought after, and that in the end, she had chosen the man she loved: you."

For a short moment, Brogan closed his eyes, and a soft smile touched his lips. "She did," he whispered and once more opened his eyes. "Although I'd hoped, I'd never truly believed she would choose me. The day she told me, I thought I'd strayed into a dream."

Henrietta smiled. "You were lucky to have found each other, just like Fiona and Liam."

Meeting her eyes, Brogan sighed, and Henrietta could see the many contradicting thoughts tearing him apart. "I never wanted anything but her happiness," he confessed as though revealing a well-guarded secret. "No matter what happened, she's my daughter and I love her."

Henrietta frowned. "No matter what happened?"

Closing his eyes, Brogan took a deep breath. "Ainsley was like Helen of Troy, a vision, a siren. Men would take one look at her and fall in love." He sighed. "As did I, and Reid as well."

"I see," Henrietta said, sensing they were getting closer to the real reason for Brogan's objections to his daughter's choice. "Did you not believe she truly loved you?"

Brogan shrugged. "I wanted to. On some days I did while on others I had doubts."

"You did not think yourself worthy of her love?"

"Compared to her, I was a no one," he confessed. "Compared to her other suitors, I was a no one as well. There was no good reason why she should have chosen me. I never expected her to. Only I could not step down without at least stating my desire to make her my wife."

"You still doubt her love, do you not? Even today," Henrietta asked, his own demons almost visible in the tortured expression on his face. "But how does that affect Fiona?"

Brogan took a slow, painful breath. "Because I am not certain that she is, in fact, my daughter."

Henrietta's eyes went wide, and yet, deep down she had suspected something like this. "You believe her to be Reid's daughter?"

Brogan nodded, a hint of relief on his face that Henrietta understood. As painful as it was to drag the past back into the light of day, it also felt good to finally voice one's concerns to another who would simply listen and understand.

Throwing his hands in the air, Brogan shook his head, his eyes wide with indecision. "I canna let her marry her own brother, can I?"

"But you're not certain, are you?" Henrietta asked. "What gave you the idea that Fiona is not your own child? Did they admit to an affair?" Remembering Reid's placid face, Henrietta doubted that the man even so much as suspected that Fiona could be his daughter.

"No." Brogan shook his head. "I didna have a chance to ask her."

Henrietta nodded. "Yes, Fiona told me that her mother died in childbirth."

Loss edged in his face, Brogan looked at her. "All of a sudden she was gone, and I..."

"I'm sorry," Henrietta whispered. "It must have been awful to lose her so unexpectedly."

Brogan nodded, then lifted his eyes. "But ye know what that is like, do ye not?"

A sad smile came to Henrietta's lips, and she nodded. "Tell me what made you doubt her love. For Fiona's sake."

Fighting through the pain, Brogan forced back the memories that so plagued him. "Although she'd agreed to marry me, many of her suitors still tried to dissuade her, convince her that she had chosen badly. Our entire betrothal, up until the morning of our wedding, I lived in fear that she would change her mind and call it off." He shook his head in exasperation. "A part of me knew I was being foolish, but I couldna help myself. I watched her. I watched them look at her, speak to her." Meeting Henrietta's eyes, he smiled. "She never gave me any reason to doubt her, to doubt the love she had for me, and I felt even more foolish."

When Brogan remained silent, his eyes distant as he relived memories from long ago, Henrietta cleared her throat, bringing him back to the here and now. "Did something happen with Reid? Something that made you doubt her after all?"

Sighing, Brogan nodded. "He had spoken to her many times, and she had merely answered him with a courteous smile on her lips, like she had all of the others. But one night, I thought I'd seen something different."

"You saw them together?" Henrietta asked, wondering what it would feel like to come upon her own husband in another woman's arms. Instantly, her stomach twisted painfully, and Henrietta had to swallow a lump in her throat. Later, she thought and turned her attention back to the man before her.

"It was a festival," Brogan remembered. "A bonfire lit the night. There was music and dancing and…merriment. Everyone was laughing and having a wonderful time as did we. We danced long into the night, but at some point, a friend in tears called for her, and Ainsley went to comfort her." Taking a deep breath, Brogan swallowed. "When I saw her again, she stood in the shadows of the castle wall…with Reid." Gritting his teeth, he shook his head. "I canna say what it was, but the way they spoke to each other sent chills down my back. So, I stopped and tried to listen. Only I couldna hear them. They were whispering, and I couldna get close enough without revealing myself."

"What happened?" Henrietta asked, uncomfortable at the level of intimacy she asked him to share with her, and yet, she had to know. For Fiona's sake.

"They were whispering," Brogan forced out, the muscles in his jaw clenched. "Their heads bent together, they whispered to each other. I couldna see Ainsley's face, but Reid's said more than a thousand words. I knew exactly how he felt for I felt the same way about her." Brogan swallowed. "He brushed a strand behind her ear, and she reached out and placed her hand on his arm. That's when I left. I couldna look at them any longer." Raking his hands through his hair, he began to pace, and Henrietta could see that his shock and pain were still as fresh as they had been twenty years ago.

"Why did you not ask her about it?"

He shook his head. "Because I was afraid of what she would say," he admitted, his eyes wide as he stared at her. "I know I should have. I even knew it then, but I couldna. I knew I should've released her from her promise, but I couldna. I wanted her more than life itself, and once she had agreed to marry me, I couldna risk losing her no matter what." Closing his eyes, Brogan shook his head. "I am weak, and now, Fiona has to pay for my weakness."

Stepping forward, Henrietta gently placed a hand on his arm.

Instantly, his eyes snapped open, and he stared at her as though shocked that he had just now shared his darkest secret with her, a foreigner, a stranger, a woman. Embarrassed, he averted his eyes and stepping back cleared his throat.

"You're not weak," Henrietta said. "You were in love, and that made you vulnerable. It is a risk, and I've spent my whole life thinking that it is not worth it." A soft smile came to her lips. "But recently, I've come to believe that I might be wrong. I haven't quite shaken off the ties of my past yet. I will need more time, but I am determined to rid myself of them and be happy. Truly happy."

Holding her gaze, Brogan nodded, a hint of hope glistening in his tear-brimmed eyes. "More than anything, I wish for Fiona to be happy."

"Then find out the truth," Henrietta counselled. "It is the only way. If you ignore what lives in your heart and your mind, you'll be trapped in this maze forever. As will she, without even knowing why."

His hands balled into fists, Brogan nodded. "Ye're right," he whispered, astonishment shining in his eyes as he looked at her. "Thank ye, my lady."

Touched at his words, Henrietta smiled. "Thank you for trusting me. I'm used to people seeing me as the enemy." As she blinked, a tear rolled down her cheek. "This is new to me," she admitted, then took a deep breath and cleared her throat. "With your permission, I'll call in my husband and ask him to send for Reid Brunwood so that we can lay this to rest before the sun sets on this day, and we can all lay down our heads tonight with a clear conscience."

When Brogan nodded, Henrietta turned to the door, but stopped when he called, "My lady?" As she turned back and met his eyes, he inclined his head to her. "I was wrong. Yer husband did choose wisely."

Feeling new tears threaten, Henrietta simply smiled at him in gratitude.

Chapter Thirty-Two
OUT OF LOVE

Pacing the hallway outside his study, Connor thought he would go mad. More than once, he was tempted to listen at the door, but then called himself back at the last moment.

When the door finally did open and his wife stepped out, her eyes red-rimmed, he was ready to strangle Brogan Brunwood without a moment's hesitation. His wife, however, stepped in his way, and as her eyes found his, he felt his hammering pulse finally calm down. Reaching for her hands, he pulled her close. "Are ye all right, Lass?" he whispered, and his gaze was drawn to the small tear that spilled over and ran down her cheek. "What did he say to ye?" he growled, ready to storm past her.

"He confided in me," his wife whispered, pride and joy ringing in her voice, and Connor's eyes snapped back to meet hers. "As hard as it was for him, he told me the truth." Sadness began to cloud her eyes as she spoke. "His story is like mine. Like me, he has demons that haunt him. Will you help us defeat them?"

Seeing determination and strength glow in her eyes, Connor nodded. "Of course, Lass. I'm yers to command," he chuckled, and the smile that lit up her face melted his heart.

"I need you to send for Reid Brunwood," she said. "There is a matter they need to discuss. If it turns out the way I think, the way I hope, then I am certain Brogan will give his consent."

Frowning, Connor stared at her. "I'm surprised, and yet, I know I shouldn't be for I've always known, from the moment ye first snapped at me, that ye're capable of great things."

An embarrassed blush coloured her cheeks, and she averted her eyes.

In that moment, all Connor wanted was to wrap her in his arms and carry her upstairs to their bedchamber. It took him all the strength he had to release her hands, find his clerk and have him send for Reid Brunwood. Maybe once this issue was resolved, he would finally have some time alone with his wife.

Fortunately, his clerk as well as Reid Brunwood were located quickly, and not even a half hour later, Connor found himself back in his study, his wife by his side. While Brogan looked emotionally exhausted, Reid glanced from one to the other, clearly confused by the change in attitude his childhood friend had undergone.

"We asked ye here again," Connor began, his eyes meeting Reid's, "because we have come to believe that the anger between the two of ye stems from a...misunderstanding twenty years ago." From what his wife had told him, Connor could only hope that her instincts had not deceived her.

Reid frowned. "A misunderstanding?" He turned to Brogan. "What misunderstanding?"

With his jaw clenched, Brogan took a slow breath, and Connor could see how much effort it cost him to remain calm. "It's about Ainsley," he forced out through gritted teeth, his hands balling into fists.

"Ainsley?" Reid's eyes went wide, and he swallowed, a shadow of the past falling over his face. Glancing from Brogan to Connor, he cleared his throat. "What about her?"

Staring at Reid, Brogan tensed even more, his eyes narrowing. "He looks guilty," he snarled under his breath before he stepped forward, anger burning in his eyes.

"Wait!" Before Connor could even move a muscle, his wife stepped forward. Gently placing her hand on Brogan's arm, she searched his eyes. "I beg you. Do not jump to conclusions. Allow me to speak to him."

As the sinews on his fists began to stand out white, Brogan met her gaze. With his lips pressed into a thin line, he nodded, then took a step back, forcing air into his lungs.

Turning around, Henrietta met Reid's bewildered look as he glanced back and forth between all three of them. "You do not understand," she mumbled, a hint of relief on her face.

Reid shook his head. "I do not. He said I looked guilty. What is he accusing me of?" For a moment, his eyes travelled to the floor before he forced them back up.

"Twenty years ago," Henrietta began, "both of you asked for Ainsley's hand in marriage."

Reid nodded. "As did many others."

Henrietta nodded, a soft smile on her face. "So I've heard." Taking a step closer, she held Reid's gaze, her eyes slightly narrowed. "And she made her choice. Ainsley chose Brogan."

Reid swallowed, and his lips thinned. "She did." He took a deep breath. "Is that what he his accusing me of? Even after twenty years? That I cared for the woman who became his wife?" Shaking his head, he looked at Brogan. "Is that the reason ye refuse to give yer consent?"

Anger still in his eyes, Brogan opened his mouth.

However, once again, Henrietta interfered. "It is not your regard for Ainsley that has haunted him these past twenty years," she began, a hint of red tinging her cheeks, "but his belief that you are his daughter's father."

Eyes trained on Reid, Connor waited, his breath stuck in his throat, and he was not disappointed.

As soon as the words had left Henrietta's lips, Reid's face fell open. His jaw dropped. His eyes widened and became as round as plates while all colour left his cheeks.

For a moment, Connor thought he would faint on the spot.

"His daughter's fa-? What?" Reid stammered. Then he turned to Brogan, bewilderment clear on his face. "Why would ye believe that? Ye were my friend. I wouldna have done such a thing." He swallowed. "I admit even after she had announced her decision, I tried to change her mind, but I would never have betrayed ye in such a way. Believe me, I never laid a hand on her. Fiona canna be my daughter for I never touched Ainsley."

A hint of relief came to Brogan's eyes, and yet, doubt remained as he glared at his childhood friend. "I saw ye," he forced out through gritted teeth. "The night of the festival, I saw ye. Ye met her in the shadows of the wall, away from prying eyes. I saw ye whispering and..."

Rubbing his hands over his face, Reid shook his head. "I did meet her, aye, but only to speak to her. As I said, I tried to convince her to choose me instead." Lifting his hands in honest regret, Reid took a careful step forward. "I'm sorry to have gone behind yer back, but...I couldna imagine my life without her. I was desperate, and I did what I shouldna have."

Reaching for his wife's hand, Connor watched as Brogan's tense shoulders began to relax and his fists uncurled. The older man took a deep breath, and yet, his eyes remained narrowed slits.

"But I..." Brogan swallowed, and Connor could read indecision on his face, unsure if he truly wanted to know the answer. "She touched ye," the older man finally said. "She stepped closer and put her hand on yer arm. She whispered to ye."

Reid nodded. "She did, but only to tell me that she loved ye." Sadness and loss fell over Reid's face with such an intensity that Connor felt the sudden need to steady the man. "No matter what I said, I couldna sway her. She spoke kindly to me though and whispered words of encouragement because I was yer friend. She didna wish for me to be sad because she didna wish for ye to be sad. What she did for me she did because of ye."

Staring at Reid, Brogan swallowed as tears began to brim in his eyes. "I didna know," he whispered. "I thought...and then when Fiona was born early, I was certain that..." He shook his head, his jaw trembling with the sudden onslaught of emotions. "I didna know."

"As much as it pains me to say it," Reid choked out, "Ainsley loved ye, ye alone, and Fiona is yer daughter." Taking yet another step toward his old friend, Reid held out his hand. "But I would be honoured to call her my daughter-in-law, Brother."

Eyes shining with a new-found peace of mind, Brogan grabbed his friend's hand, nodding his head vigorously. "And I shall be honoured to call Liam my son-in-law."

Still holding his wife's hand, Connor turned to her, awe shining in his eyes as he looked down at her tear-streaked face. "Ye're an amazing woman," he whispered as she sagged into his arms, all strength leaving her body after the emotional upheaval of the past few days. "Ye saw what no one else did, and ye did not only secure a happily-ever-after for two young newly-weds, but ye also brought two old friends together who had been separated by a misunderstanding twenty years ago." Skimming a hand over her cheek, he smiled. "I don't mean for it to sound condescending, but I'm proud of ye."

Smiling, his wife closed her eyes and rested her head against his shoulder while Connor held her close, knowing how lucky he was to be married to the woman he loved. While Reid had lost Ainsley to another man, Brogan, too, had lost the woman who held his heart to this day long ago. It was a crippling fate, and Connor could see its aftershocks on the two men's faces as they embraced for the first time in twenty years. They would never get Ainsley back; she was lost to them forever, but the future still held promise.

Chapter Thirty-Three
SUSPICIONS

When they walked out into the rose garden later that afternoon, Liam and Fiona met them with solemn faces, which instantly changed when they beheld the expressions in their fathers' eyes. Joy swept them into each other's arms, and tears of happiness streamed down their faces.

"Thank ye so much," Fiona sobbed, embracing Henrietta again and again. "I knew if anyone could help, it'd be ye."

Looking slightly uncomfortable with all the attention, Henrietta dropped her eyes to the ground, mumbling something unintelligible before ushering the overjoyed bride back into her husband's arms. The newly-weds' fathers thanked her as well, if slightly less exuberantly, but in the end it was Brogan's courteous nod that brought fresh tears to her eyes.

Stunned himself, Connor watched as the older man inclined his head, his eyes shining with deference and respect. Standing beside him, her arm securely tucked in the crook of his own, Henrietta took a slow breath and a slight tremble shook her slender frame as she, too, gave a courteous nod of the head, answering Brogan's silent message with her own.

"Ye're one of a kind," Connor whispered, and turning to face him, his wife raised her eyes to his. "Not too long ago, ye yerself were trapped in a web of past fears and doubts, and now, ye use yer gained wisdom with such ease that I find myself speechless."

A mischievous grin lifted the corners of her lips. "For someone who claims to be speechless, you ramble on quite a bit."

Connor laughed. "Ye're a smart woman, Lass, and an honest one. I will have need of yer counsel in the future." Pulling her closer, he held her eyes as his own grew serious. "I need ye, Lass, as does the clan. Ye belong here. This is yer home, and we are yer people, yer family. I need ye to know that."

Taking a slow breath, his wife swallowed. "I do feel at home here. I never thought I would, and yet, there is still a part of me that wants to leave," Connor inhaled sharply, "and find a place where I can be who I am."

He opened his mouth to interrupt her, but she stopped him.

"I know what you think," his wife said, "and you're right. A lot has changed since I've faced my past. However, at my core, I still am who I've always been." As though in apology she shrugged her shoulders. "Men may not generally be bad, but the world we live in favours them greatly and gives them power and control over women." She shook her head, a disgusted snarl curling her lips. "I wish things could be different, and I'm not certain if I can ever be truly happy as long as this imbalance exists."

Connor sighed, wishing that things could indeed be simple. "Change has always come slowly," he said, holding her hands tightly in his, "and always at a high price. If ye truly want the world to change, Lass, then ye'll have to be the one to change it." He smiled at her. "As ye've changed mine. Are ye willing to fight for it?"

In celebration of the newly-weds, a spontaneous festival was held in the courtyard that night, and for the first time, Henrietta did not feel as though she did not belong. As not only Liam and Fiona but also Reid and Brogan sang hymns of praise of her for reuniting them, people began to look at her with different eyes. Slowly the last remnants of their mistrust vanished and were replaced by open curiosity and the desire to get to know her. That night, Henrietta laughed and chatted with people she had barely spoken a word to before.

"I'm incredibly proud of ye," Rhona beamed, wrapping her in a tight embrace, "and I hope ye can forgive an old woman's meddling."

"Meddling?" Henrietta asked, glancing from Rhona to Moira and Deirdre.

Rhona sighed, a mischievous grin on her wrinkled face. "After all, it was me who sent Connor after ye that night. Otherwise, he wouldna have found ye."

Henrietta laughed. "Morag said you would."

"That old tattletale," Rhona grumbled, winking an eye at her before laughing out loud. "I'm glad to see ye smile. It suits ye, and it makes my son smile as well."

Glancing at her husband, Henrietta bit her lower lip when she caught his gaze.

"Do not be embarrassed," Deirdre chided before her own eyes travelled over to Alastair where he stood speaking to Connor. "They affect us as much as we affect them, or at least that is the way it oughta be."

"Ye're wise for someone so young," Rhona mused. "If only I had been back then." Then she chuckled and shook her head. "Now, go and dance with yer husbands."

Deirdre immediately set off as though pulled to Alastair's side by an invisible bond. Henrietta remained behind and hugged her mother-in-law. "Thank you for all your help. I don't know what I would've done without you."

"Oh, don't ye thank me, Child," Rhona chided. "We're all so happy to have ye here with us; are we not, Moira?"

"Certainly," the young woman agreed, her eyes, however, lacked the enthusiasm Rhona's held. "I was truly impressed with how ye reunited Reid and Brogan. I never thought that possible."

"Thank you," Henrietta said, her own words a mild echo of the insincerity she'd detected in Moira's, and she couldn't help but wonder at what point things had changed between them.

"Good evening, fair ladies," Connor greeted them, an exuberant smile on his face. "Would ye care to join us on the dance floor?" Pointing behind himself, he glanced at Alastair and Deirdre, just now standing up with other couples, Fiona and Liam among them, to dance the night away. "It promises to be a fine evening."

Out of the corner of her eye, Henrietta saw Moira take a step forward, her face aglow, when her features suddenly froze. Clearing her throat, Moira blinked before the polite smile was back on her face, and she nodded to Connor good-naturedly, "Go ahead, dear Cousin, and dance with yer wife."

"Aye, by all means," Rhona chimed in, giving Henrietta a soft push so that she stumbled forward into Connor's arms. "Do not mind us unmarried women."

Laughing, Henrietta allowed her husband to escort her to the central area in the courtyard used for dancing that night. However, looking back, she found Moira's eyes on her and thought her initial impression confirmed.

Maybe out of habit, Moira had thought that Connor had wanted to ask her, his cousin, to dance. Had Moira also thought that he would marry her? Had she wanted him to? Or had she merely expected him to because of tradition?

As her husband led her into the dance, Henrietta's mind was occupied with the contrasting glances she had caught of Moira, and deep down an old fear re-awakened, whispering a warning and reminding her that some people did have hidden agendas and did not openly display their true sentiments. Although Henrietta had come to realise that she had been rather obsessed in her distrust of people, she had to admit that at least a healthy dose of distrust was wise.

"Where are ye with yer thoughts tonight, Lass?" her husband whispered in her ear, his eyes searching her face with a hint of concern in them. "Ye look troubled."

Swallowing, Henrietta sighed, "I'm afraid I can't help it."

"Can ye tell me what troubles ye?"

"I don't know if I should." It was bad enough that her past constantly interfered with her own emotions, leading her astray and threatening to destroy the fragile bonds she had managed to establish to other people. However, Henrietta did not want her ungrounded fears to ruin the relationship her husband had with his cousin. Maybe Moira simply felt jealous and needed some time to come to terms with the current situation. Henrietta ought to give her the benefit of the doubt.

"I'm yer husband, Lass," Connor objected. "Yer troubles are mine whether ye share them with me or not."

Touched, Henrietta smiled up at him.

With his broad shoulders and tall stature, Connor Brunwood was a bear of a man, built to carry the heavy broadsword of his ancestors and slay enemies in battle. However, his kind words often betrayed a soft core underneath his sturdy exterior. Few things escaped his watchful eyes, and he constantly surprised her by knowing exactly how she felt and what she needed to hear to heal her wounds. Out of respect and consideration and maybe even out of love-if she dared to believe it-he often put her needs before his own, giving her the time and space she needed to discover whether or not she truly cared for him.

By now, Henrietta knew that she did. But did she love him? Did she truly want to spend the rest of her life by his side? Of course, she was his wife, so by societal rules, the choice had already been made. However, even without him saying the words, Henrietta knew that her husband needed to know if she stayed by his side out of obligation or love.

As much as she wanted to put his mind at ease, Henrietta was not sure. At least, not yet, and so she refrained from saying anything on the matter lest she give him false hope.

"Moira seems sad tonight," Henrietta finally said. Although it was not the essence of her thoughts, neither was it a complete lie. After all, Moira did seem sad.

Glancing at his cousin, her husband sighed, then nodded. "Aye, she has been as of late," he confirmed. "A few days ago, she came to speak to me."

"She did?" Not having expected that, Henrietta's eyes narrowed.

"She said she was concerned about ye," her husband elaborated, "and wondered if there was anything she could do to help. Of course, I didna give her any details about our marriage, but from the way she looked at me, I could tell that she was deeply concerned."

Frowning, Henrietta glanced at the tall woman, standing by the refreshment table. A scowl on her face, she sipped her wine as Angus Brunwood approached her from the side. Pouring himself a drink, the old man met her eyes, and quick words were exchanged before he hobbled away, casting a hateful glance at the dance floor.

When Moira looked up and saw Henrietta watching her, she quickly dropped her gaze to the ground before meeting her eyes once more, a practised smile now on her face.

A strange sense of foreboding came over Henrietta, and a shiver went down her back. Turning back to her husband, Henrietta couldn't shake the feeling that Moira was watching them. "I understand that she would be concerned about us," Henrietta lied. "However, you said she was sad. Not because of us, would she?"

Connor shrugged. "She didna say. I've known her for a long time though. We practically grew up as brother and sister, and I know when something bothers her. The way she looked at me made me think that something was weighing heavily on her mind. She wouldna say though." Searching her face, her husband's eyes narrowed. "That is not what's bothering ye, Lass, is it?" he enquired. "Will ye not tell me what's on *yer* mind?"

Henrietta sighed. "Honestly, I'm not quite certain what is on my mind," she admitted, "and I do not wish to alarm you in case my suspicions prove wrong."

"Alarm me?" Instantly, the arms that held her tensed. "What suspicions?"

Henrietta shook her head. "I need a little more time. Please! Trust me."

Taking a deep breath, her husband eyed her wearily. "Whatever it is that troubles ye, is it something dangerous? Something that can harm ye?"

Taken aback, Henrietta frowned. The thought that Moira might try to harm her physically had never crossed her mind. "No, it's not," she said, trying to set his mind at ease, and yet, once spoken, his words stirred on her fears, and she could not help but wonder.

After a rather restless night, Connor spent the morning in his study, dealing with everyday clan business. His mind, however, constantly dragged him back to the previous night.

When Brogan and Reid had reconciled so unexpectedly, giving their consent to their children's marriage, Connor had inadvertently taken this as a good omen, his own hopes soaring into the sky. The night had started out so promising. His wife had been truly affected by the men's reconciliation, and Connor had seen without difficulty the sense of pride and confidence that had come to her. She had shed tears of joy, clinging to his arm as though he were the only one with whom she would want to share such an emotional moment.

Later, he had seen her laugh and smile from across the courtyard, and he had been drawn to her side like a moth to a flame. Connor remembered the glow in her eyes vividly, and his heart had skipped more than one beat at the thought of the wonderful night that awaited them.

Only then everything had fallen apart as old fears had once more reared their ugly heads. Connor knew that he could not expect her to overcome fears born out of a lifetime of abandonment and abuse in a matter of days, and yet, his heart had hoped that she had come to love him, that he was enough to make her feel safe, and that her days of sadness and fear were finally numbered.

He had been wrong though, and for a moment, Connor doubted that things would ever change.

As a knock sounded on the door, he cleared his throat, determinedly pushing aside all thoughts of hopelessness, and called to enter.

"May I speak with ye," Moira asked, closing the door behind her. "'Tis rather urgent."

"Certainly." Setting aside the papers before him, Connor turned to her, trying to determine what awaited him. "Is something wrong?"

A suppressed smile on her face, Moira could barely keep the skip out of her step as she came to stand in front of his desk. "On the contrary, dear Cousin. I've come to elicit yer assistance in a matter of rather dubious nature."

Connor's eyes widened in surprise before they narrowed into slits, eyeing his cousin carefully. "I have to say that yer words do not match yer tone, dear Cousin. Pray tell for what is it ye seek my assistance?"

Moira chuckled, "Ye know me too well." Taking a step closer, she looked at him with soft eyes, the expression on her face serious once more. "I saw ye dance with yer wife last night," she began, sympathy in her voice, "and from the looks of it, I thought ye could use a little assistance."

"Assistance? I thought ye were here to seek *my* assistance?"

"Aye, and aye," Moira said, an amused curl to her lips. "I know that yer marriage has not been easy for the both of ye, and I remembered that Henrietta told me how much she enjoyed fencing with ye."

"She told ye that?" As Connor began to understand for what Moira wanted his assistance, he felt a new hope swell in his chest.

"She did, and I believe it would do ye both good to get away and be with each other." She grinned. "And I thought we'd make it a surprise."

"A surprise?"

"Aye, ye grab everything ye need," she explained, "and head to the meadow by the cliffs while I lure yer wife away under a pretext and then lead her there." Clapping her hands together like a little girl, his cousin smiled at him. "What do ye think? Would she enjoy that?"

As a deep smile spread over his face, Connor felt his shoulders relax as last night's tension slowly evaporated. "Aye, I think she'd enjoy that." Rising from his chair, he walked around his desk and took his cousin's hands into his own. "Thank ye, Moira. I owe ye a debt of gratitude for all yer efforts."

"Ye're welcome," she whispered, her eyes shining like diamonds, and for a moment, Connor wondered if his instincts had deceived him for today she did not strike him as sad at all. "As irritating as ye can be, ye know I love ye dearly, dear Cousin, and there is nothing I wouldna do for ye."

Hugging her tight, Connor glanced over Moira's shoulder and out the window at the brilliantly shining sun. As dark as the day had begun, now it promised to be the very day he had hoped for all along.

Chapter Thirty-Four
REVELATIONS

As the sun shone warm on her head and the wind brushed gently over her cheeks, Henrietta followed Moira down the small trail, leading them deeper into the forest. Kerr stepped carefully over raised roots and around tree stumps, and Henrietta gently patted the mare's neck. "I wish I was as sure-footed as you are, sweet girl."

Glancing at the woman riding ahead of her, Henrietta wondered about Moira's motives for asking her to ride out together. All smiles, Moira had seemed unusually eager for Henrietta to join her, and despite a sinking feeling in her stomach, Henrietta had not been able to decline. After all, what reason could she have given? Moira was being perfectly nice, and Henrietta did her best to convince herself that her husband's cousin was merely trying her best to befriend her-as awkward as this whole situation felt.

"'Tis not much farther," Moira called over her shoulder as she guided her gelding through the thicket.

Trusting Kerr, Henrietta glanced around. "Where are we going? I don't believe I've ever been here."

"'Tis a lovely place near a stream," Moira said, an affectionate smile on her face.

Maybe a little too affectionate, Henrietta thought before she called herself to reason and tried to rein in her fears before they could run off with her sanity. "That sounds lovely."

Glancing around her nervously, Henrietta sighed in relief when the forest began to thin out and they came upon a small clearing at the bottom of a steep rock wall. A thin waterfall cascaded down its face and pooled into a small stream that ran through the green meadow, its fresh waters sparkling in the sun.

"Oh, how beautiful!" Henrietta exclaimed as her eyes feasted on the landscape before her. "I don't think I've ever seen anything so marvellous."

"'Tis breath-taking, is it not?" Moira asked and slid out of the saddle. "I've come here since I was a little girl. 'Tis my favourite place in the world."

Letting Kerr graze freely, Henrietta walked up to Moira, who stood on the banks of the small stream, eyes travelling upward to the top of the waterfall.

"When we were young, we'd spent our summers here, daring each other to jump off the edge," she mused in memory, but Henrietta gasped. "Of course, no one ever did. It would've been suicide, but it was fun to dare each other."

Wondering about her husband's bond to his cousins, Henrietta said, "From what Connor said, you have quite a few cousins, is that right?"

Moira nodded, then met Henrietta's eyes. "Aye, sometimes I feel as though there are too many to count, but I've always felt closest to Connor and Deirdre." A smile came to her lips that had a challenging curl to it. "We've known each other all our lives and know the other almost as well as ourselves."

Drawing in a deep breath, Henrietta felt her fears confirmed as she held Moira's daring glance. "That sounds wonderful," she said, forcing a lightness to her voice that she did not feel. "I suppose growing up together as you did almost makes you siblings. No wonder Connor speaks of you as though you were his sister."

At her words, Moira's eyes narrowed and the smile slowly slid off her face. "He thinks of me as family, aye," Moira hissed, "but I only have one brother, Alastair. Connor is merely my cousin, and the bond we share is of our own making, shaped by years of shared experiences."

"I'm sorry," Henrietta said, now sensing open hostility emanating from every pore in Moira's body. "I did not mean to offend you. Connor will always be your cousin," she took a step closer, her eyes fixed on Moira's, "but he is my husband."

Instantly, all pretence of civility fell from Moira, and open hatred filled her eyes as she glared at Henrietta.

Standing on the small slope leading down into the valley, the two women stood facing each other. While Moira seethed with anger, her hands balled into fists, every sinew in her body tense to the point of breaking, Henrietta stood with her head held high, shoulders squared, aware of the struggle coursing through her opponent's body. Should Moira choose to attack her, Henrietta would not hesitate to defend herself. However, she would not allow Moira to bait her into acting first.

Laughing, Moira shook her head. "Ye're merely an outlandish distraction," she snarled. "He will come to his senses soon enough and see that I was born to be his wife."

Although Henrietta was far from losing control, she was surprised to detect an unfamiliar emotion swell in her chest, the desire to defend what was hers. Never in her life had she felt territorial about anyone, never experienced the need to keep others at bay, at a safe distance from those she loved.

Accepting the challenge issued, Henrietta took a deep breath, her eyes narrowing, focused on the threat standing an arm's length in front of her. "He chose me," she said, her voice almost a whisper but laced with a determination she had never felt before, "when he could have chosen you."

Moira's jaw tensed as her teeth ground together.

"Whether you were born to be his wife or not does not matter," Henrietta continued as pride burst from her soul and swept through her body, "he merely sees you as his cousin. He told me so himself only yesterday. He never wanted you as his wife, not the way he wants me."

"Do not pretend to know him," Moira snarled. "The few glimpses ye've caught of him are nothing compared to the lifetime we've shared together."

"You're right," Henrietta admitted. "You probably know Connor better than me. However, you are his past while I am his future." At her own words, a fierce longing grew in her heart, and Henrietta knew beyond the shadow of a doubt that she wanted him. She wanted to be his wife. She wanted to stay by his side. No matter what the consequences.

"Not if I can prevent it!" Moira barked, her eyes frantically looking around as though searching for something to come to her aid. "He is mine! I will do whatever necessary to protect him from ye!"

Goose bumps rose on Henrietta's arms as the sun disappeared behind dark clouds, and once again a sense of foreboding gripped her heart. Her eyes shifted from the snarl on Moira's face to her surroundings, trying to glimpse the threat that lay out there. "What did you do?" she demanded when none emerged from the tree line in her back. Eyes narrowing, her gaze snapped back to Moira. "What did you do?"

With her hair whipped about by the growing wind, Moira looked like a fury as she stared at Henrietta in triumph, an ugly snarl on her face. "I did what I had to," she bit out. "Ye don't belong here. Not with him. Not with us. I tried to tell ye before that he wasna right for ye, but ye wouldna listen. Now, 'tis too late."

"Too late for what?"

"To return to the place ye came from," Moira snapped, "in peace. But ye wouldna. Ye made me do this."

"Do what?" Henrietta demanded, her eyes still scanning the tree line as well as the valley stretching out toward the other side of the rock formation to her right. To her relief, she could not detect anyone approaching. "Are you planning to kill me?" Henrietta asked straightforward, her mind reaching out to search for the dagger she carried on her person at all times. Yes, there it was in the right inside pocket of her jacket. If Moira had completely lost her sense and would try to take her life, Henrietta would not lay down without a fight!

Moira laughed. "Not me," she hissed, and her gaze narrowed as she leaned forward and stared into Henrietta's eyes. "That's a man's job."

Shocked, Henrietta stepped back, and her hand flew up to her jacket, whipping out the dagger with practised ease. Glancing around herself, she demanded, "Who? Who is helping you?"

For a moment, Moira seemed to be taken aback as she stared at the sharp blade in Henrietta's hand. Then a slow smile came to her face, and she shrugged. "Do ye truly not know? After all, there is no one in Greyston Castle who hates ye more. Maybe even more than me." Glancing down the slope, Moira turned her head, eyes searching the meadow as it stretched to the far horizon, and a frown came to her face. "Where is he?" she mumbled as her eyes narrowed in concentration, her head jerking from side to side. "'Tis the right place. He promised he'd be here."

"He?" Henrietta demanded once more, the muscles in her body growing heavy with the tension she forced on them. "Alastair? Is it Alastair? Is your brother helping you?" Could she have been wrong about Alastair? Yes, he disliked her, but would he truly betray Connor and take the life of his chief's wife? Old fears soared to the surface, and Henrietta feared she'd misjudged him.

"Puh!" Moira spat. "My brother is loyal to a fault. He would never do anything he'd deem a betrayal of Connor."

"But you would," Henrietta said, shaking her head. "How can you betray him? I thought you cared for him."

A disgusted snarl on her face, Moira hissed, "I love him, and ye're wrong if ye think I would ever betray him."

"But you are!"

"I am not betraying him," Moira spat. "I am liberating him, setting him free of yer harmful influence so that he can reclaim his rightful place." Taking a slow breath, Moira lifted her head and stared into the distance. "I've always known that he was meant to be chief of Clan Brunwood. Even as a child. And so when the time came, I made certain, he would be named tanist."

Staring at the wild look on Moira's face, Henrietta gasped, "You? It was you who spread those rumours. You're the reason Alastair was passed over. How could you do that to your own brother?"

"I did nothing," Moira hissed. "This was meant to happen. I saw it in my dreams. Connor is the rightful leader with me by his side as his wife."

Dreams! The word echoed in Henrietta's mind as she remembered what Rhona had told her. *I rarely act upon my dreams now. A part of me feels that what is meant to happen will, and my dreams merely intend to prepare me for what is to come, not change the outcome. Too much knowledge about the future causes more harm than good.* Did Moira have the gift as well? Had she seen a glimpse of the future? A future in which Moira was Connor's wife?

Doubts rushed back into Henrietta's heart as she stared at the woman before her. Was Moira telling the truth? Had she seen such a future in her dreams? Had it been her obligation to act as she had to ensure that these things would come to pass?

Once again recalling Rhona's words, Henrietta realised that her mother-in-law would have disagreed. *Whatever my dreams are meant to do, I believe that you two were meant for each other.*

Standing up straight, Henrietta squared her shoulders. "You have no right to shape the future, everyone's future, based on your own wishes," she said with determination, "for you cannot know what your dreams are meant to do. Who is to say that what you see is truly meant to happen? Maybe your dream was simply trying to sway you from a wrong path. Maybe it was simply a dream, revealing your heart's desire. But nothing more."

"Ye're an outlander," Moira hissed. "Ye know nothing of our customs, our history, our beliefs. Ye could never understand the gifts this land bestows on those who are worthy. The English have always taken what is not theirs, invading other countries and forcing them under their rule. Ye canna know what it's like to have everything taken from ye that makes ye who ye are. One day, Scotland will rise again, but only with men like Connor leading us into a better future."

As the hatred in Moira's voice touched Henrietta's heart, it answered with pity and regret while the words the young woman had spoken stirred a memory, and a vaguely familiar face began to form in Henrietta's mind.

Angus.

Countless times, the old man had glared at her, the same hatred burning in his eyes that Henrietta now saw so clearly in Moira's. He had despised her for being English, called her the enemy and…and Connor a traitor.

Instantly, Henrietta's head snapped up and she strode toward Moira, her eyes hard as she met the young woman's frantic gaze. "Is it Angus? Is he whom you're waiting for?"

Moira's eyes narrowed, then she nodded. "He will come as will those that follow him."

"Those that follow him," Henrietta mumbled, her eyes once again returning to her surroundings, searching for approaching riders, weapons readied in their hands.

Only there was nothing. No one. All remained still. Peaceful even.

Gripping Moira's wrists, Henrietta snarled into her face. "You're a fool! He's not coming! He doesn't want me! He wants Connor! He used you to get to him!"

Staring into Henrietta's eyes, Moira's mouth fell open, and the shock drained all colour from her face. "He w-wouldna," she stammered. "Connor is our chief. Angus would never harm him. Ye're the enemy. Ye're English. Ye're-"

"I may be the reason he is after Connor," Henrietta snapped, "but Angus knows that killing me will not change the man who holds the clan's future in his hands." Shaking her head, Henrietta held Moira's gaze as it slowly began to waver, the hatred in her deep blue eyes replaced by a dawning fear. "I am not the problem. I did not intentionally infiltrate your clan in order to overthrow your chief. Connor chose me. He brought me here, and Angus sees that as a betrayal, a weakness, and he can only ensure the clan's future by eliminating the real threat." Henrietta swallowed. "Connor."

"No!" Moira gasped. "Ye're wrong! He wouldna!"

"Then where is he?" Henrietta demanded, gesturing at the open land around them. "Do you see him? If so, point him out for I cannot detect another presence besides ours."

With wide eyes, Moira turned her head from side to side, her eyes searching the four directions of the compass, only to come up empty.

"He is not coming!" Emphasising every word, Henrietta tightened her grip on Moira's wrists. "He betrayed your trust. He knew that your hatred for me would blind you to his true purpose." Holding Moira's gaze, Henrietta waited for the first spark of understanding in her blue depths. "Where is Connor? Angus wouldn't attack him at Greyston. You lured him away, didn't you? Tell me where he is!"

Staring at her with unseeing eyes, Moira remained quiet as tears began to brim in her eyes.

"Now is not the time to weep, Moira!" Henrietta growled, shaking the trembling woman vigorously. "Angus will kill him! Are you truly that spiteful that you'd rather see him dead than married to me?" Staring into Moira's eyes, Henrietta felt tears of her own threatening, but she forced them back down. If there had ever been a time when she had needed her strength, it was now.

"Moira!"

"He's by the cliffs," the wide-eyed woman whispered, "waiting for ye."

A lump formed in Henrietta's throat as she realised that if things came to pass, he would die thinking she had betrayed him. "The cliff top by the ruins?" Pushing all other thoughts aside, Henrietta forced herself to focus on the here and now. Connor was still alive. There was still a chance to save him.

Moira nodded.

"Listen!" Henrietta hissed into her face. "You may have a chance to make this right, but only if you do as I say." When Moira hesitated, Henrietta snapped, "Do you want him dead? Tell me here and now!"

Moira swallowed. "No. I never meant for this to happen."

Henrietta took a deep breath as hope gave her the strength she needed. "Then ride back to Greyston and tell Alistair what happened. If there is anyone we can trust to be loyal to Connor, it is him. You said so yourself."

Slowly shaking off the trance that had come over her, Moira nodded.

"But make haste!" Henrietta commanded as they rushed back to their horses. "There won't be much time!" Climbing onto Kerr's back, Henrietta grabbed the reins as her mare pranced nervously.

"What will ye do?" Moira asked, pushing herself up and into the saddle.

"I'm his wife," Henrietta said more to herself than the woman beside her. "I belong by his side."

"They will kill ye!"

Sliding the small dagger back into her jacket, Henrietta met Moira's eyes. "I won't let them kill the man I love. Not without a fight!" As Kerr shot forward, chasing after the sun, Henrietta glanced back at Moira, who set off in the opposite direction.

The man I love.

The thought echoed in her head and heart as Henrietta leaned forward, flattening herself to Kerr's back. She could only hope that she would get there in time, that she would not arrive too late.

"The man I love," she whispered, and a smile came to her face.

Chapter Thirty-Five
YER OWN KIN

Gazing down at the sea as the waves crashed against the rocky shore, Connor inhaled deeply and closed his eyes, savouring the fresh scents carried inward by the winds.

This was truly a wonderful place, he thought, remembering how he had come upon his wife here not too long ago. That day he had thought she was about to jump off the cliffs, but he had been wrong. It had been a day of strong emotions, some painful, some liberating, but they had guided her away from the death drop and toward a future with him.

As his eyes swept over the ruins, foundation boulders of an ancient castle, Connor smiled. Time was fleeting and wasted in the blink of an eye. Trapped in a circle of fear and doubt, one could spend years waiting and hoping until one would come to realise that a lifetime had passed and one had not lived. Not at all. Not even a little.

Shaking his head with determination, Connor promised himself that he would not waste another day. He would be patient with his wife, but he would not waste another minute living in fear of the future. He would tell her how he felt and what he wanted.

With a smile on his face, Connor set down the small picnic basket he had brought and then began to unfasten the foils latched to the back of his saddle. In his mind, he pictured her face upon seeing the weapons, and his heart rejoiced at the thought of facing his wife in a playful battle.

In the distance, a horse whinnied, and Connor turned his head.

Like a terrace at the top of the world, the old castle ruins sat on a hill, locked in by the cliffs and the sea on one side and a thick-growing forest on the other. Only a small stretch of even land, here and there dotted with trees and bushes, allowed for a farther view.

Turning in that direction, Connor spotted a rider approaching, and suspecting that it was Moira leading the way, he squinted his eyes, searching for his wife close by. As the riders came closer though, Connor realised that they were not women, but men, coming toward him at high speed.

At first, they rode in single-file, but then they fanned out, riding side by side.

Watching them, Connor frowned. He could not put his finger on it, but something about them made him uneasy. It was almost as though they had spread out to cut off his only escape route.

After a moment of hesitation, Connor mounted his gelding, disconcerted with the disadvantage of remaining on foot. Shifting his weight, he moved his hand backward, running it over the sheathed foils still latched to the back of his saddle.

As he watched the riders approach, Connor's mind raced with the myriad of reasons he could gather for their unusual behaviour. Nothing made sense. This was a time of peace. War was long gone, and there hadn't been a violent incident in these parts in years.

Out of the corner of his eye, a movement caught his attention and Connor's head snapped around, his eyes narrowed scanning the tree line.

At first, he only detected faint movements of leaves and branches that could have been caused by the wind. As he looked harder though, the shadows in the forest took on the shape of men on horseback.

Instantly, all doubt fell from him, and his mind screamed one word: *trap!*

Pulling up the reins, Connor searched his surroundings, trying to find a way out before he was completely surrounded by enemies he knew nothing about. Were they thieves lying in wait to rob wealthy travellers? If so, what were they doing so far off the main road? Had they known he would be here? After all, this was an isolated area.

Once the riders coming down the stretch of flat country had reached the outer borders of the ruins, more riders emerged from the forest, all together forming a half-circle completed by the cliff face in his back.

A military mind had planned this, Connor thought as he watched the riders approach. Clad in dark colours, they wore hooded cloaks, black masks covering the upper half of their faces, and here and there, Connor spied old broadswords hitched to their belts.

Frowning, he shook his head. After the massacre at Culloden, Scots had been forbidden to carry their most trusted weapons. Most had been confiscated. Many had been hidden throughout the land. His father's still lay hidden at the bottom of a fake wine barrel in the cellar of Greyston. Years ago, Ewan Brunwood had instructed his young son in secret, but always returned the weapon to its hiding place as soon as their lesson had been over.

Once more eyeing their broadswords, Connor knew that things had taken a turn for the worse. Aside from the fact that he was severely outnumbered, his enemies' weapons would chop his foils into kindling with a single strike.

Knowing that there was no chance for escape, Connor sat tall on his gelding that pranced nervously. He lifted his chin and slowly let his gaze wander over the half-circle of riders now slowing to a trot, trying to identify their leader. "I am Connor Brunwood," he called, voice hard with authority, "chief of Clan Brunwood. State yer name and purpose on this land."

Moments passed, and only silence answered him as the riders pulled to a stop at the remnants of the old outer wall of the ancient castle.

As Connor stared at their silent faces, Henrietta's face flashed before his eyes, and he remembered why he was there in the first place. His gaze travelled up toward the horizon in the distance, but to his relief, he could not spot another approaching rider. Praying that his wife was safely back at Greyston, he returned his attention to the riders before him.

Although they all seemed rather stoic, barely moving a muscle, many had their heads slightly inclined to the right as though waiting for a signal to attack. Allowing his eyes to travel in the same direction, he glanced from rider to rider until he came upon one that bore the presence of a leader.

While he was clad in the same clothes, his posture was more set, wider and more dignified. In a strange way, he reminded Connor of his father.

Shaking off the unwelcome memory, Connor addressed the shrouded leader, "I demand to know who ye are and what intentions bring ye here."

The leader inhaled deeply, and a conceited smile curled up the corners of his mouth. "Ye've no right to demand anything, Lad."

"Allow me to remind ye that ye're speaking to the chief of Clan Brunwood, and ye're on my land."

The leader snorted, "Ye've got no rightful claim to that title. Ye stole it like a mere thief, and we've come here today to right that wrong."

As the leader's hateful voice echoed in his ears, Connor's mind conjured the memory of an old man, sitting by the fire as he spoke to a group of young lads, telling them stories of righteous battles and conceited enemies, of triumph and defeat, of justice and revenge.

For a moment, Connor closed his eyes and the man's snarling face drifted to the front of his mind. "Angus," he whispered before he opened his eyes once more and met the leader's disdainful gaze. "Angus Brunwood," he called across the stretch of land separating them. "Are ye mad, old man? With all yer stories of honour and valour, I never would have thought I'd live to see the day that ye betray yer own kin."

Angus' face darkened, and his eyes narrowed. "'Tis not I who is the traitor," he spat. "'Tis not I who turned away from my own kin and allowed the English to dictate the future of our clan. Ye," his hand whipped out, and he pointed an accusing finger at Connor, "are the traitor!"

Filled with rage, the desire to throw himself at Connor plainly visible on his masked face, Angus leaned forward and almost slid off the horse when his limp leg failed to maintain his balance. Clenching his jaw, he curled his fingers into his gelding's mane and bellowed, "Kill him!"

As adrenaline shot through his body, Connor watched the riders draw their swords and kick their horses' flanks before they came galloping toward him.

Clenching his teeth with grim determination, Connor drew both foils, the only weapons at his disposal and prepared to meet them. If he was to die, he would not die without a fight!

A foil in each hand, he urged his gelding behind one of the taller boulders, his knees directing the horse while the reins lay slack on its mane. He heard the approaching riders, their horses' hoof beats thundering on the ground, and glanced around the edge of the boulder.

As expected, the first rider reached the tall boulder just as Connor whipped out the foil and neatly slit his throat. The man tumbled to the ground, his hands futilely reaching up, and gasped for breath before he finally lay still.

Dodging other attackers, Connor retreated to the inner courtyard where tall walls remained, turning the area into a narrow maze. Like threading a needle through the small gaps in the walls, Connor dealt many a rider cuts on arms and torso with his slim foils, here and there severing a major artery, before he, too, felt a blade's steel cut his skin.

A broadsword came out of nowhere, digging itself into his left shoulder.

Connor groaned in pain, and the foil fell from his hand. Clutching his shoulder, he urged his gelding on, flattening himself to the beast's back as it shot past another attacker, the man's sword slicing through the air a hair's breadth above his head.

Holding on for dear life, Connor allowed his gelding to take the lead, trusting the beast's survival instincts as it reared and kicked, dodged an attacker here and almost ran over another there. However, before long his opponents started to target his horse, and when the large gelding received a cut down its flank, Connor slid from the saddle and gave the mighty beast a slap, sending him off.

Watching the black gelding race off toward the forest, Connor raised himself on shaky legs, the remaining foil clutched in his right hand. As a group of riders approached, Connor slid down the side of the castle's old foundation, the rocks cutting into his back and legs, and stumbled along the narrow path between the edge of the cliff and the towering wall of the ruins.

Unable to follow him on horseback, most of the riders circled back while one slid out of the saddle and pursued him.

Gritting his teeth against the pain in his shoulder, Connor dragged himself onward, his eyes focused on the tree line. If he could make it to the forest, maybe…

Lunging himself from above, an attacker tore Connor from his feet, and they rolled down the path, almost going over the edge.

Connor growled in pain and almost dropped his remaining weapon. He lay on his back, gasping for air, when he heard the soft crunch of shoes on gravel.

Bundling what was left of his strength, he rolled over and raised himself on his knees, the foil braced before him.

A pleased smile on his face, his attacker lifted his broadsword, which gleamed in the sun as though mocking the thin blade that was Connor's only protection from the man approaching him with confidence in his step. "Ye were never worthy," the man snarled and lifted his sword with both hands.

Knowing that his knees wouldn't hold him, Connor raised his own blade as the sword came crashing down toward his head.

The second he heard the soft *clink* as his foil was cut in two, Connor lunged forward. He landed on his injured shoulder and almost blacked-out. His muscles clenched against the onslaught of pain, and he rolled over, once more evading the deadly swing of his opponent's sword.

Laughing, the man sneered, "Ye canna escape me." Then he lifted his sword once again, and this time, Connor had nothing to defend himself with as his foil lay broken beside him in the grass.

As the man stood above him, the sword pointed downward at Connor's heart, Connor closed his eyes and whispered a silent goodbye to his wife.

Above all, regret filled his heart. If only…

Laying in the grass, Connor waited for the piercing pain that would end his life when a soft whir reached his ears, followed by an agonising grunt.

As his eyes snapped open, Connor stared in wonder at the small dagger sticking in his attacker's chest.

Gaping down at the small weapon, the man drew in a strangled breath and a trail of blood flowed out the side of his mouth. His eyelids drooped, and he sank to his knees before he collapsed onto the ground beside Connor.

Chapter Thirty-Six
THE TRAITOR'S WIFE

Stunned for but a moment, Connor craned his neck...and for yet another moment, he thought he had died after all.

For right there on the slope leading down from the forest line stood his wife.

The second their eyes met, Connor saw something on her face that almost stopped his heart.

Then she rushed toward him, her skirts billowing in the wind. "Are you all right?" she asked, her eyes sweeping over his face before coming to rest on his shoulder. Gritting her teeth, she swallowed, then forced a deep breath down her lungs.

Connor simply stared at her. "What are ye doing here, Lass?" he stammered, his heart torn between joy and fear.

"We need to go," she whispered, ignoring his question. Then she rose to her feet and stepping around him knelt down beside his attacker, who lay dead in the grass. To Connor's surprise, she reached out her hands and with a soft grunt pulled the dagger from his chest. Then, she grabbed the broken foil and hurried back to his side. "Can you walk?"

In that moment, hoof beats echoed from the other side of the wall.

"Ye need to go, Lass," Connor hissed, fear stealing into his heart.

"Not without you."

"Go!" Connor snapped, yanking back his arm as she tried to help him to his feet. "They havena seen ye yet. If they do, they'll kill ye as well. Go!"

As she looked down at him, her eyes narrowed and a new determination shone in them that Connor hadn't seen before. "Why do you think I came here, you mule-headed fool?" she snapped. Then she reached for his good arm once more and pulling him up hissed, "You're coming with me whether you like or not. Either you walk or I'll knock you out and carry you. These are your choices!"

Clenching his teeth against the pain, Connor leaned against her, willing his knees not to give up their post. "Ye're mad, Lass!" he whispered, staring into her eyes. "D'ye even know what ye're saying?"

Her lips thinned then, and she nodded her head. "I do," she said, her voice strong and proud, "for I do not wish to live without you." She swallowed and took a deep breath as though gathering courage. "I love you. I'm just sorry that it took you nearly dying for me to realise it."

Still staring at her, Connor felt as though he had strayed into a dream. As though his wound had been healed magically, the pain subsided and a new strength filled him. His knees grew stronger, and the strength in his right arm returned.

"Don't stare at me like a fool," his wife snapped as she gathered the collected weapons in one hand and pulled his right arm over her shoulders with the other. "Move your feet."

"Aye," Connor breathed as his heart filled with joy. If only her love for him had not come at this unfortunate moment. If only *she* hadn't come here, Connor thought, and yet, he could not bring himself to regret what had happened. Despite the threat to their lives, he had never been this happy.

"We need to try and make it to the forest," his wife grunted out as he leaned on her heavily. "I hitched Kerr to a tree for they would've spied me too easily on horseback. Without her, I was able to crouch low to the ground."

Looking down, Connor saw the grass and dirt stains on her dress, and still a part of him could not believe that she had truly come for him, that she was willing to risk her life to save his.

Hurrying down the narrow path along the outer wall of the ruins, Connor glanced over the edge at the rolling waves down below, then upward, hoping that not another attacker would jump on them from above. Voices as well as hoof beats sounded close by, only held at bay by the massive wall. But what if they reached its end?

"They'll be waiting for us," Connor moaned, "before we can even make it to the tree line."

"We have to try," his wife countered. "It's our only option, and I still have my dagger and the broken off foil."

Connor grunted. "It'll never be enough. There are too many of them."

"Do you have a better idea?" she snapped.

Growling under his breath, Connor sighed, "I do not."

"Then stop fretting!" his wife hissed as she glanced up at him with gentle eyes. "Trust me. I'll get you out of here."

A soft chuckle rose from his throat, and Connor nodded. "I do trust ye, Lass."

"Good."

"Where did ye learn to throw a dagger like that?" he asked, savouring the last few moments he would probably ever have with his wife.

"My brother," she said, pulling him forward and behind a tall growing bush once the path widened. Should their attackers come upon them, at least they would gain time by not revealing their position directly. "Although he taught me how to fight, he always told me I didn't have the strength to win a sword fight with a man," she whispered as they trudged through the dirt, branches scraping their skin. "As mad as I was, I suppose a part of me did believe him, and so I taught myself to hurl the dagger."

"Ye're full of surprises, Lass," Connor whispered, then froze as a horse's whinny sounded only a few steps ahead of them. Pulling his wife down, he sank to his knees behind the bushes, gritting his teeth against the pain. "D'ye see him?" he whispered, trying to see through the dense foliage.

Craning her neck, his wife tried to see above the thicket, her eyes narrowed in concentration. Then she nodded, and her hand slid down to the pocket that held her dagger.

Connor swallowed as conflicting emotions raged through him. Although he knew how capable women were, he, too, had grown up with a code of honour instilled in him from the moment he had been born. A husband was to defend his wife, not the other way around.

And yet, Connor had to admit that right then and there, his own abilities were nowhere near his wife's. Although he was a formidable sword fighter, he knew he did not have the same precision that his wife possessed when it came to hurling a dagger.

And so Connor swallowed his pride and took a deep breath, praying that his wife's hands were steadier than his own.

Crouched low, his wife stepped around the bush and pushed aside a few branches, her eyes trained on the rider circling the area, his eyes on the ground searching for tracks. Apparently, their enemies had not yet come upon the trail they had surely left in the soft ground.

Holding his breath, Connor watched as his wife slid the dagger from her pocket, gripping the hilt with only two fingers while the others merely stabilised the weapon's position as it rested almost gently in the palm of her hand. Then she drew back her arm, the dagger rising above her shoulder, its sharp end directed at the still circling rider.

Although his eyes were trained on the shiny blade, Connor barely saw the moment his wife's arm flew forward, sending the dagger spiralling through the air until it buried itself into the rider's back.

The man grunted in pain, then slid off the horse and hit the ground with a low *thud*.

Still holding his breath, Connor waited, praying that the man wouldn't get up or worse cry out for help.

When the fallen rider remained still, his wife rose from her crouched position and pushing aside the branches of two closely grouped bushes made to step through the thicket.

"What are ye doing?" Connor hissed as his eyes searched their surroundings. "There could be more."

"I don't see any," his wife simply stated. "I need to retrieve my dagger. It's the only reliable weapon we have." Then she slipped through the thicket and, for a moment, was lost to his sight.

With his heart pounding in his chest, Connor held his breath until she reappeared only a few steps away, carefully approaching the fallen rider, his horse grazing by his lifeless body.

Stepping closer, she kicked his leg and when he failed to respond, she knelt down beside him and once more pulled the dagger free.

Watching her, Connor marvelled at the strong and yet fragile woman who was his wife, and he realised that they complemented each other perfectly. Where he was strong, she was weak, and where he was weak, she was strong. If he had ever believed in fate, it was in that very moment when his slender wife pulled her bloodied weapon from a man who had threatened their lives. She had defended them, defended him, and Connor couldn't be more proud. They were truly meant for each other.

"Can you walk?" his wife asked, her gentle voice tearing him from his thoughts.

Blinking, Connor looked up into her face and smiled. "Aye," he said and dragged his tired body through the bushes while she held apart the branches.

As Connor's eyes slid over her, he noticed new stains on her dress that hadn't been there before. Bright red, they gleamed in the sun, covering her lower sleeves as well as the front of her dress. From their pattern, Connor assumed that she had brushed her hands down her skirt in order to wipe off the man's blood.

"Let me help you," his wife said, once more tearing him from his thoughts.

Again, Connor blinked and found her standing before him, leading the fallen rider's horse by the reins. Glancing around, she bent forward and linked her hands. "Get on," she told him, and Connor smiled.

Today was truly a strange day, and he wondered about his own sanity as his thoughts repeatedly tore him from the danger at hand and led him to new musings. After all, not too long ago, she had snapped at him for offering to help her on the horse. And now, here she was offering him the same assistance she had so rudely refused herself.

A smile on his face, Connor shook his head, then walked up to the horse, slid his booted foot into her hands and allowed her to lift him into the saddle. From looking at her, Connor would never have guessed at the strength that lived in her chest as well as her arms!

Once he was seated on the prancing horse, his wife quickly swung herself into the saddle before him, taking up the reins. Slowly, she directed the horse toward the thicker-growing copse to the side of the cliff that ran all the way down to where it stretched into the forest where Kerr waited. All the while, her eyes searched their surroundings, narrowing whenever movement caught her attention.

With his good arm wrapped around his wife's middle, Connor managed to stay upright although the horse's movements brought new pain to his shoulder.

"There he is!"

The call tore through the air, and for a moment, Connor froze as did his wife, staring at the lone rider who had spotted them.

Gesturing wildly, he shot forward, his horse quickly bringing him closer, as more riders appeared on the horizon.

Grunting under her breath, his wife kicked the horse's flanks and they set off toward the forest. Connor doubted they would make it. However, it still was their best option.

Cries echoed behind them as their pursuers cursed his name, and for a moment, Connor contemplated sliding off the horse so that his wife could make her escape.

Only she wouldn't, would she? She would circle back and die trying to save his life.

When they had almost reached the forest, a tiny spark of hope sprang to life in his chest, but was instantly crushed when Connor spotted yet another group of riders emerging from the tree line. There were only three of them, but counting the twenty-odd riders already pursuing them, there was no way they could overcome such an opposing force.

His wife reined in the horse as her eyes glared at the three riders blocking their path.

Even despite their masks, Connor could see their surprise, and he realised that his wife had truly remained undetected until then. If only he could have persuaded her to leave when she still had the chance!

"'Tis her," one of the riders hissed, "the English wench! The traitor's wife!"

The second his hand lowered to reach for his sword, Henrietta once more drew her dagger, already stained with the lives it had taken that day, and flung it forward with such speed that the man only saw it when it had already sunk its blade into his chest.

His comrades gaped with open mouths as the rider slid from the saddle, staining the soft brown ground crimson red.

Recovering from their initial shock, the two remaining horsemen drew their swords, angry snarls on their faces as they advanced.

"We need help," his wife whispered under her breath as she reached for the broken foil. "Alastair, where are you?"

"Alastair?" Connor asked in surprise before his wife flipped the foil in her hand, her fingers now holding the thin blade. As she drew back her arm, the approaching riders stopped, their eyes widening as they stared at the small weapon.

"Let us pass," his wife demanded, "or you can choose which one of you will be next." Voice hard, she glanced down at the fallen rider before once more meeting the others' eyes.

Despite the hatred clearly visible in their eyes, the two riders remained still, indecision clouding the angry snarls on their faces.

The moment they looked as though they were about to comply, a familiar, angry voice commanded from behind them, "Kill them! Kill them now!"

Chapter Thirty-Seven
A LOYAL MAN

Where was Alastair? Henrietta wondered. If he didn't come soon, their lives would be forfeit.

If it hadn't been for Angus, the two riders blocking their path might have allowed them to slip by, but now that last little hope lay crushed at their feet.

The broken foil in her hand, Henrietta turned the prancing horse, her eyes gliding back and forth between the two men guarding the rim of the forest and the approaching riders, their drawn swords glistening in the bright afternoon sun. Her eyes narrowed as she judged their speed, and she realised that they had no intention of slowing down and would simply run them down.

The only chance they had was to buy some time for Alastair to arrive. How long had it taken Moira to return to Greyston and relate what had happened? And how long would it take Alastair to come to their aid with the full force of Clan Brunwood?

The answer was: too long.

Realising that her hope was futile, Henrietta still couldn't bring herself to surrender. One look at Angus' angry face had told her all she needed to know. Driven by misguided revenge, the old man had no intention of taking prisoners, but sought to eliminate a man whom he deemed a threat to his clan.

Behind her, Connor took a deep breath, and his good arm tightened around her middle.

More than anything, Henrietta wanted to lean back and enjoy the soft embrace he offered, but the moment couldn't have been more wrong. If she didn't think of something soon, all would be lost.

Whatever my dreams are meant to do, I believe that you two were meant for each other.

As Rhona's words echoed in her mind, Henrietta drew forth the last bit of courage and hope left to her. There was not much in the world that she had ever believed in, but in her heart, she knew that she belonged with her husband just as much as he belonged with her, and now that she had finally found her place in the world, she would not surrender and die.

As her eyes narrowed, targeting the lead rider thundering toward them, Henrietta's arm drew back, then flung forward and released the broken foil like a bolt of lightning striking the ground and tearing it asunder.

The broken blade struck the lead rider square in the chest, knocking him to the ground while his horse raced on.

Too stunned to react, some of the riders following close behind did not manage to dodge his fallen body and trampled over him, their gaping mouths betraying the shock that rattled them to their bones.

After the initial surprise, most of the riders slowed their horses, their eyes drawn to the trampled body of their fallen comrade. However, before long shock turned to anger, and Henrietta could see the desire for revenge on their faces.

Connor had to have seen it, too, for his arm tightened around her as he whispered in her ear, "We need to run. It's our only hope." He nodded to their left. "Into the forest."

Swallowing, Henrietta agreed before her eyes travelled into the distance one last time. Nuances of red and purple streaked across the sky as the sun slowly dipped lower, painting a breath-taking picture of hope and strength and promise

And there in the near distance, something moved.

Henrietta's eyes narrowed as she squinted them against the setting sun. Holding her breath, she tried to focus, and her heart jumped into her throat as she saw an army charging down the plains toward them. The faint thundering of hoof beats echoed to her ears, and relief washed over her like a spring rain.

"He's here," Henrietta gasped, gesturing toward the approaching warriors of Clan Brunwood.

Behind her, Connor exhaled slowly, and although she could not see his face, she could almost feel the tension falling off him. His arm holding on to her relaxed, and for a moment, he rested his forehead against the back of her shoulder. "Alastair," he whispered, joy and relief plain in his voice.

Then Connor raised his head and cleared his throat. "I offer ye one last chance to stand down," he commanded, voice hard as it echoed across the small meadow. "I am the chief of Clan Brunwood, and those loyal to me," he gestured to the approaching warriors, "will not take kindly to traitors of their own kin."

Grouped rather disorderly in the middle of the meadow, the riders gasped as they spotted the approaching clansmen, their faces betraying the shock they felt at seeing the situation changed so dramatically. They had been prepared to ambush a single man, who unarmed posed little danger to their own lives. However, now they were facing a large number of trained warriors, and all of a sudden courage failed them.

As Angus raged and ranted, issuing commands left and right, his face turning red as he found himself ignored by his own followers, Henrietta exhaled slowly and, for a moment, closed her eyes.

Only now did she realise how frightened she had been.

"Are ye all right, Lass?" her husband whispered in her ear, his good arm pulling her closer once more.

Henrietta nodded, turning her head to look at him. "I am," she said, smiling at the renewed promise of a future she wanted. "I've never felt better."

"Surrender or die!" Hard like stone, Alastair's voice echoed across the clearing, instantly followed by the clatter of swords hitting the ground. His warriors spread out, surrounding the now unarmed riders while their commander sped onward, only pulling up his horse once he'd reached his chief's side. "Are ye all right?" he asked, his narrowed eyes gliding from Connor's injured shoulder to the blood stains on Henrietta's dress.

"We're alive," Connor said, a beaming smile on his face. "Thank ye, Cousin, for coming to our aid."

Alastair rolled his eyes as though he considered such an expression of gratitude an insult.

"How did ye know?" Connor asked, his eyes shifting from his second-in-command to Henrietta. "Ye knew he would come, didn't ye, Lass?"

"Well," Henrietta began, knowing that everything that had happened that day was not easily explained.

"Yer mother sent us," Alastair interrupted.

Henrietta's head snapped around. "Rhona?"

Alastair nodded. "I canna say how she knew," he admitted, "but I know not to doubt her word." Meeting Connor's eyes, he inclined his head in respect. "She told us there'd be an ambush here. She told us to come to yer aid, yers and yer wife's."

As Alastair's gaze shifted to hers, Henrietta met his eyes, and once again, he inclined his head in respect, his usual distrust and disregard for her vanished as though they had never been.

Smiling, Henrietta nodded, glad that they would have the chance to begin anew with a blank slate. They might never become friends, but they had both stood by Connor's side and always would, and that alone made them allies.

"Ye're a fool!" Kicking his horse's flank with his good leg, Angus drifted toward them, his face an angry snarl. "He's a traitor! Not only did he steal yer rightful claim to the chiefship, but he also handed over the rule of Clan Brunwood to the English. 'Tis because of men like him that the clans fell."

Surprised, Henrietta watched as Alastair simply ordered to have Angus taken back to Greyston and locked up. He did not, however, respond to the old man's insults in equal measure. His face remained calm as he instructed his men to collect the surrendered swords and return Angus' followers to the castle as well. "Ye're in need of medical attention," he said, eyeing Connor's shoulder with concern. Then his gaze travelled to Henrietta. "Are ye injured as well?"

Henrietta shook her head, but it was Connor who spoke. "'Tis not her blood."

Glancing at the fallen riders here and there dropped in the grass, Alastair nodded, acknowledgement in his gaze.

"She saved my life, Cousin," Connor said, "more than once. If it hadn't been for her, ye would now be the chief of Clan Brunwood."

For a long moment, Alastair held her husband's gaze before he grinned, shaking his head. "Then I suppose I owe her two debts of gratitude for I certainly am glad not to be the one who'll have to deal with Angus in the future."

Connor chuckled, and Alastair joined in.

Watching the two cousins, Henrietta thought the future had never seemed so bright. Whatever lay ahead, they would manage for they had not only each other but loyal friends and family, who would stand by them no matter what.

Chapter Thirty-Eight
A PAINFUL TRUTH

Back at Greyston, her husband rested comfortably on their large bed while a myriad of concerned people were grouped around him. The second they had entered the castle grounds not only Rhona and Deirdre had rushed to their side but also Moira.

Henrietta had exchanged a quiet word with the woman who had almost destroyed her new-found happiness, and Moira had assured her that as soon as Alastair was ready to leave his chief's side, she would speak to her brother and confess her role in Connor's ambush.

Although she could not say why, Henrietta believed her.

"Ye need bedrest, Lad," Morag instructed with a stern face, her capable hands setting his left arm in a sling to give his injured shoulder the rest it needed. When Connor was about to object, she added, "Do not argue with an old woman for ye shall not live to regret it."

Inhaling deeply, Connor closed his mouth although his annoyance with the healer's instructions was plainly visible on his face.

Sitting down on the other side of the bed, Rhona squeezed her son's right hand, her eyes brimming with tears.

Deirdre, too, looked as though she was about to cry as she clung to her husband's arm, repeatedly gazing up into his face as though to assure her that he was still there.

Understandably, only Moira stood apart, her head bowed, wringing a handkerchief in her hands. Guilt and remorse drew down the corners of her mouth and rested in her eyes, and although she stayed for the duration of the healer's visit, she seemed incredibly uncomfortable, frequently casting painful glances at Connor's injured shoulder.

"Now, everyone out," Morag instructed, sweeping her arm out toward the door. "The lad needs rest."

Although reluctantly, everyone complied, whispering well-wishes on their way out.

"They're such wonderful people," Connor mumbled after the door had closed behind them, "but them staring at me with those sad eyes makes my skin crawl."

Henrietta laughed and climbed onto the bed. Laying down on her side, she propped up her head on her elbow, her eyes searching her husband's face.

"What?" he asked, grinning. Then his eyes narrowed. "Yer eyes don't look sad," he observed, a question in his tone.

Henrietta shrugged. "That's because I'm happy," she whispered, a hint of embarrassment creeping into her cheeks. "Not to mention, your injury isn't all that bad."

Smiling, her husband laid his head back against the pillow, wincing slightly as he moved his shoulder. "Did ye mean what ye said, Lass?"

Since she knew exactly what he was referring to, Henrietta bit her lip and inhaled deeply through her nose, gathering the courage she needed to portray her feelings so openly. "I did." Then she lifted her gaze and met his eyes.

A deep smile came to his face, and his own eyes glowed with such warmth that Henrietta felt the slight chill leave her hands. "Not that I'd doubt yer words, Lass," her husband said as his eyes searched hers, "but a part of me was afraid that ye only said it to…eh…to motivate me." Holding her gaze, he waited as once again a question hung between them.

Although her fears screamed at her to take a step back, Henrietta was tired of doubting and questioning her own feelings every step of the way.

Sitting up, she held Connor's gaze, and although tenderness lived in her heart, she grinned at him, a mischievous twinkle in her eyes. "Why would I have bothered to try and save you if I didn't love you?" Mockingly, she shook her head. "You're not making any sense. Maybe the blood loss has addled your mind."

Her husband laughed, then reached out with his good arm and took her hand in his. "It feels good to laugh," he said before his face became earnest. "However, all the laughter in the world canna erase what happened today." He held her eyes. "What did happen?" he asked. "I think ye know more than me, Lass."

Henrietta swallowed, unsure how to begin.

"When I saw ye standing on that hill," her husband continued, slowly shaking his head as though trying to determine whether or not he was dreaming, "I thought I'd died and gone to heaven. Ye were like an angel, come to save me."

With cheeks flashing hot, Henrietta smiled shyly.

"How did ye come to be there?" Connor asked. "And why was Moira not?"

Again, Henrietta took a deep breath and then told her husband everything that had happened that day beginning with Moira's revelations to the moment Alastair had appeared on the horizon.

Apprehension had been on his face from the second Henrietta had opened her mouth. However, with each word, the tension in his body grew, and his face turned a darker shade, anger and disappointment marking his eyes.

"I canna believe I didna see it," he growled. "My own cousin!" He shook his head as though unable to believe the truth. "We grew up together. She was like my sister."

A smug part of Henrietta smiled at his words, relieved that no corner of her husband's heart had ever felt for Moira the way it now felt for her.

"I cannot explain it," Henrietta said, wishing that there was something she could say to heal the sting of betrayal he felt. "I can only say that everything that happened has led us here." Squeezing his hand, she looked deep into his eyes, willing him to understand the enormity of the words she was about to say. "I am who I am, and yet, certain choices are my own. The life I want is not the life I thought I wanted."

The darkness that had fallen over his face slowly receded.

"I am still afraid," she confided, "but not too afraid to admit that I love you, that I am happy to be your wife and...that I love that you love me back." A shy chuckle escaped her, and she cleared her throat. "I have misjudged myself, you, Alastair and many others. I did not see Moira's true intentions either. Not until it was too late."

"Not too late," her husband corrected as he pulled her forward until she rested against his good shoulder. "Ye came for me, Lass. Ye risked yer life to save mine, and that means more than words could ever express."

"I couldn't have done it without Alastair."

Connor nodded. "Aye, he came in the nick of time." A frown drew down his brows. "Didn't ye say that Moira was to alert him? But he said that my mother sent him."

Smiling, Henrietta nodded. "I did send Moira to speak to Alastair. There was no other choice. If I had gone back to the castle myself first, I would never have made it to you in time. I knew there was a good chance Moira wouldn't get to Alastair in time either and that he would arrive too late."

"But he didna."

Henrietta shook her head. "He didn't." She swallowed, weighing her words. "I didn't have a chance to speak to your mother after our return, but I believe that she saw what would happen in her dreams."

Her husband took a deep breath. "There are rumours about her visions, her uncanny ability to know what will happen, what was. I never asked her, and she never spoke of it. But she told ye, didn't she?"

Henrietta nodded, a soft smile on her face. "She told me that we were meant for each other, that she saw us in her dreams and that that was the reason," looking up into his eyes, Henrietta took a deep breath, "why she sent you to England...to find me."

Her husband's eyes opened wide. "She didna tell me that."

"She didn't," Henrietta agreed, "because she believed you would not like to hear that your life was pre-determined. She thought you would seek to prove her wrong and thus miss your chance to..."

"To find the woman I love?" he asked, finishing her sentence. "She's right. I probably would have, and it would have been the biggest mistake of my life." His arm tightened around her then, and he planted a soft kiss on her head. "There is much to talk about in the days to come, but right now, I know everything I need to."

Pulling the blanket up and around them, Henrietta rested her head on his good shoulder, her arm wrapped around his middle the same way his arm lay draped across her shoulders. Safe and warm and loved, she closed her eyes and fell asleep, listening to the rhythm of her husband's beating heart.

Chapter Thirty-Nine
ANSWERS OF OLD

A fortnight passed, and Henrietta could not have been happier. She woke every morning with a smile on her face, reaching out an arm to assure herself that her husband was there, right beside her, sleeping peacefully. His shoulder was healing nicely, and he grew more daring in his expressions of his love for her. Henrietta, too, enjoyed every moment she could spend with him, rarely leaving his side, and so she often accompanied him in his duties as chief of clan Brunwood.

Step by step, Henrietta found her way around the castle and its people, seeing that if she met them with an open mind and heart, they would do the same for her. She also learnt that Angus and the men that had followed him to the cliffs that day were a minority within the clan. Most adored her husband and trusted him to have their best interest at heart, which was all the more reason for the people of Greyston to welcome Henrietta into their hearts.

After the story of the ambush had made its rounds through the castle and the village, people started looking at her with different eyes. Many walked up to her with smiling faces, thanking her for saving their chief while Connor stood beside her, pride shining in his eyes as he gazed at her lovingly.

Life was good, and for the first time, Henrietta felt truly loved and wanted and welcomed into a family, not just tolerated. Rhona was the mother she had always longed for while Deirdre became the sister she never got to know. Even Alastair had the occasional smile for her; his initial disregard vanished into thin air.

After confessing her deeds to her brother, Moira had been confined to her room. For Alastair's sake, Connor had been lenient, and as of yet, a final decision with regard to her punishment had not been reached. At the same time, Angus and his followers had been expelled from the clan, which judging from the old man's face was a fate worse than death.

Everything else had returned to normal, and Henrietta slowly found her place within the family as well as the clan. She could not imagine ever living another life, and the thought that her uncle had not forced her hand in marriage was her worst nightmare.

At least during the day.

For the past fortnight, Henrietta's dreams had often awoken her in the middle of the night. Again, she found herself dreaming of that one fateful day her parents had died, and yet, something was different.

Before, her dreams had been true nightmares, torturing her with vivid images of her mother's bloodstained body. Fear and pain had pressed down on Henrietta, almost suffocating in their intensity as they entered every fibre of her being, making her distrustful and afraid.

In those dreams, she had been a little girl, terrified by the thunder and lightning that assaulted the house. However, the dreams that woke her now did not stir her emotions to such an extent as before. In a strange way, she felt as though she were an unaffected observer.

Through calculating eyes, Henrietta watched herself as a little girl as she tiptoed out of her room to get her little brother from the nursery. Then she headed downstairs and hid in the pantry.

While she sat in the dark, Angus's snarling face often drifted before her eyes, and she squeezed them shut, waking herself in the process.

"Are ye all right, Lass?" her husband asked, his dark eyes filled with worry as they slid over her. Reaching out his good arm, he pulled her closer. "Another dream?"

Gasping for breath, Henrietta nodded. "The same as the night before." She shook her head. "I do not understand why this would bother me still." She turned pleading eyes to her husband as though all she needed to do to rid herself of her dreams was to convince him of her rightful claim. "I've dealt with my parents' death, my fears and distrust. Why do I still dream of that night?"

"Ye said yer dreams had changed," Connor reminded her. Sitting up, he wrapped an arm around her, holding her tight while her fingers dug into the blanket, hoping to stem their trembling. "Maybe it has nothing to do with yer fears, Lass. Maybe there is something else buried in yer mind that ye seek to uncover."

"But what? I can't think of anything."

"What did ye see?"

Taking a deep breath, Henrietta closed her eyes, trying to remember. "I was a little girl again, only it was as though it wasn't me. I wasn't scared, not like I was before. I got out of bed, went to get my brother and then hid in the pantry." Squinting her eyes, Henrietta frowned. "Angus."

"What?"

"I saw Angus."

"What? The night yer parents died?"

Henrietta shook her head. "No, just in my dream. His face...he...looked familiar somehow."

"D'ye think ye've seen him before?" her husband asked, his brows drawn down. "Before coming to Greyston?"

Henrietta shrugged. "I don't know. I cannot remember." Again, she explored the image she'd seen. "I think not. I think it was only the expression on his face that looked familiar."

"What expression was it?"

Shivering, Henrietta shook herself. "Disgust. Hatred. Hostility." Turning to look at her husband, she said, "The way he always looked at you, especially that day at the cliff top. His eyes stared at you as though you had no right to live, as though you had no right to be the man you are. He looked at you as if you were the enemy." Shaking her head, Henrietta sighed, "I cannot believe I didn't see it earlier."

"Don't blame yerself," her husband whispered, pulling her into his arms. "No one saw, much less understood what went on inside his head. Ye couldna have known."

Nodding, Henrietta felt herself dragged back to the night of her parents' death.

"Only that is not it, is it?" Connor asked. "Ye don't wake up from that dream because you feel guilty. It's something else, isn't it?"

Henrietta nodded. "If only I knew what."

"Ye said the expression on Angus' face reminded ye of something or rather someone."

Focusing on the expression in the old man's eyes, Henrietta closed her own and hoped her subconscious would succeed where her waking mind had failed.

Slowly, ever so slowly, the image cleared and broadened, depicting not only eyes but then also a proud nose, a moment later complemented by thin lips pressed together in anger.

Henrietta swallowed. "My uncle," she whispered, and the blood froze in her veins as the image expanded further.

"Yer uncle?" her husband repeated, an angry growl in his voice. "He looked at ye like that?"

Staring into the night, Henrietta shook her head, goose bumps crawling up her arms and legs. "Not me," she whispered as a new fear spread through her heart. "Tristan."

Chapter Forty
A GUARDIAN ANGEL

"Yer brother?" Connor asked as the significance of her words eluded him. "I don't understand."

Suddenly unable to sit still, Henrietta slid out of bed, her feet restless. Pacing the length of the room, she mumbled under her breath as she tried to remember the details of her dream. "I sit in the pantry, my baby brother in my arms, and listen. All I can do is listen. I hear my father's angry shouting and my mother's sobs. For a long time, that's all I hear. Then everything is quiet. Until..."

Watching her with worried eyes, Connor sat at the edge of the bed, wishing there was something he could do. "Until?"

Then she turned to him, her eyes wide with shock and fear that he rushed to her side, his hands coming around her arms, holding her upright as her knees gave out.

When she sagged against him, tears streaming down her face, Connor picked her up. Wincing at the renewed pain in his shoulder, he carried her to the bed and sat her down. Then he knelt in front of her, holding her cold hands in his. "What is it?" he pressed, unable to bear the silence any longer.

His wife took a slow breath and blinked, her eyes finally seeing him. "He's in danger."

"Who? Yer brother? Why?" Connor asked before her words once more echoed in his mind. "Because yer uncle looked at him the way Angus looked at me? That doesna mean he'll try to-"

"But he already did!"

"What?" Shaking his head, Connor took a deep breath, then squeezed her hands to make her look at him. "How d'ye know, Lass? What did ye remember?"

His wife swallowed and once more took a deep breath, collecting her thoughts. "I don't know why I didn't see it before, but...the night my parents died, I remember hearing their voices, then silence and then...a shot rang out. Everyone thought, including me, that my father had slit my mother's throat and then shot himself."

"Ye don't think that's what happened?"

Shaking her head, she stared at him. "I always thought I remembered wrong. I was a child, barely five years old." Again, she shook her head. "But I didn't."

"Tell me," Connor pressed, his own heart filling with dread.

"I remember hearing footsteps, going upstairs," she whispered as though speaking too loudly would bring about a disaster. "I remember hearing those footsteps as they entered every room before returning downstairs. I remember someone cursing under his breath," she swallowed, her eyes drilling into his, "after I heard the gunshot." Staring at him, she shook her head. "My father was already dead. Who was that?"

Gritting his teeth, Connor felt his muscles grow tense. "Ye think that someone entered yer home and killed yer parents...and then went upstairs looking for ye?"

Henrietta shook her head. "Not for me. I'm no one. I barely had a dowry to my name. No, not me. My brother." Pulling her hands from his, she rubbed them over her face. "He was the heir to my father's title, his estate. The moment my father passed on, Tristan became Viscount Elton."

Staring at his wife, Connor voiced the thought that had been hanging in the room ever since Tristan's name had been mentioned. "Ye think it was yer uncle? Ye think he killed his own brother and would've killed his nephew had...had ye not hidden him in the pantry?"

Toward the end, his voice trailed off as the truth of his words finally sank in.

"Please, tell me I'm insane!" his wife begged as she seized his hands once more. "Please, tell me that my brother is not in danger!"

Holding her pleading gaze, Connor swallowed. "There's nothing I'd rather say, but I'm afraid there's merit to yer words, Lass."

Burying her face in her hands, his wife sobbed. "I know. Deep down, I've always known." Meeting his eyes, she shook her head. "I never trusted my uncle. He has always been a ruthless man, only looking out for his own good." Squeezing her eyes shut, she sighed. "Tristan was right, and I did not believe him."

"Believe him what?"

"He would always get into fights, into all sorts of trouble," she said, more tears streaming down her face as shame filled her eyes. "Again and again, my uncle had to bail him out. I cannot say how often Tristan was injured. Once he almost died. We all thought he was too reckless, too carefree, unable to act as the responsible man we all wanted to see. But it was all a lie." Wiping the tears from her face, Henrietta looked down at him, her eyes hard. "It was my uncle. All this time, Tristan begged me to believe him, and I never could. Not fully."

Connor rose to his feet and sat down beside her. "D'ye truly believe this possible? That yer uncle tried to kill him again and again, and yet, Tristan always survived?"

His wife shrugged. "I suppose when Tristan was a child, my uncle's hands were tied. He couldn't have killed him under his own roof. But when he became a man, there were other options. It was always a stranger in a tavern or a thief lurking in a dark alley. I don't know how often Tristan was called out to a duel or robbed."

Connor frowned, determined to examine this issue rationally before allowing his wife to come to the conclusion that began to seem inevitable. "And he always survived? How? That seems as unusual as all these *accidents* themselves!"

Henrietta frowned. "I'm not certain. Occasionally, he would mention a friend. I don't even know his name, but sometimes Tristan would speak of this friend when I was particularly worried about him."

She lifted her head and met Connor's gaze. "Once he even called him his guardian angel."

Connor nodded. "I see. Then I suppose it has been that friend who's been standing between yer brother and an early grave."

Henrietta swallowed, and her eyes widened. "What if my uncle tries again?"

"We need to put a stop to this," Connor declared, then took his wife's hands and looked deep into her eyes. "We'll go to London and find yer brother, and then we'll deal with yer uncle."

Staring into his eyes, Henrietta nodded her head vigorously. "Yes. Thank you. Yes."

Rising to his feet, Connor stepped toward his closet. "Get dressed," he said over his shoulder, pulling on his breeches and reaching for a shirt. "I'll have the carriage readied."

"No." On her feet, Henrietta stepped forward, already pulling the nightgown over her head. "We'll be faster on horseback."

"Are ye certain, Lass?" Connor asked, trying hard not to look at his naked wife as she changed into a riding habit. "It'll be a long journey."

"I'm certain."

"All right," he agreed. "I'll have the horses readied and have a quick talk with Alastair, informing him of our absence. Then we'll be off."

"Thank you," his wife mumbled again and again until he walked out of their bedchamber.

Fear and hope fighting over dominance of his heart, Connor hurried down the corridor. There was no time to lose. Who knew if his wife's uncle hadn't already succeeded? He could only hope that they would not arrive in London too late.

Although Connor didn't know his brother-in-law, he would do everything in his power to spare his wife the loss of her brother. She had been through enough, and he wasn't certain her heart could bear losing Tristan.

By God, they had to save him.

Epilogue

London 1806 (or a variation thereof)

Five months earlier

His head throbbed unbearably as Tristan Turner, Viscount Elton, stumbled out into the night. Drunken laughter followed him out the tavern door, and he momentarily covered his ears to shut out the noise.

The man's fist had come out of nowhere, and Tristan rubbed the aching place on his face where it had connected with his jaw. Had he truly leered at the man's wife? What kind of a man would bring his wife to a tavern? Tristan couldn't even remember seeing her. There had been a barmaid. Had she been the man's wife?

His head buzzed like a beehive, and all he wanted in that moment was a good night's sleep.

Turning down the street, he squinted his eyes as even the dim light from the street lamps increased the throbbing in his head and stumbled over an uneven cobblestone, almost falling flat on his face.

Tristan cursed under his breath and stopped in his tracks, trying hard to keep upright. The night sounds of the city echoed to his ears, and strangely he wondered what it would feel like to be blind, unable to see what lay ahead. As he listened to the distant sounds of hoof beats and cart wheels, dim voices and music, Tristan felt the skin in the back of his neck begin to prickle.

His eyes snapped open, and he craned his neck, glancing at the shadows that surrounded him.

Had he heard someone breathing behind him? Or had it only been the wind?

Tristan couldn't be certain. After all, trouble seemed to find him no matter where he went or what hour of the day it was.

Stumbling on, he hoped that he would find a hackney carriage, but looking out through narrow slits, Tristan thought the street appeared almost deserted.

Footsteps echoed behind him, and Tristan spun around.

Instantly, his headache pounded mercilessly and he cringed.

"Don't you look handsome," a familiar voice laughed. "Who did you offend this time?"

Sighing in relief, Tristan took a deep breath, waiting for his heartbeat to slow. "Apparently, I leered at another man's wife."

Derek chuckled, "With the husband present, I assume?"

"You would assume right," Tristan admitted although he could do without his friend's teasing.

After a small eternity, Derek finally stopped laughing. "I've known you to do stupid things, but still you never cease to amaze me."

"If that is the kind of compliment you offer to the ladies," Tristan snapped, "it's no wonder they all turn you down."

Derek's face sobered, and he swallowed, his eyes shifting to the ground.

"I'm sorry," Tristan mumbled. "It's been a long night. I did not mean to insult you."

"I know," Derek said. "Let me help you home."

"Thank you." Allowing his friend to guide his steps, Tristan sighed. "What would I do without you?"

Derek chuckled, "Die an early death, I presume!"

"I suppose you'd presume right."

Epilogue Two

Scotland, December 1811

Five Years Later

"Am I mistaken," Henrietta asked, her lips curled into a smile as she glanced at her sister-in-law Beth, "or do you stay longer each year?"

Beth laughed as they sat together in the large hall of Greyston Castle, tying evergreens together into large arches to be hung in doorways and over windows. "Are you saying you do not want us here?" she teased, glancing over at their children.

Both their eldest daughters rode on their fathers' shoulders, tying little red ribbons to the evergreens already hung in the large entryway, while the younger one scrambled around their feet, picking up the ribbons that fell.

Henrietta sighed as she watched her husband, balancing their oldest daughter Bridget on his shoulders while trying not to step on little Aileen's fingers as she crawled over the stone floor, picking up one ribbon after another.

At this speed decorating all the evergreens would last long into the night.

"I admit having all these little hands and feet under one roof is exhausting," Beth continued as she watched Tristan with their daughter Ellen.

At almost four years old, the little blond-haired girl was a bit on the shy side and always needed a few days to warm up to her extended family when they came for a visit over Christmas-as they had every year for the past five winters. However, once she had settled in, her exuberant nature took over, matching Bridget's wild temper in every way.

Ellen and Bridget were a match made in heaven. Both shared the same radiant flaxen hair and deep blue eyes, the shade of dark waters that ran deep. Although Ellen was a bit more hesitant and cautious in her ways, they both throve on excitement and adventure, daring each other into the remotest corners of the castle, hunting ghosts and goblins...or on occasion their little siblings.

At almost two-years-old, Aileen was more tender-hearted and often misunderstood her elder sister's teasing, her green eyes going wide as she shrieked in alarm whenever the two elder girls chose to scare her with yet another gruesome story.

"Mummy, look how pretty!" Ellen called over, pointing at the red ribbon she had just tied to a branch. However, in doing so she leaned sideways as she sat on Tristan's shoulders, which almost made him lose his balance and he stumbled to the right to catch himself.

"Would you sit still?" he growled, grasping his daughter's legs to keep her from sliding off. "Or we shall trade places!"

Connor laughed, his booming voice echoing through the large hall as Ellen and Bridget giggled. "I wouldna recommend that. Yer little one will snap like kindling."

Grinning, Tristan sighed.

"I never get tired of watching them," Beth mumbled, her gaze lovingly tracing over her husband and daughter before it shifted to her little ten-month-old son, sleeping soundly on the settee beside her. "Ellen never slept as he does," she observed, meeting Henrietta's gaze.

"Life always seemed to hold too much excitement for her to truly close her eyes."

Henrietta chuckled. "I know what you mean," she said, glancing at Bridget, who at that moment tried to climb onto her father's head.

"Dane is different," Beth said, brushing a gentle hand over his forehead, which brought forth an angelic smile. Still, he slept on undisturbed, not minding the ruckus around him in the least. "He sleeps like a rock." Lifting her gaze, she looked at Henrietta, a touch of concern in her eyes. "It frightens me sometimes."

Henrietta frowned. "Why?"

Beth shrugged. "Sometimes he seems so still as though..."

Swallowing, Henrietta nodded, remembering how Deirdre's little daughter-the first child she had been able to carry full-term-had slipped away during the night at only three months old. It had broken her parents' hearts, leaving them mere shadows of themselves.

Henrietta wished she knew what to do, how to help them.

"Mummy?"

Blinking, Henrietta found Aileen standing beside her, her big green eyes filled with longing, as she tugged on her sleeve. "What is it, sweetheart?"

Inhaling a deep breath, Aileen glanced over her shoulder, looking at her elder sister with longing eyes. "Me, too."

Henrietta smiled. "Then go and demand your turn," she encouraged her daughter, seeing her shy little smile and the hesitation in her eyes. "They will not bite you."

Pressing her lips together, a determined gleam came to Aileen's eyes. Then she nodded her head and turned toward her father and sister, her little legs carrying her forward step by slow step.

"She seems too fragile sometimes," Henrietta said, watching her youngest face down her fears and claim her prize.

"Oh, she'll do fine," Beth counselled. "Look at her. She might be afraid, but she does not back down."

Henrietta nodded, watching her little girl as she made herself heard and was then rewarded by her father. With ease, he lifted Aileen onto his shoulders as Bridget sat by his feet, pouting. "Now, don't ye fret,"

Connor chided his eldest. "'Tis very unbecoming. Aileen deserves a turn. Now, be a good sister and pass up some of the wee ribbons."

Henrietta and Beth laughed. "Will you come visit us in the summer?" Beth asked when they had finished with the evergreens. "I'm certain the girls would love to see each other more often. As would I."

Henrietta nodded, delighted with the suggestion. "I'm certain we can arrange it. Thank you for the offer. It would be wonderful to see England again after all this time."

"Do you ever miss it?"

"I miss you, all of you." Glancing around Greyston Castle, Henrietta smiled. "But this is my home now. I've never felt quite the same anywhere else. I feel at peace here."

Beth met her gaze. "I'm happy for you."

Henrietta sighed, resting her hands on her hips. "Well, then. It's time to go find the perfect yule log. Will you watch the children while we're out?"

Beth nodded, a deep smile on her face. "You still insist on cutting down the tree yourself?"

Henrietta grinned, feeling her limbs ache with the need to move. "I cannot help it. Holding that axe makes me feel strong, powerful, in control." Glancing at her husband, she felt her smile deepen. "He would never take that from me." Her gaze returned to Beth. "Maybe that's why I feel so safe here."

"Then go," Beth said, a knowing smile curling up her lips. "And don't worry about your little ones. After all, we're family."

Henrietta nodded. Yes, family. Finally, that word had come to mean what it ought to. Family were people who loved one another, protected one another and strove to make one another happy.

Family no longer meant fear and pain and doubt.

That was in the past, and she would ensure that her daughters would never know what she had learnt as a young child. No, her daughters grew up with a kind and caring father and a mother who would never be afraid to stand up and protect them.

Wasn't that the true meaning of family?

THE END

Thank you for reading *Abandoned & Protected*!

In the next installment, *Betrayed & Blessed - The Viscount's Shrewd Wife*, we will learn what happens after Henrietta and Connor leave for London and we'll finally get to know Tristan.

At a masked ball, he meets a mysterious lady. Will Beth turn out to be his true love when the masks come off?

Read a Sneak-Peek

Betrayed & Blessed
The Viscount's Shrewd Wife

Prologue

England 1786 (or a variation thereof)

Twenty Years Ago

An icy wind howled through the night, attacking the tall, fortress-like manor from all sides. Windows rattled in their hinges here and there as the onslaught continued, not yielding, but clinging tightly to the dark stone that had faced down many such attacks and not succumbed.

It was a night on which only the foolish or reckless would venture from the safety of their homes.

Or the desperate.

Pulling the heavy, black cloak more tightly around her shoulders, Ellen Cartwright, Countess of Radcliff, stood in the large kitchen located in the back of the monstrous building and gazed down at the sleeping child in her arms.

Lost in her dreams, her daughter smiled as Ellen brushed a gentle hand over the little girl's forehead, her golden locks slightly swaying as her mother rocked her.

Taking a deep breath, Ellen wrapped her arms more tightly around her precious girl, pulling her closer as though any moment she might

PROLOGUE

slip from her arms and vanish. "My sweet, little Beth," she mumbled into the child's hair as her arms began to feel the two-year-old's weight. Slowly, she forced them to relax, allowing the carrying cloak she had fashioned for the child to bear most of the burden. As her arms relaxed, the straps cut into her shoulders, and she had to brace a hand on the table beside her to keep from falling over.

The moment she leant forward and her hand touched the rough wooden surface, a jolt of pain cut through the left side of her ribcage, and for the hundredth time, Ellen prayed that her ribs were not broken...only bruised.

"Do you truly not want to wait?" her mother-in-law asked as she came walking into the empty kitchen, a dark bag in her hands as she stepped toward Ellen, deep concern in her gentle eyes. "You are not feeling well. What if you cannot hold her for long? What if-?"

"No," Ellen interrupted, drawing in a shaky breath. "It has to be tonight. Everything's in place." Gritting her teeth, she straightened her back and met her mother-in-law's eyes. "I can do it, Clementine," she said, knowing that she had to. It was a simple as that. "I can do it."

As a tear rolled down Clementine's weathered face, the older woman reluctantly slung the bag over Ellen's head and shoulder, careful not to disturb the sleeping child. Then she gazed down at her granddaughter, gently brushing a stray curl from her little face, and whispered, "Be safe, my little angel."

"I will protect her," Ellen said as though saying the words would make them true. Deep down, she was terrified, and yet, she needed to be strong. Fear would not serve her. Only strength would see her daughter safe.

"I know." Nodding her head, her eyes brimming with tears, her mother-in-law gently cupped her wrinkled hand to Ellen's cheek. "I hate to see you go," she whispered, "but neither can I stand to watch you suffer any longer." She hung her head. "I'm sorry for everything that's happened. I wish...I don't know what happened that changed him so. I wish I did."

Ellen nodded, her own throat constricted at the thought of leaving behind the only mother she had ever known. As much as she despised her husband, next to her daughter, his mother was the person she loved most in this world and leaving her broke her heart. "I need to go," she said, reminding them both of the inevitable. "Will you...will you see me outside?"

A soft smile came to her mother-in-law's face. "Wild horses couldn't keep me away."

Pressing her lips together, Ellen forced the tears back down as she turned toward the door, her mother-in-law by her side, her arm wrapped around her shoulders.

Silently, they stepped out into the dark night, the wind tearing at their clothes, and walked around the side of the building to the stables, leaving behind the looming manor and its sleeping inhabitants.

For weeks, Ellen had planned the night of their escape, but without her mother-in-law's help she would never have succeeded.

Only together, they had been able to convince her husband to allow her to remain in the country when he had been called back to London for business. By then, Ellen had known that *business* generally referred to another night of gambling and drinking until the wee hours of the morning. However, by then, she did not care any longer.

In her mind's eye, she still saw the pale bruises on her daughter's little arm after her father had dragged her from his study.

Oblivious to her father's temper, little Beth had ventured around the house after escaping her nurse's attention and then discovered the many wonders hidden in her father's desk.

Upon discovering her in his study, papers strewn about, some crumpled, some torn, he had been furious, his head turning red, as he had yanked the crying child out into the hall.

It had been the first time his rage had been directed at his child. The first time she had felt her father's uncontrolled temper. The first time his anger had marked her skin.

It had been in that moment that Ellen had known that she had to leave.

Alone in the country, far from her husband's watchful eyes, she and Clementine had arranged for them to start a new life. In her bag were papers that would attest to her marriage to a fictitious man, to their daughter's birth as well as to his untimely death. As a young widow,

PROLOGUE

Ellen planned to start over again and give her daughter the one thing every child needed the most: safety.

Long before Beth had fallen asleep that night, her grandmother had added a sleeping potion to the servants' food, and by the time Ellen had sneaked downstairs to ready the horse, most of them had been sound asleep in their beds. Then she had returned to gather her things and latch her daughter to her body so that she could ride with greater ease.

Although the wind howled around them, the earth was dry as it hadn't rained in over a week. And yet, the sky had been heavy with dark clouds all day, promising a storm on the horizon.

The opportune moment had come.

Ellen knew it. She couldn't hesitate now.

If she left tonight and covered sufficient ground, the hard soil would show no hoof prints that would lead others to her location. And if luck held and the storm came in a day or two, it would impede the search for her even more. After all, what she needed most was a headstart to put as much distance between herself and her husband before she could start looking for a place to begin a new life.

Leading her trusted mare from the box, Ellen turned to her mother-in-law. "Thank you for everything you've done," she whispered as tears streamed down her face, and she quickly wiped them away before they fell on her daughter. "You saved us both."

Closing her eyes, Clementine took a deep breath, then strode forward and wrapped her daughter-in-law and granddaughter in a desperate embrace. "I wish I could've done more. I wish you didn't have to go." She stepped back, her eyes brimming with tears. "But I am grateful that you're strong enough to go. I don't know if I could've done it."

Pride swelled in Ellen's chest, giving her strength. "It is a mother's duty to protect her child," she said as she had so many times since making up her mind.

Her mother-in-law nodded. "It is." Then she pulled a small envelope from her shawl and slipped it into Ellen's bag. "To help you get started."

Ellen's eyes widened. "I couldn't. I-"

PROLOGUE

"For my granddaughter," Clementine interrupted, her eyes determined as she held Ellen's gaze. "After all, it is also a grandmother's right to protect her grandchild."

"Thank you," Ellen whispered, feeling new tears sting her eyes. Before they could spill down her face, she stepped forward, gave Clementine a quick hug and then led her mare out into the night. Handing the reins to her mother-in-law, she mounted the horse, careful not to wake her sleeping daughter.

"Be safe," Clementine said over the howling wind, her hand squeezing Ellen's as she returned the reins into her grasp. "Be safe."

Holding her mother-in-law's gaze for a moment longer, Ellen nodded. "I will. I promise." Then she kicked her heels into the horse's flanks, and a moment later, they were swallowed up by the night.

Forcing herself not to look back, Ellen guided her mare away from Beechworth Manor and across the fields, grateful for her good sense of direction as she planned to stay off the main roads as much as possible.

If everything went well, her husband would never find them.

She could only hope that her luck would hold.

For her daughter's sake.

Series Overview

LOVE'S SECOND CHANCE: TALES OF LORDS & LADIES

LOVE'S SECOND CHANCE: TALES OF DAMSELS & KNIGHTS

LOVE'S SECOND CHANCE: HIGHLAND TALES

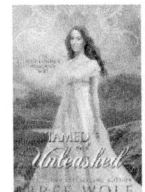

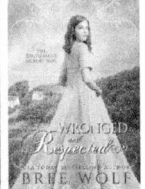

SERIES OVERVIEW

FORBIDDEN LOVE SERIES

HAPPY EVER REGENCY SERIES

THE WHICKERTONS IN LOVE

For more information visit www.breewolf.com

About Bree

USA Today bestselling and award-winning author, Bree Wolf has always been a language enthusiast (though not a grammarian!) and is rarely found without a book in her hand or her fingers glued to a keyboard. Trying to find her way, she has taught English as a second language, traveled abroad and worked at a translation agency as well as a law firm in Ireland. She also spent loooong years obtaining a BA in English and Education and an MA in Specialized Translation while wishing she could simply be a writer. Although there is nothing simple about being a writer, her dreams have finally come true.

"A big thanks to my fairy godmother!"

Currently, Bree has found her new home in the historical romance genre, writing Regency novels and novellas. Enjoying the mix of fact and fiction, she occasionally feels like a puppet master (or mistress? Although that sounds weird!), forcing her characters into ever-new situations that will put their strength, their beliefs, their love to the test, hoping that in the end they will triumph and get the happily-ever-after we are all looking for.

If you're an avid reader, sign up for Bree's newsletter on **www.breewolf.com** as she has the tendency to simply give books away. Find out about freebies, giveaways as well as occasional advance reader copies and read before the book is even on the shelves!

Connect with Bree and stay up-to-date on new releases:

- facebook.com/breewolf.novels
- twitter.com/breewolf_author
- instagram.com/breewolf_author
- bookbub.com/authors/bree-wolf
- amazon.com/Bree-Wolf/e/B00FJX27Z4